First published
Jemmett
31 I
Grea
Aylesbury
Buck HP17 9TP

Kindle version worldwide 2023
Jemmett Affection

Text © Anthony Randall & Doug Goddard 2023

The moral rights of Anthony Randall and Doug Goddard
to be identified as authors for this work have been asserted
in accordance with the Copyright,
designs and patents act, 1988 and the duration
of Copyright and rights in Performances Regulations 1995.

All rights reserved. No part of this publication may be reproduced, stored in a retrieval system, or transmitted, in any form or by any means, electronic mechanical, photocopying, recording or otherwise, without prior written
permission of the publisher and copyright owner.
Nor be otherwise circulated in any form of binding or cover
other than that, in which it is published and without a similar condition including this condition being imposed on the subsequent purchaser.

Cover design by Aspire Book Covers.

Acknowledgements

This book would be unreadable without the impeccable diligence of
Rebecca Carter, who corrected a million grammatical errors.
Karen Slade, for her astute observations and amendments, and preventing
us from using some ridiculous words.
And, Sylva Fae, for her constant support, help, advice and beta reading skills.
We thank you all.

This book is dedicated
To the following

Vladimir Kara-Murza
Alexe Navalny
And
The hundreds of political prisoners
Incarcerated in Russian Prisons

Simon Wiesenthal

The White Rose, German anti-Nazi group
Formed in Munich 1942

Your courage and dedication
Has been duly noted

Contents

1.	9
2.	28
3.	43
4.	57
5.	69
6.	85
7.	112
8.	126
9.	140
10.	152
11.	167
12.	191
13.	212
14.	229
15.	247
16.	271
Epilogue.	291

White Avenging Rose

To the Russian people

Your next presidential election on Sunday, 17th March 2024, will be a one-horse race.

Grandpa Putin has already decided that he'll win by eighty per cent, and the Kremlin has begun to hand-pick his challengers, certain people they consider safe opponents.

So, although he has not yet decided to run for president, he will, and will win it, leaving you stuck with him for the following six years, still alienating your country and ruining your economy.

One hundred and eight million Russians are eligible to vote. Your future is in your hands.

After nearly two years of fighting in Ukraine, thousands of men, women and children from both countries have been killed, maimed and rendered homeless.

Your people are still being ostracized from the world's stage and thousands of Russian mothers are seeing their sons brought home in body bags.

The current situation will not have changed in 2024; it will almost certainly be worse.

The democratic process must be allowed to prevail, and all one hundred and eight million voters should be allowed to cast their votes unhindered and without prejudice or coercion.

The two things that old-man Putin fears the most are losing the support of the Russian people, and losing the war in Ukraine, which will lose him the backing of his inner circle and the Russian people anyway.

Both are inevitable.

The election will go ahead as scheduled, but it is down to every one of you to decide your destiny. Make the right choice.

Nothing gives the fearful more courage than another's fear.

Please vote.

The Authors

1

Living under the same roof as Russian and Ukrainian medical students for the past four years had given me advantageous insight as to what was happening politically in both countries. So it came as no surprise, that on Thursday, 24th February 2022, the Russian army entered illegally into Ukraine en mass, with President Putin declaring to the world that this was not an act of war, but purely a 'special military operation'.

These words fooled nobody, and Putin's rhetoric was clear long before he congregated a hundred thousand troops on the border. He wanted to commandeer the whole of Ukraine. A giant and very lucrative piece of the former Soviet Union; the fundamental, idealistic communist state he was hell-bent on resurrecting.

As the troops rolled in, to begin with virtually unopposed, Putin's vitriolic declaration underlined a plain truth to me. Any dialogue with the man, either now or in the future, would be futile, and an alternative solution would have to be found. This, without doubt, would almost certainly entail removing Putin from office.

I arrived back home late, just before seven o'clock, to find all of my housemates gathered around the TV in the ancient wooden conservatory at the rear of the property. A room that doubled as our lounge and affectionately known as The Raft.

They were glued to a news channel, anxiously watching in disbelief the horrors of the Russians, advancing like a Blitzkrieg across the wintery landscape, obliterating anything that stood in its path.

The tanks and armoured vehicles, each painted with a large white letter Z on the body, were flying Soviet flags and transporting hordes of young smiling soldiers atop, foolishly brandishing peace V-signs toward the media. All of them bolstered with lethal disinformation.

A reporter was saying that some of the soldiers he had spoken to didn't know they were even in Ukraine and that this wasn't a war; they were just here to protect the people from a Nazi uprising.

Arouna, who was from Ukraine, squatted in the middle of one of our tired old couches, flanked by our Spanish mother-hen, Safira, and Victoria, a Londoner. All three women were close to tears. Understandably, Arouna, who was the most upset, was being comforted under the wing of Safira.

On the other battered couch, Lukas, our German anaesthetist, sat wide-eyed and still, next to our Muscovite, Nikolay. I had never seen the Russian lad so distressed. He was usually the life and soul of a party, but this evening, overwhelmingly feeling the shame of his county's conduct.

Nikolay had not heard from his family in ten weeks. Neither had his two uncles, one who lived in London and the other in Brussels. The Russian embassies had clammed up, but due to 'security reasons', nothing was forthcoming from any of them.

Three mobile phones scattered untidily on the small coffee table in front of the lad showed the extent of his anguish. He could be reached on any one of three numbers, should anybody have any news. They'd been lifeless for days.

The two armchairs were occupied by Jack, a Welsh respiratory student and house comedian, and Beau, a

British-born Hong Kong Chinese, whose parents had come over to work in hospitals twenty-five years ago. Beau was studying Neurosurgery.

Nikolay spotted me first, paused in the doorway, "You okay, Abel?"

Under all this stress, he still had the compulsion to care for others. It's the way with medical students; why they walk this line.

All eyes were now looking my way.

"Yes, mate, fine, just can't believe what I'm seeing."

At that moment it was like walking on thin ice. Which housemate should I console first?

Arouna was now fully sobbing and Nikolay looked as guilty as hell. She stood up and yelled at him, "Your bloody people, you have no right to do this!"

Nikolay looked down at his shoes, while Arouna steamed out of the room, hastily followed by Safira.

Jack stretched an upturned palm towards Nikolay. "It's not his fault, is it? He's not invaded anybody. Not for a while anyway." The last remark was a half-arsed attempt to lighten the mood.

"Still no word from your family Nik'?"

He shook his head in slow motion.

There was a pregnant pause. It seemed nobody had anything to say right now.

I broke the speech drought, "I'm having a beer. Anyone want one?"

Nobody was in the mood, so I sauntered off to the kitchen to find solace in a cold long-neck.

I'd just flooded the dim kitchen with fridge light when Safira strutted in.

"Pass me the Pinot blush, please, Abel. Arouna and I are going to get smashed."

I handed her the Rosé. "Don't you two have work tomorrow?"

"Yeah, but fuck it, we need something to numb the pain, and all the morphine's at the hospital."

I half smiled as she grabbed two glasses from a cabinet.

Safira and I shared a fridge. There were four in the kitchen, and two gas stoves, which was more than adequate for all eight of us to not get in each other's way.

The owner of The Lemon Grove, Cedar Avenue, Oxford, had restored the four-storey Victorian detached property sympathetically to its original standard, and had taken great care over the details, but had converted eight rooms into ensuite bedsits, so that each of us had a very large, retro, personal space to relax in, plus a big kitchen and the Raft to use as communal rooms, should we want to hang out.

The kitchen had retained its original indoor washing line, a wooden rack and pulley system that could be hoisted up into the high ceiling, out of the way, which was very handy on a winter's day like today. I did have some socks up there, but it was mostly adorned with skimpy knickers. Like the flags of the house residents, it sported a multitude of colours.

"Has Arouna heard from her family recently?"

"Yes, her mum and sister are waiting for a train to take them to Kyiv. Their town is being heavily bombed. When Arouna's father has seen them safely to the capital, he and his son will head to the Donbas to retrieve Marko's mother from Sievierodonetsk, an area that is largely populated with Russian-backed separatists. Hopefully, the family will all convene together in Kyiv."

The situation with Arouna's family had gotten to Safira, tears were welling up in her eyes again, so I changed tack.

"What are Spanish people saying about the war?"

"Disgusted, of course!" She threw her arms up and out, as if to say 'what the hell'. "I spoke with my father in Fuengirola yesterday. He cannot believe what a fool this Putin is. The repercussions are going to be felt around the world."

"How does he feel it will affect Spain?"

She shrugged her shoulders so that her neck almost disappeared.

"Well, only yesterday a news reporter was on the TV in Marbella, talking to an estate agent who sells villas to well-off Russian clients. On average he sells thirty or forty properties a year. Already he has had twenty-eight asking to put their villas on the market. The party is over, said the estate agent."

She looked at me for a reaction. All I could do was raise my eyebrows.

"How do you think this ends, in Ukraine?" Her eyes were hooded.

I stared at my bottle of beer and thumbed at the label, whilst trying to conjure up something profound.

"I just hope that there are more good Russians than there are bad ones." I feebly uttered.

"*Ruego que también,*" she murmured. "I pray that also."

Safira left me at the table, grabbing her wine before disappearing down the gloomy hallway.

If I was honest, all I could see ahead for the Ukrainian people was death, desolation and misery. I took a swig of beer.

***

Trying to creep through the house noiselessly at five in the morning, I took on the persona of a primitive hunter-gatherer stalking prey through a leafy jungle, shifting the weight to the edges of my feet, intent on not making a sound.

But the creaky stair treads let the side down and sent antelope and deer fleeing in all directions.

A light was on in the kitchen, and the smell of freshly brewed percolated coffee suggested that one of my housemates was on an early shift at the hospital.

I was wrong. Arouna was seated at the kitchen table in her orange dressing gown, feverishly texting to some unknown recipient. She had a second phone charging on the worktop behind her.

The coffee mug in front of her was two-thirds empty and looking decidedly tepid. I asked her if she wanted a new cup, to which she just nodded, then said "please," her mind, definitely elsewhere.

It was an unwritten rule in our house. Whoever was up first would put the ageing percolator on and make a full pot. Because most of the early risers that followed on would still be half asleep and incapable of functioning until they'd had their first caffeine shot.

It wasn't always me. It depended on where I was travelling to, but today I was off to a meeting with the MOD down in Dorchester, Dorset. So I would need to fill up my thermal mug with some strong Java for the long journey.

The anguish she was suffering was evident on Arouna's face, as was the lack of sleep. Yet she possessed the inner strength and resilience to hold it together under extreme pressure. This is what made her an ideal candidate for her chosen vocation. Arouna was just a year away from becoming a fully-fledged GP.

The strain she was under right now was testing her resolve to the max.

She put her phone down to receive a fresh mug of roasted beans.

"Any news?" I inquired.

"Last night, my mum and Lena were going to sleep on the floor of a crowded train carriage, sitting in the station at Poltava-Kyivska. I don't want to call them yet, they may still be asleep."

"Sure, sure… Will they be safe in Kyiv?"

She gave me an incredulous look. "Of course not! That bastard wants to destroy my whole country. I will have to get them out."

"Your mum and sister? I thought your dad and brother were going to get your grandmother and bring her back to Kyiv so that the family could be together?"

"My dad and brother won't leave. They are patriots. They will stay and fight for Ukraine, as will all the men. That fucking dictator will not take my country. He does not know the strength of my people. We will fight to the death, with sticks and stones if need be."

I'd never seen this side of Arouna; she was usually so happy-go-lucky and took everything in her stride.

I narrowed my eyebrows. "So what are your plans for your mum and sister?"

"From Kyiv Pass, they can get a train straight to Warsaw, where thousands of refugees are being processed. From there, they can get busses to France, hopefully, Calais, then a ferry to Dover; I can get them from there."

"They'll need visas to get into England."

"Absolutely. I am working on that now… When they get here, would you have any problem if they stayed in my room until I can find them better accommodation?"

I shook my head once to clear the cobwebs. "Of course not, they can stay as long as it takes. I'll even pick them up from the coast if you like."

She softened. "That would be very kind of you."

We had an eclectic collection of cars on the drive. Beau had a little clapped-out Ford KA, Jack, his cherished 1967 red VW camper van, and Lucas, a pale green Vesper scooter. We all had push bikes, but mostly everyone else walked to work or took an uber if they were going further afield. Both Jack and Beau were insured to drive my Volvo if they needed it.

I was trying to stay positive for her. When our landlord converted his deceased parents' house into bed-sits, he had made three bedrooms on the ground floor, and they were huge, with extremely high ceilings. Arouna had one of these, at the front of the house, and would have no problem fitting in another two beds.

"Don't worry about getting extra furniture. We'll take of that. There's plenty of stuff at the reclaim warehouse. We'll just have to get new mattresses and pillows and stuff."

She was stoic. "They'll sleep on the floor if they have to. I'm more concerned about my father and brother. Neither of them has any military experience, and Olek has only just turned eighteen."

Tears were welling up in her eyes again. I wanted to allay her fears with some reparative all-conquering speech, but all I could muster was, "Would you like me to bring you back a stick of rock from the coast?"

She smiled at me, more out of pity than anything else.
"And where are you going today?"
"Dorset, close to Weymouth."
"You love your job, don't you, Abel?"
It was my turn to smile. "Yes, I really do."
Inexplicably, I found myself holding her left hand. "Now I want you to take the day off and get some sleep," I said, a bit too patronisingly.
"You're sounding like one of us now?"
"Well, the whole Avenue thinks I'm a doctor, so I may as well live up to the part."
This time her smile was almost radiant. She threw my hand back at me. "Go on, you'd better get going, or you'll be late."
She was right, I'd spent way more time in the kitchen than I had intended, and the MOD will not be kept waiting.

It was still dark outside, and bitterly cold. No snow on the ground like there was in Ukraine, thankfully, but dank and dreary. A shiver rocked me before I got into the Volvo and reminisced about warmer times during the height of the pandemic, when people were out in the street every Thursday evening, banging on pots and pans and clapping for the NHS.

We used to get boxes of chocolates, flowers and cards left on the doorstep, sometimes on the bonnet of my car. It was hard to drive home at times without being congratulated down the Avenue. I tried to tell them above the furore that I wasn't a doctor, but it fell on deaf ears. I lived with seven medical students who were at the time working exhausting shifts under incredibly difficult circumstances at the hospital. And we all had to isolate ourselves from each other at home, but we somehow came through it without any of us contracting Covid.

My housemates found it highly amusing that I was considered one of them. My profession couldn't be further away.

When I tell people I have the best job on the planet, I truly mean it, even if they don't believe me at first. But, I drive the length and breadth of Great Britain ear-marking suitable spots for creating new woodland environments for the Forestry Commission.

Since 2010, we have planted over fifteen million trees in the UK, the equivalent of thirteen thousand hectares of new forest, and I'm very proud of that fact.

Today, if all goes well with the MOD, Weymouth council, several building contractors and soil experts, thirty-two thousand indigenous broadleaf saplings will be allocated to new areas where trees haven't grown in centuries. And I was dead excited to be involved.

By half past four, it was all sewn up, almost twenty-eight hectares of grassland re-assigned for woodland creation. Planting will begin in the autumn.

I hadn't eaten since lunchtime, so when I arrived back in Oxford just before eight, I was ravenous.

Cooking myself dinner tonight wasn't a desirable prospect, so I took a favoured option. The go-to place when the cupboard was bare, or we just couldn't be arsed to cook, Sid Squids. Probably the best fish and chip shop in the county.

He only opened his doors Thursday to Saturday between five and eight-thirty, and only sold three things, Cod, Haddock, and chips. All of which were amazing.

I bagged a large Cod and chips with a huge gherkin on the side, which was dutifully wrapped the old-fashioned way in several layers of imitation greaseproof paper, salt and vinegar already added. I stuffed the package inside my padded anorak, to keep me and it warm, and then headed for Cedar Avenue.

The Victorian lamp hanging on the front porch burnt brightly, a warm beacon on a dreary night, guiding us weary travellers in with a promise of home. It always brought a smile to my face.

Unusually, for this time of night, inside, the entire house was in darkness, like it had been dipped in chocolate. I flicked on the hall light and meandered down to the kitchen, turned its lights on, then retrieved a plate and a glass from a cupboard, a knife and fork from the drawer, and a bottle of Bergerac Blanc from the fridge.

Sid's portions were way too big for me to eat, and I knew through experience that one of the others would be grateful for a free meal at some point this evening, so I divvied the fish and chips in half, put mine on the plate and placed the other half in the oven, which I switched on low.

The battered Cod was exquisite. Chunky, white, juicy flakes of fresh fish in a light crispy coating, perfectly fried. No wonder the guy had awards in his shop window.

Midway through the meal, I heard footsteps coming down the stairs. Nikolay had radar for cooked food and an infinite appetite. He appeared in the doorway with a searching look on his face.

I raised a little laugh. "There's some in the oven. Help yourself."

"Actually, I'm not hungry; I've just come down for a drink."

"Oh, a glass of wine?" I offered.

He grimaced like I'd slightly offended him, and then went to his own fridge. Pulling out a litre bottle of vodka and a carton of orange juice, he said, "I prefer a proper drink."

Understandably, I thought.

He chugged vodka into a half-pint tall glass, until it was nearly full, then topped it up with a splash of OJ. Nikolay did like his vodka.

I was curious, "Where is everybody tonight Nik'?"

"Victoria and Safira have taken Arouna to a wine bar, to help take her mind off things. Jack and Lukas have gone down to The Swan to watch a comedian, and Beau is staying over at his girlfriend's."

"You didn't fancy going out?"

"No, I'm not in a good place."

I knew my housemate very well. We'd bonded over the past three years. I was kind of like his older brother, and the first person here he'd opened up to about being gay, so I guess he must have had a lot of trust in me.

But something was off, more than just being embarrassed by his country's dastardly actions. Something deeper was troubling him.

How Nikolay arrived in England was sad, but intriguing.

By the age of twelve, he knew he was different, and so did his parents. Both his mum and dad had brothers who were gay. Each of them fled Russia in the 1970s to avoid the stigma and persecution of homosexuality by the government and the populace as a whole.

For his safety, at the age of thirteen, Nikolay was sent to a private boarding school in England, spending the holidays with either of his uncles. He would often joke that he had three sets of parents.

He had an older brother, Dmitri, who was eight years his senior, and like Nikolay, had followed their father into the medical profession. They were all Oncologists.

They also had a nineteen-year-old sister, who was by all accounts a right handful, a rebel and an activist. If it wasn't for her father and brother being held in high esteem within their profession, then, I was told, Anna would have been detained for her antics long ago. Many of her friends were now behind bars for protesting against the ruling establishment.

Nikolay downed half his drink in one protracted gulp and sat there staring at his glass.

I stopped eating. "What's up, mate? You seem really down."

"If I tell you something, Abel, can you keep it to yourself?"

I straightened my back. "Absolutely, you can count on me, scout's honour."

He looked at me quizzically and then nodded a few times.

"As you know, I lost all contact with my family in Moscow about ten weeks ago. Uncle Dima went to the Russian embassy in London, and uncle Sascha to the embassy in Brussels. Both of them received the same answer. That my father and brother had both volunteered for service in the medical core of the Russian Army. All the embassies could tell them was that both men were okay and that for security reasons, no contact with the outside world could be made."

I screwed my face up. That sounded amiss.

Nikolay continued. "We all knew that Putin was planning some kind of military operation months ago, amassing all those troops on the border. But there was no way my brother and father would consider enlisting. It would be ludicrous to take two of the finest oncologists in Russia away from mainstream medicine to do meatball surgery on the frontline. They are experts in their field and people need them in Moscow. This is not right, Abel. I do not believe what the embassies are saying. They are lying,"

My friend was getting quite agitated; his fists were like tightened balls on the tabletop.

"Sounds a bit fishy, mate." I looked down at my cooling dinner; it wasn't the right thing to say. "What about your mum, any idea where she is?"

"Not a clue. I can only presume she is with them. None of my relatives knows a thing."

His eyes were bloodshot now and full of tears. I felt helpless.

He carried on. "I had this horrendous dream last night; I woke with a start just after two o'clock, drenched in sweat and couldn't stop shaking."

He paused, reflecting on his nightmare. "...I'd walked into this massive field hospital tent of a front-line MASH unit, knee-deep in bloodied bodies, intestines, amputated arms and legs, and torsos. The stench was unbelievable. Dying soldiers were moaning and crying for their mothers. Civilians were amongst the carnage. Wounded men, women, and children screaming in agony, tangled in a quagmire of slippery limbs, flesh and guts."

I was wincing. It sounded like the epitome of hell.

"You know what I can't get out of my head Abel, are my socks. I was up to my ankles in blood and body parts and I could feel haemoglobin soaking into my socks and squelching around my toes. And all I was worried about was it ruining my socks."

I felt the cold goo in my own shoes and curled my toes in sympathy.

"My father and brother were in the centre of the tent, each with a casualty on their table. My brother had the torso of a young blonde woman on his table, devoid of arms and legs, her serene face turned towards me, cold blue eyes looking directly into mine. Whilst she was tugged and pulled about, she never made a sound. On my father's operating table, a soldier, naked apart from his boots, had a massive stomach wound and his entrails were hanging out, reaching to the floor. My father suddenly looked up at me, drenched in blood, and started yelling, 'Help me, Nikolay, for god's sake, help me!', but I could not move. I was paralysed…"

He stopped talking and stared wide-eyed at his empty glass.

I got up, went to the fridge, retrieved his vodka and orange, and poured him another hefty concoction.

He took the glass immediately and shakily raised it to his lips, swallowing another mighty glug.

I tried to reassure him by saying that it was just a bad dream, and had no connection to real life. It was only his mind animating his deepest fears. I told him that I bet his father and brother were just fine, in a military hospital in Russia somewhere, just as a precaution should things go awry.

What he said next was far from what I expected.

"That is only part of the nightmare. They are okay, for the moment."

"What do you mean, have you spoken to them?"

He took another swig of vodka. "Let me explain. After my dream, I had a shower, put my sheets in the washing machine, and then re-made my bed. I fixed myself a drink, and then I phoned Sergei. It was three o'clock in the morning, but I just needed to talk to someone."

Sergei was Nikolay's partner. They'd been together three and half years and seemed suited. I'd met Sergei on several occasions; he was effervescent and fun to be around, but also being a surgeon, he had a serious side.

Sergei's father was English, and his mother was Latvian. He grew up in Latvia on the family farm, until he was seventeen, and then he moved to England to study medicine.

Right now, he was back in his homeland, attending his mother's funeral. It was said that she died of a broken heart due to his father also passing away less than a year ago from a gruesome tractor accident.

The farm was vast, employed fifteen staff members, and bordered Russia. It was known locally as the English farm. Yet apart from his sisters, nobody there now spoke of a word of the Queen's own.

Sergei had two sisters, who had both married second-generation Russians, and both of them had three children each. All the adults worked on the farm, so the obvious thing to do was to let them run it. Not being Sergei's bag, he hadn't decided on whether to sell his shares in it or just take a cut of the profits. It would be a decision he'd make before returning to the UK.

Being an English-owned farm next to the Russian border had never been a problem in the past, but what with recent developments, Latvia being a part of NATO, and having Russian descendants owning it; things were a little jittery and not so black-and-white.

Sergei was asleep in his old bedroom when Nikolay called, but surprisingly calm at having been wrenched from his slumber. He listened patiently to his partner's tale and then suggested that he could contact a friend, code-named 'The Fox', in Khimki, who ran a dark-web chat room throughout Russia and the Baltic states. It was a site where many gay men found companionship, especially those from the military where homosexuality is increasingly frowned upon under Putin's traditionalist dominion.

The encryptions used by the site made ID tracing very difficult, and so far its users had remained anonymous. The Fox had put up a message which read, 'has anyone seen Dr's Maxim and Dmitri Plotnikov? I want to thank them both for saving my life.'

It was in the hope that someone in the army would see it, and respond.

Nikolay paused, closed his eyes to compose himself, took a couple of deep breaths, and then continued.

"Two hours ago, Sergei phoned me back. The Fox had been in contact. A user of the site codenamed The Scalpel had left a message saying that my father and brother were still at the hospital they worked in. This guy works there too, as a nurse. He was able to tell us that both of them were carrying out their usual routine, seeing patients and performing operations. But under constant guard wherever they went, even to the toilet, a guard would escort them. They were also chauffeured to and from work accompanied by security. So it would be impossible to pass a message on to them. Also, The Scalpel wouldn't be returning to work for three weeks because he had contracted Covid 19."

I could tell from my friend's body language that there was more to come. He emptied his tall glass and stared at me, searching for a reaction. I had nothing to offer him.

"You haven't sussed it yet, Abel, have you?"

His tone was low in register and sombre.

I shook my head.

"Why would two of Russia's leading oncologists have such a tight security detail around them? My father and brother aren't a threat to anyone. Quite the opposite, they save lives."

With a large clunk, the penny finally dropped. I needed just one word, "Putin… You think Putin's got cancer?"

He cocked his head to one side in the affirmative.

"It doesn't quite make sense to me, Nik'. If Putin's got cancer, why let his oncologists go about their daily routine? Surely he'd want them at his house, at his beck and call."

"You are wrong, my friend. Putin is no fool. He knows it is better to have Russia's leading physicians practising in the oncology department, rather than have them biting their nails under house arrest. That would definitely expose his secret."

This was massive. If Putin did have cancer, depending on the type, of course, and at what stage, and it became public knowledge, it would change the whole course of the war in Ukraine. And stabilize the fear on the world stage.

"What does Sergei think you should do?"

"He told me to talk to you, my oldest friend here in the UK; he said you'd know what to do."

I don't know what made him think I was qualified for that role. I knew nothing of Russian state security, little of Russian politics, and even less about diagnosing fatal diseases. But, there were six other medical students in the house, and one of them was another oncologist.

"I reckon we should have a house meeting. You should tell everyone the whole story. Let them brainstorm it and see what they come up with. They're all clever people."

Nikolay hadn't eaten all day. He had no appetite. But vodka wasn't going to sustain him. So I made him an offer. If he could eat the remaining half of my fish supper that was in the oven, I would arrange for the entire household to come together tomorrow night for a meal and a discussion on the possible state of Putin's health.

He agreed. So while he retrieved a plate and the food from the oven, I buttered him a couple of slices of bread and sliced up a lemon. What was left of my meal would have to be heated up in the microwave.

We talked some more while we ate, mostly about Sergei's family farm. It was one of the largest in Latvia, with fifty per cent of it covered in ancient woodland. They roamed British White Park cows in the forests, an old hardy breed that will eat almost anything.

It is estimated that forty per cent of Latvia is still established forest, and as a true conservationist, I was eager to visit the country one day.

As I was getting ready for bed that night, despite the planet being on the edge of a possible third world war, I had to chuckle to myself. Putin's excuse for starting this war was that he didn't want the UN on his doorstep, seeing that Ukraine had applied for membership. But a little bit of England runs not twenty miles from his borders in the Baltic.

2

My best friend, Charles, and I have been rowing double sculls since university. This year, we had decided, will be our last.

Charles was expanding his firm of solicitors, and I have been working twelve or fourteen-hour days of late. So, finding time for our hobby was becoming increasingly difficult.

Having decided to finally hang up our oars, we wanted to go out on a high and try to win a trophy at this year's Henley regatta. This meant putting in some serious practice sessions on the river.

Hence, we found ourselves shivering our nuts off at eight in the morning, carrying our scull down to the frosted, slippery jetty in front of the boat club.

The coldest day of the year so far had created a quintessential winter scene, ice dusted, glinting in the places that were touched by the early sun. Vapour rising from the river, warmer than the air above and dormant vegetation, suspended in a deep freeze.

The Thames was a mill pond today. No other craft were mad enough to venture out, and it seemed to me sacrilegious to be disturbing the peace with the racket we were making, sliding back and forth in our seats, the oars clanking in the rigger, the blades cutting through the water and the strained noises from the sheer effort.

As coots honked their disgust and ducks took flight from our path, it seemed immoral to be cutting through their world uninvited, violently smashing through the environment. But unlike the Russian insurgents, we weren't leaving a trail of death in our wake, just ripples that quickly dissipated into the river's calm equilibrium.

We weren't practising for the race right now, just strength-building and perfecting our timing. After rowing for two miles upstream, we turned about and repeated the exercise back to the club.

It was a mighty strenuous workout; we were steaming by the end of it, like a couple of red deer in the rut. But, I was going to miss these early mornings out on the river. On a glorious day, there was nowhere else I'd rather be.

We hosed down our scull, locked it up in the boat house and stowed away our gear. By now, fellow rowers, canoeists, and river enthusiasts were turning up. The frost had all but gone, and the low sun was turning a cold start into a rather pleasant day.

Charles was taking an important call, so I just waved him goodbye before getting into my Volvo and starting the engine straight away. With the heater on full blast, I examined the coffee in my thermos flask. It was still half full, and thankfully still pretty warm.

While sipping the coffee, I checked my phone for messages. There was a text from Safira, and it wasn't good news.

A Russian missile had hit Arouna's Nan's apartment block, killing the woman, her neighbour and both of their little dogs. Understandably, Arouna was distraught.

Safira added that she needed some stuff for the meal tonight, and could I pick up some decent potatoes, two punnet of mushrooms and two tins of pineapple chunks from Lidl, on the way home?

She signed off as she always did with '*Amor y Besos*', love and kisses in Spanish.

I texted her back with deep condolences for Arouna, asking Safira to give her a hug from me, and of course, I would do the shopping.

However, I was a trillion, trillion times pissed off as to why I had to be sorry for Arouna's loss, when the man who had caused it walked around without conscience or scruples.

Charles had finished his phone call and was walking back to his Mercedes, parked alongside my car. He turned to say bye and caught an angry look on my face.

"You alright. Abe," he mouthed.

I wound my window down.

"Just a bit fucked off, mate."

I relayed Arouna's awful news back to him and vented my feelings toward Putin's unprincipled impunity.

Charles was upper-class, five years my senior, and had been, in many ways during our friendship, my mentor and guru, but I never expected this pearl of wisdom.

"Remember these words, Abel," he said, "Oligarchs, Shakespeare and one Russian can only take so much beetroot and vodka."

It was an odd statement.

"See you next week, old chum," he assured me, and then slid into his top-end motor to reverse out of the bay before I had a chance to digest his proverb. But he stopped before he took off, wound his window down and said, "thirty-seven thousand pounds."

I curled a lopsided smile. "You're getting there," I replied.

The reason for the offer originated at last year's Henley regatta. Charles and I had each bought fifty pounds worth of raffle tickets, the first prize of which was an oil painting depicting the regatta in Edwardian times, valued at fifty thousand. We both wanted it, of course, and by chance, which floored me, I bought the winning ticket.

He was envious from the start and offered me ten grand straight away. I refused, of course, as it was worth so much more, and he has been upping the ante, periodically, ever since. But he's still not there yet.

Charles has plenty of money. He has made a fortune in the conveyance of high-end property for the rich and famous, including as it happens, many Russian clients.

Once I had picked up the groceries from Lidl. I stopped at a florist and bought some yellow roses and blue delphiniums for Arouna. Then I drove to a reclaim unit in a retail park, which sold used furniture.

I was looking for a set of oak bookshelves for my room, but they didn't have any. What I did spot, however, was an assistant putting together a set of adult bunk beds, which according to the chap, could also be used separately, as singles.

They were priced at a very reasonable hundred and eighty pounds, and looked brand new. The plastic was still on the mattresses. So I took a chance and bought them for Arouna's mum and sister for when they eventually arrived.

The whole kit fit into the back of my Volvo with the tailgate open, so I could take them home straight away.

The gift would serve two purposes. One, she wouldn't have to worry about sorting bedding out herself, and two, setting it all up and rearranging her room would help to take her mind off what was happening in her own country for a short while.

By seven o'clock that night, Nikolay and I had rounded everyone up, and we were all seated around the kitchen table, enjoying our starter, a fiery bowl of patatas bravas.

Arouna was trying to eat and fight off the tears. She thanked us all for agreeing to let her mum and sister stay with us for a while, and especially me for buying the beds.

"We're all here for you," I said.

Jack added, "And for your country." Which, we were all quick to support.

Safira's mushroom risotto was something else, really creamy and smooth. I was hoping for seconds, but alas, it looked like so was everybody else.

Nikolay and I were sharing a bottle of Rioja; I was just topping up his glass when he gave me the nod. I nodded back.

The time was right to ask our wise group of student doctors for their valuable opinion.

I put my spoon down and stood up.

"My dear friends," I began, "Nikolay and I have concluded on a topic, but we would like a second opinion. Actually, it's more of a diagnosis we are after, one of which you guys are more than qualified to provide."

All six of them were staring at me, wondering what I was going to ask of them. I continued. "Would you all be willing, tonight, to put your professional heads together and help us out?"

They all made gestures as to say why not, none of them had pressing plans this evening, which was fortunate.

It was Nikolay's turn to stand. He went on to tell our housemates of the situation he was in and the determination he had made, all the while looking to me for reassurance.

The bottom line was, could they deduce whether the most hated man on the planet right now has cancer, based purely on circumstantial evidence?

I suggested that they all retire to the Raft, to debate the matter in full and try to arrive at a hypothesis.

Nikolay and I would bring in the desserts, which were lemon cheesecake, tinned pineapple and cream, coffee and brandy to follow.

I also volunteered to do all the washing up, which aroused a small round of applause and thanks.

The doctors wasted no time. When I brought in the desserts, they had already drawn up notes on a whiteboard, they all had their laptops engaged, notepads were drawn, and the conversation was laced with words that I did not understand.

I retired to the kitchen, washed some more dishes and then made the coffee, took that into them, and returned to my pot washing detail.

By the time I served the brandy, the vodka and the odd whiskey, and then went back and finished a third lot of washing up, two hours had passed. I poured myself a well-earned Napoleon from a bottle I had on the go, then went and joined my friends.

"Has the smoke gone up the chimney?" I asked, referring to the tradition following the appointment of a new Pope.

They all knew what I meant.

Beau, the most senior student doctor, took the floor, beside the whiteboard, crammed with incomprehensible jargon.

"Based on the evidence available to us, we believe that Putin has a seventy per cent chance of having lung cancer."

"Right…" I elongated the word. "So you're not convinced then?"

Beau gave a steely response, "Given that we don't have the man here to examine, this is all purely hypothetical, but all the indicators we've seen point in that direction."

"If we did have the man here," said Arouna coldly, "I'd ring his fucking neck."

Nikolay hung his head and stared at the floor.

To appease my analytical mind, I asked, "And what drove you to this conclusion?"

"Apart from the situation Nikolay's father and brother are being forced to accept," replied Beau, "we considered two other factors. One, Putin is sixty-nine, a non-smoker and a health freak. But he has had to endure a lifetime of secondary smoke from his cohorts, especially during the Soviet era. Russians are heavy smokers, around forty-three per cent of the population still smokes cigarettes. It was sixty per cent the year before, and cigarettes are cheap over there, about £1.10 a packet."

Nikolay acknowledged the fact with a nod.

I'd read about the new laws Putin had brought in, which banned anyone born after 2015 from buying cigarettes. The offence would be treated the same as buying illegal drugs. And, he outlawed anyone from smoking near or around him, making it an imprisonable offence. The paranoia must have been brought on by something.

Beau continued. "A life of continuing stress would compound his vulnerability to illness, the silent killer, weakening the body's immune system. He's under plenty of stress right now, and it is fully accepted now that stress and traumatic shock are major factors for kick-starting cancers."

Safira picked up the mantle. "Abel, this reckoning of seventy per cent would increase significantly if Putin went into hospital for a surgical procedure. And that would be hard to keep a secret. Too many people would witness the event: porters, anaesthetists, nurses etc. Nik', couldn't Sergei's spies find out a little bit more information on what's going on over there?"

"I'll call him tonight. I think that The Scalpel is going back to work on 17th March. He can do some discreet snooping from then on."

"Cool," she replied.

Victoria, the quietest member of the group, had her legs tucked under her on the couch. The light from her laptop screen illuminated her body a florescent blue. "If Putin is dying from lung cancer, the world needs to know," she said.

Jack agreed, "She's spot on if the Ruskies… No offence Nik'…"

Nikolay shook his head as if to say none taken.

"If the Russian people knew that their president was on his way out, he'd lose his status straight away. They wouldn't respect a weak leader."

"Absolutely," added Nikolay, "neither would the military. News like that would undermine his authority and cause an entire regime change, probably ending the war."

Safira was agitated. "We have to do something," she blurted.

"What us?" said Jack, "what can we do?"

"We can tell the world what we know!"

"But what do we know, really?" Jack waved his arm at the whiteboard. "This is just speculation."

Nikolay intervened, "My father will know the truth."

"Yes," said Arouna, "but if you can't get to speak to him, how the hell is he going to tell anyone? That's if he is willing to, because it will certainly put his and your family's life in danger."

Nikolay nodded solemnly, chewing the inside of his cheek.

Silence prevailed.

Lukas spoke first. "Obviously, your family needs to leave Russia, Nikolay, go into hiding."

"Yes!" blurted Safira, "Then, when they are safe and well, Doctor Plotnikov would be free to confirm our diagnosis.

"But where would they go?" Nikolay looked completely lost.

I stepped in. "Well, the way I see it is that we need more information. Perhaps this Scalpel and his friends can provide us with what we need. Then maybe, between us, we can come up with a plan to get Nikolay's family to safety. Because letting the world know that Putin is a dead man standing seems like an imperative thing to do."

Jack was sceptical. "Sorry, mate," he said to Nikolay, "I'd like to help, but aren't your dad and brother under armed guard? What can we do from here?"

Beau was even more pragmatic. "It hurts me to say this, but I feel useless too. I have no friends in Europe who could possibly help. If you could get your family back here though, I'd be willing to help with that."

The other four were more enthusiastic, especially Arouna, who had both Russian and Polish friends. Lukas had relatives in the Netherlands

Despite our two negative friends, we decided to give The Scalpel until the 24th of March to get back to us. In the meantime, we should pool all our resources to see if we could devise an escape route.

***

For the next two and a half weeks we ate in the Raft, eyes glued to the TV.

Every news channel was devoted to the events unfolding in Ukraine, and not much else. It was as if there was no other news, life on hold, the world teetering on the brink of total war.

Except for just a few, and China abstaining from comment, it seemed that most countries were releasing statements condemning Putin's actions. Sanction after sanction followed, freezing Russian assets, banning imports and exports, seizing Oligarchs foreign wealth, and choking the finances of Russia's war machine.

All of the major western companies pulled out of the country and closed down their franchises. Governments and corporations alike were cutting ties, in an attempt to sway the public away from Putin's rhetoric.

It was having some effect. Students were protesting in the streets and being arrested, and mothers of soldiers were posing questions to their local governments.

But with little consequence on the war front, the tanks kept rolling on, the missiles and shells kept falling, and civilians and soldiers were dying by the hundreds.

Each evening, after the news, we'd switch the TV off to debate the horrors we had witnessed. Arouna naturally was the most upset and animated. She was finding it hard to go to work and keep a rational head on her shoulders. But I admired how she was keeping it all together.

Nikolay too was under a lot of pressure. He had no excuses, nor could he come up with any reasoning for what his president was doing, only that these were the actions of a madman with impunity and a loaded gun.

Russia's minister for foreign affairs, Sergey Lavrov, and the leader of the Russian diplomatic mission to the UN, Vasily Nebenzya, were both arrogantly and emphatically in denial of any atrocity inflicted by the Russian military. That there was even a war going on at all; just a special military operation, to help the Ukrainian people cleanse themselves of the rise of Neo-Nazi militias, which were gaining strength and popularity, and had to be eradicated for the sake of national security.

But when the help you are offering consists of laying to waste villages in your path, murdering and raping civilians, bombing hospitals and schools, and killing pregnant women and children, then I think, the terminology of your campaign has to fall in line with war crimes and genocide.

The Russian public too was subjugated, misinformed and denied world media reports, given only the state TV's biased coverage and fabrication. When interviewed, the average Joe would either curse America or had little or no knowledge of what was actually going on in Ukraine.

But it seemed to us that, inevitably, it would be the Russian people who would decide the outcome of this war. Once the sanctions took hold, and the coffins started to pile up in their thousands for no gains whatsoever, disquiet, it was reasonable to believe, would begin and turn into a deafening roar that would roll over and flatten the lies and propaganda spouted by the federal government.

Nikolay had been in contact with Sergei regularly, and although he had no news yet on the well-being of his family, The Fox had reported on the first rumblings of discontentment and hostility brewing amongst the populace. Directed solely at Putin, expressly amongst those under the age of thirty, of whom the majority believed that the invasion of Ukraine was wrong.

The gay fraternity also, an element of society that has long since been persecuted by the communist party and beyond, were ready to stand up and rebel against Putin's governance.

The Fox described the state of Russia as being millions of tinderboxes, poised to explode. Even those closest to the president, his advisers, aides and oligarchs wanted to be rid of him. They knew it was a pointless war that Russia could never win. All it would take was to ignite those millions of tinderboxes was someone ballsy enough to strike a match.

***

Courage comes in many different forms. On the 14th of March, Russian journalist Marina Ovsyannikova, who worked for the main evening newscast called Vremya, on Channel One, appeared behind the news anchor, Ekaterina Andreeva, during a live broadcast, holding a placard which read, in a mixture of English and Russian, 'No war. Stop the war. Don't believe the propaganda. Here you are being lied to. Russians against war', and shouting, "Stop the war. No war!"

Which, of course, made international headlines and went viral on the internet. She was arrested, held without access to her lawyer, fined thirty-thousand rubles and later released.

We watched a clip of the heroic act on our evening news open-mouthed. Fully expecting this brave lady, whom it turned out was born in Odessa, to be bumped off or at least imprisoned for the rest of her life considering that Putin was handing out fifteen-year sentences for just saying the word war. But neither happened. Miraculously, she was let off with just a slap on the wrist.

The world and the Russian public were watching, and it was by far the wisest thing to do, as far as Putin was concerned, to play it down. What war? Nothing to see here!

What transpired next changed all eight of our lives irreversibly.

Lukas was the first to comment, "She reminds me of one of the White Rose students."

It was a term I was unfamiliar with, as so it seemed, was everyone else.

"Who?" said Safira.

"The White Rose, a German anti-Nazi group during World War II. Google it," he prompted.

In 1942, medical students from the University of Munich formed a group to discuss their opposition to the Nazi regime. They produced a series of leaflets expressing their beliefs under the name the White Rose, advocating passive resistance to the Nazi war machine.

The first leaflet concluded with the statement 'Do not forget that every nation deserves the government it endures'.

Six leaflets were published over eight months and were sent to prominent individuals across Munich, then, later distributed by hand. Followed by graffiti on buildings with slogans such as 'Down with Hitler' and 'Freedom'.

Three of the members, Hans and Sophie Scholl and Christoph Probst were caught throwing leaflets from the university windows on 18th February 1943. They were quickly tried, found guilty and by the 22nd, all astonishingly were beheaded.

In the months that followed, the rest of the group was rounded up, and two more members, Willi Graf and Alexander Schmorell were also executed.

The pathos in the room was so substantial I could practically feel it in my mouth.

The courage these young people displayed against the Third Reich was formidable. Naively implemented perhaps and with tragic consequences, but may have been the hidden voice of tens of thousands of German people had they been given the choice.

For the past three weeks, our group had been discussing ideas on what it would take for the Russian people to step up and overcome their fear of the despot in charge.

A catalyst may have just been presented to us via Google.

"Why don't we do that?" suggested Lukas.

"What, get ourselves executed?" Jack replied cynically.

Lukas frowned at him. "Print some anti-Putin leaflets. We don't have to distribute them. I bet The Fox and The Scalpel will know plenty of people who could do that. No, we just have to get them printed and out there somehow. It could start something."

"He has a point," said Safira. "If the Russian people were given the actual truth of what was happening in

Ukraine and notice of the ill health of their president, then many millions would turn against him."

Beau wasn't convinced; his face was contorted with concern, "And what if it comes back on us? The FSB has been known to carry out some dastardly deeds abroad. I'm not that keen to splash on some Novichok aftershave that's shoved through the letterbox."

"We would have to find a way to make our involvement untraceable," I said. "There must be ways."

"And who's going to pay for it?" asked Jack.

"We all will," said Arouna, "It can't cost that much if we all chip in."

"A leaflet campaign," said Lukas, "a war without death."

The debate went on for some hours. By bedtime, we had at least all decided to consider Lukas' proposal. We agreed in principle that we ought to be doing something.

3

So, the general consensus was if this war was to be ended as soon as possible, with the least amount of bloodshed and misery, Putin would have to be ousted.

Preferably, by his own people, because, if NATO and its western allies were seen as the aggressor, a huge chunk of Russian society would buy into the disinformation and poisoned rhetoric, that they were the ones suffering from unprovoked attacks, and back their autocrat president into total war.

The leaflet distribution seemed to me to be a drop in a hoodwinked ocean. Maybe opening Russian minds to the true realities of what was happening beyond their closed borders, and perhaps the dire health of their President, would enlighten a few young minds to the possibilities that they were being conned, and that a fresh government was the only answer to world stability. But I for one doubted it would change the indoctrinated minds of the older masses.

According to Nicolay, Russian people are weak and comfortable in their duped state of being. Happy with the bullshit fed to them by state media and have no real understanding of what a nuclear war would look like, or a realisation that it would be a mutually assured destruction war. So, they had no fear of the west's second strike capabilities if Putin did actually lose the plot and launch his ICBMs.

We stayed up late each night after work, in the Raft, discussing Russian politics, which I knew little of, and ways in which we might, as a small foreign group, be able to have some sort of influence on the outcome of the war.

Getting the Plotnikovs out of Russia was our immediate priority and would certainly strike a hefty personal blow for Putin, as well as being internationally embarrassing, but it wouldn't stop the war, just enrage the vertically challenged tyrant further.

Even if he were ousted, or happened to die, who would replace him? Someone from within the Kremlin who is just as bad? There seemed to be several candidates waiting in line.

The Prime Minister, for instance, Mikhail Mishustin, 56, an economist, was appointed by Putin in 2020, a position he accepted without a single person voting for him.

Sergei Sobyanin, the Mayor of Moscow, 64, a communist and anti-gay antagonist, has banned Pride marches in Moscow.

Sergei Shoigu, the Defence Minister, 67, a part of Putin's inner circle, is largely seen as the architect of the Ukrainian invasion.

Sergei Lavrov, the Foreign Affairs Minister, 74, is known to have just two objectives: to veto things for the greater glory of Russia and to take Americans down wherever possible. A member of the Obama administration once labelled him as 'nasty and acerbic'.

A glut of Sergei's, none of which were ideal alternatives.

We learnt that there were at least eight political parties represented in the lower house. Putin didn't belong to any of them; he was an independent, in his own party.

All the other parties were, of course, theatrically in opposition, carefully managed soft opposition and most of them conveniently pro-war. The largest of which is the conservative party, Yedinaya Rossiya (United Russia), which held three hundred and twenty-five of the four hundred and fifty seats in the State Duma.

This lot is led by Nationalist Dmitry Medvedev, the former president and prime minister, who came from the same city as Putin, St Petersburg.

It is stated that he resigned as president in 2012, to allow Putin to make significant, sweeping constitutional changes. Notably, amending the presidential term limits in 2020, from a cap of just two terms to an additional six, effectively giving Putin the job for life.

However, the newspaper *Kommersant*, reported that it was Putin who had sacked Medvedev, and that the resignation was not voluntary but forced; since these changes give power to the president to dissolve the government without explanation or motivation.

Putin also signed a bill in 2020, giving lifetime prosecution immunity to all ex-presidents, covering his arse nicely.

The biggest threat to Putin's presidency came in 2018, when the Liberal Democrat party of Russia, led by former businessman, Sergei Furgal, won many state-wide and local elections, gaining a majority in the Legislative Duma of Khabarovsk Krai, the City Duma of Khabarovsk, the City Duma of Komsomolsk-on-Amur, and two seats in the State Duma in 2019.

Furgal was elected Governor of Khabarovsk Krai in a landslide victory, gaining 69.57 per cent. His win was largely attributed to an anti-establishment sentiment shared on both the left and right of the political spectrums. According to the Moscow Times, "Protest-minded voters in the region back then were ready to vote for anyone who'd defeat the candidate backed by the regime." Putin had personally backed the incumbent, Vyacheslav Shport, so Furgal's refusal to quit the race was seen as unforgivable.

He was arrested in July 2020 on charges of involvement in multiple murders of several businessmen in the region and nearby territories in 2004 and 2005. He could face life in prison if convicted. Furgal has denied all the allegations, which date back to the period when he worked as a businessman with interests ranging from imports of consumer goods to timber and metals before he launched his political career.

After the 1991 Soviet collapse, Russia plunged into violent turf battles between rival criminal clans for control over business assets, and contract murders of businessmen were a regular occurrence during the 1990s and the early 2000s.

Alexander Khinshtein, the head of the information and communications committee in the lower house of parliament, said Russian law enforcement agencies had long been aware of Furgal's alleged criminal connections. "I'm not surprised about his arrest. I'm just surprised that it happened so late," he tweeted.

Furgal's supporters believe the arrests are purely politically motivated. Furgal was too much of a threat to Putin's stronghold over the country.

The LDPR is now run by the ultra-nationalist, right-wing conservative, Leonid Slutsky, and unsurprisingly is pro-war.

According to what we understood, none of the puppet opposition parties in Russia had the will or the strength to stand up to Putin and, right now, since the invasion of Ukraine began, powerful and prominent people, some in charge of large corporations with plenty of capital to raise any sort of political crusade, are dying under mysterious circumstances. Suicide seems to be the favourable cause of death, with fifteen 'do it yourself' individuals at this point in time.

Lukas posed an unexpected question. "How difficult do you think it would be to form a new political party, Nik'?"

The Russian's eyes widened, he inhaled and stiffened his back. "I've no idea, Luk, but I know some people who probably would."

Arouna gave them both an incredulous look, "Who's gonna be stupid enough to do that? You may as well just put a target on your back."

Her tone was curt and dismissive.

Beau, forever the analytical, most cerebral amongst us, washed away Arouna's ungracious assertion, with an expansion on Lukas' enquiry.

"What if, hypothetically, a clandestine party could be formed outside of Russia, and recruit members in secret, ready to stand up against Putin when the time was right?"

The cogs in my mind started to whir. "That sort of thing would have to be super stealthy. There are eyes and ears everywhere, and communication could never be electronic. Sorry to put a downer on it, but something like that would take years to evolve."

"Not necessarily," proffered Nikolay, looking like a man holding all the cards.

"What do you know?" asked Jack, smiling suspiciously.

"There's a meeting held twice a week in a damp rundown chapel in Harrow, Middlesex. It's run by a brother and sister, Andrei and Milana Fyodorov. They are activists in exile who oppose Putin vehemently. Both their parents rot in Russian prisons for standing up for their political rights. They would know how to create a new political party, and who to have in it."

Safira shot out an outstretched, palm-up, arm towards Nikolay. "There you go," she said. "Let's get involved with that!"

"Hold on a minute," I said, gathering my thoughts. "How many people attend these meetings, Nik'?"

"I've been there a couple of times. Maybe thirty or forty people go regularly. It's interesting stuff, things you'll never hear on the news. Andrei and Milana are excellent speakers, and they are both fluent in English."

"Surely they are both known to the Russian government?" said Jack.

"Of course, but they are over here, talking to a small gathering of ex-pats, nothing for the Kremlin to get excited about."

The room fell silent for a moment.
Then Jack spoke up again. "This is all way above our heads. We're medical students. We know nothing about politics, especially Russian politics…"

"Well I know a little," interrupted Nikolay, "and that's why I suggested the Fyodorovs. They certainly know what they are talking about."

Victoria, always the quietest one in the house, cut in, "I know Harrow quite well, didn't realise there was a Russian community there though, but I haven't been back in a while. What if we all go to one of their meetings, listen to what they have to say, and maybe put forward the idea of them forming an underground political party?"

The girls were all nodding in agreement.

It took a little time, but eventually, we arrived on a date which we could all make, a week on Sunday.

***

Nestled between two houses of an endless line of 1930s built semi-detached properties, stood a forlorn, red brick chapel, long since used as a Methodist place of worship. It was now almost solely used as a makeshift Russian Orthodox Church.

It was a narrow building of two stories, with a couple of front-facing Lancet arched windows and an entrance to the right-hand side with a wooden door, much in need of a coat of paint.

We arrived in two cars, my Volvo and Jack's camper van. Parking was a nightmare along Eastcote Lane. Every household, it seemed, owned at least four cars, so we were forced to find separate spots down a side road and walk back to the chapel.

It was a cold elephant-grey afternoon, with solid low clouds, a bitter north wind and light rain in the air, the type that was not heavy enough for intermittent window wiper speed to cope with, but annoying.

As planned, we had missed the morning service. Most of us weren't religious anyway, and we could do without the tedium.

Andrei and Milana were expecting us, and waiting just inside the entrance, where the old radiators were at least giving off some flimsy heat, making a stark temperature contrast to the bleak dankness outside. I immediately unzipped my walking jacket and unwound my woollen scarf.

They greeted Nikolay first, both of them kissing him on his cheeks, the rest of us more formally with a handshake. When they got to Arouna, an exchange in Russian took place. It appeared amicable; they then kissed each other just as they had with Nik'.

Milana, I was informed was twenty-nine and her brother thirty-two. She was very attractive, had long, blonde, straight hair, with a centre parting, full lips, apple cheeks, thin eyebrows and steel-grey seductive eyes.

Andrei, however, could have come from different stock. His face was typically Slavic, oval, with narrow hazel eyes, a pale complexion and a pointy little chin. But, his smile was disarmingly warm, and he seemed overly happy to have us there, supporting their group.

"Come be seated," he said, gesturing towards vacant pews in the centre of the chapel. "Our talk is just about to begin."

The Fyodorovs filed to the front. My friends filed past me to their seats. "You speak Russian?" I said to Arouna as she passed.

"Most of us do." She shrugged. "Mine is a bi-lingual country."

The talk went on for half an hour, in both Russian and English, for our benefit, I surmised. They spoke of their disgust for Vladimir Putin, the shame he has brought down on all Russian people, the way he has crippled the motherland, ruined the economy, chiselled the constitution to his own needs and, through mindless jingoism and outdated nationalism, has made the country the most hated Rogue State in the world. And not even a peer competitor, just a failed state with few friends.

According to Milana and Andrei, Putin's regime was decaying and his reign depended on the Ukrainian outcome. The political elite would not stand for too many failures. Many of them desire change; they want to jump off the ensuing inevitable train wreck. The military hierarchy is sticking with him now, as is his inner circle, but rumours were rife of discontent within the lower house of parliament, and the Fyodorovs were intent on capitalizing on this.

It was just what we wanted to hear. After the applause from the small gathering of mostly young Russians habiting west London for a multitude of reasons, Milana and Andrei made their way through the handshakes towards us.

Nikolay patted Andrei on the back. "*Khoroshaya rech, molodtsy*," he said. Which I gathered meant, "Good speech, well done."

Andrei reverted to English. "We have to spread the word. In no way does Putin represent the opinion of the entire Russian population. Millions of ordinary Russians despise what he is doing to our country. We want change, not war; we want peace, economic growth and international trade deals, not this totalitarian, despotic nationalism crap. Nobody wants to live behind a fucking iron curtain again."

This was the fighting spirit needed for a new political party. I felt that now was a good time to approach the subject.

"How well are you connected to opposition groups active in Russia right now?"

Andrei's eyes contracted into mere slits. "Are you FSS?"

My face dropped. He meant the Federal Security Service.

"What? No, I plant trees," I said innocently.

Andrei laughed. "I'm just kidding. Forgive my sense of humour. We Russians are naturally suspicious."

His mood switched again to an accusing one. "You're here to infiltrate our group, yes?"

He laughed again; he was like Jekyll and Hyde.

Milana stepped in. "Stop it, Andrei." She turned to me. "He's such a prankster, thinks he's funny. Why do you ask, Abel?"

"Well, I think I can speak for every one of us here." I gestured towards my friends. "When I say that we are shocked and appalled by what is happening in Ukraine, to the people of Ukraine, Arouna's family directly, and also what is happening with Nikolay's family in Moscow. You know their predicament?"

Milana nodded solemnly.

I continued. "Well, we have spent many nights watching TV, absorbing all of the misery, discussing the grief and trying to come up with a way to help end it all as soon as possible, if at all possible…"

Safira interrupted my rambling. "We've come up with an idea," she blurted.

"Well, two ideas and an opinion, to be precise," added Beau.

"Yes," continued Safira, "three things…"

She went on to tell Milana and Andrei our theory on Putin's medical condition, about the proposed leaflet drop, and the concept of forming a new political party to counter Putin and eventually oust him at the next general election. The brother and sister shared an agreeable expression.

Andrei slanted his eyes once more,

"You honestly think that Putin has cancer?"

"It's a logical conclusion," replied Beau, "given that he has confiscated two of Russia's top oncologists to act as his personal physicians. Why else would he do that? And he's practically outlawed smoking."

"If this is true, our people need to know. They would not tolerate a weak man in charge," announced Andrei.

"Your leaflet drop could be a way of spreading the news," suggested Milana, "but you'd have to be certain of the facts. How are you going to secure a diagnosis?"

Nikolay stepped in. "By getting my family out and back here. Then we will know the truth."

"You have a plan to break them out of Russia!?"

"We do. It is imminent."

Milana scoffed, more out of shock than mockery.

"Well, good luck with that, my friend."

There was a pause, Milana inhaled deeply.

"So, you'd like to form a new Russian political party?" she said wide-eyed. "I don't wish to be condescending, and I really do appreciate your concern, but do you have any idea of what you are talking about? The cost alone would be astronomical."

"Besides," said Andrei, "to register a new political party in Russia, you would have to live there, be a resident for the past twenty-five years, and not have any foreign citizenship at all. You would need to be at least thirty-five years old, have fifty-thousand members in your party, fifty-thousand! You'd need five-hundred representatives in half the country's regions and a further two hundred and fifty members in the other half. I know. I've looked into it. This is not something you can do overnight."

Arouna spoke, "We have two years before the next general election in Russia. Surely all that can be done in the time available?"

"With whose money?" Andrei inclined a questioning nod.

"We have some money," I said, "not a lot, but it's a start."

"How much?" Andrei probed abruptly.

"Well, if I sell my painting to Charles, I reckon I'll get thirty-five thousand. We have five thousand in the kitty at the house for emergencies, and every one of us can put in a further thousand, which makes forty-seven thousand."

Milana was aghast. "I don't wish to be rude, but the magnitude of expense you can expect from forming a new party and running a campaign would run into the millions. Forty-seven thousand would not last a day!"

Beau rolled his eyes. Jack suppressed a laugh.

"Besides," added Milana, "Putin would not hold a general election that he had not previously rigged in advance. Standing up to him would be suicide, literally."

Andrei looked pained. "Not necessarily, sister. Russia's military, as we know, is self-deceiving, and so is the government. The decision-makers do not reflect reality; they just tell the Kremlin what they want to hear. Nobody takes the blame or the responsibility voluntarily. It's a house of cards built on deceit."

"This is not news," she responded.

"No, but, contrary to his recent incoherent rambling statements, his mad national addresses, and his self-justification for illegally invading a sovereign nation, unprovoked, Putin started this war for one reason alone, to win the next general election. He can not hope to win the popular vote based on his economic success, because the economy is shrinking along with his popularity. No, so if he can lie his way into making the people believe he is fighting to protect the motherland from a fascist uprising that will certainly infiltrate our country, then a win in Ukraine will definitely boost his legitimacy as the nation's leader."

This was an angle we hadn't heard until now.

I addressed the pair of them. "So, what you are saying is that Putin is quite weak right now, not just with his illness, but in his position, and growing weaker as each day passes without a win?"

"Yes," said Andrei, "his power is deteriorating."

"So, supposing he doesn't, in fact, die from his illness, and that his own government don't kick him out of office for ruining the country, and he makes no gains in Ukraine? A new political party could take advantage of all this, rise up and take over."

"In theory, yes, if he's weakened enough and loses the backing of his gangsters."

"So, the White Rose party could become a reality?"

"The who?" Milana enquired.

"Oh, it's the name we have given to the new party. Have you heard of the White Rose anti-Nazi party in Germany during the second world war?"

"No."

"A story for another day perhaps. The White Rose is the symbol of courage we have adopted."

"I like it," she said with a gladdening smile.

Beau spoke up again. "Hypothetically speaking, if we can find more money, would you be willing to help us find the right people in Russia to get the ball rolling on a new party?"

Milana shrugged. "Of course. We know some people, but as I said, you're going to need billionaire backing. You're going to need some like-minded oligarchs, but, bear in mind, those people are ruthless. They'll only put money into something with a profit at the end of it, or preferably some power."

We said our goodbyes and promised to be in touch, should we find funding. But deep in our hearts, I think we had all sunk a little lower this afternoon.

Outside, Jack was the first to speak. "Well, that's that fucked then. Know any multi-billionaires, anyone?"

"I don't," I replied, "but I know a man who does."

I texted Charles, telling him that I would be in his area tomorrow morning and wondered if he would like to meet up for a coffee? He pinged back straight away saying to come to the office; he'd have coffee and pastries waiting for when I arrived.

I then sent an email to my boss saying that I wasn't feeling too great and wouldn't be in tomorrow. He was fine with it. My assistant Michelle was more than competent to stand in for me at the drop of a hat.

4

Charles had invited me to his new premises in leafy Hampstead Heath many times. I never seemed to find the time to make the trip. I was always miles away, doing ultra-important conservation work or rehabilitating a tract of open land.

Today, however, I had put on a very different hat and forced a gap in my diary.

The grandeur of the white stone neoclassical Georgian mansion had both the taxi driver and me thinking we had the wrong address. Surely this building was far too plush for a solicitor.

But no, apparently not, this was Triant House, a gated, pristine property overlooking the misty but picturesque Hampstead Common, complete with joggers and arm-linked couples walking their dogs.

I viewed the ranks of cars which filled the lot. There was nothing here under an eighty-thousand-pound price tag, and every one of them was showroom clean.

It appeared that the lawyer game paid handsomely in these parts.

In-between a pair of fluted marble pillars, the gold glass doors opened automatically at my approach. Inside the red-carpeted reception, two terminally pretty young women smiled at me from behind a v-shaped, white marble block counter.

They were both blondes, had their hair tied up into high buns, wore bright red lipstick, and each was wearing a smart, white blouse. I couldn't see the bottom halves of the women, but I presumed they had legs.

"Good morning," they both said in unison.

I repaid the gesture. "Abel Llewellyn, to see Charles Pettifer."

The girls shot each other a glance. Evidently, my reputation had preceded me.

One of them rang it through.

As I waited for Charles to appear, I sat on a gilded, red cushioned, regency chair and admired the splendour of this once private residence's, hallway. Mostly it was clad in white marble, with gold fittings, red furnishings and amber glass. Conspicuously opulent, but it made a lavish first impression.

Charles sauntered down the expansive central staircase, gazing at the screen of his phone. He got to the mid-way landing, put his phone away and beckoned me to join him.

When I reached his position he said, "You don't have to sit in reception, Abe. Just come on up next time; we have a splendid lounge to languish in."

"I was admiring the fittings."

"I wouldn't say that within earshot, old boy. They'll have ya balls off!"

"Oh, the girls, no, umm, I did actually mean the décor, although your ladies are rather beautiful."

"They are cousins. Mellissa has worked for us for years, and Rebecca joined last year. It was their idea to dress alike; it brings a, um, quirkiness to all that ostentatious bling downstairs, and clients love it. They're very astute girls actually; it's a privilege to have them here."

"I bet."

We entered his office through glass doors, a wide room with a panoramic view of the common, decorated in the same livery as the foyer.

Charles stood facing out of the expansive window in his expensive suit, fists on hips, and awe in his eyes. "Look at that," he said delightedly. "Makes my nut-sack tighten every time."

"It's a splendid environment, Charles. Must have cost a packet?"

"I have very wealthy clients, mate. They like to pay a premium for a decent service."

"So I see," I said, nodding around the room.

Helen, Charles' PA, entered the room behind me, carrying a silver tray laden with coffee cups, a cafetiere, sugar bowl, milk jug and a plate of pastries. She'd been with the firm for a decade, and I knew her well.

I rushed to help her. "Morning, Helen. Here, let me take that off you. You alright?"

"Yes, Abe, couldn't be better. And you?"

"Mustn't grumble," I fabricated.

I placed the tray on Charles' enormous glass desk, and Helen did the honours.

When she left, Charles sat in his leather swivel chair, reclined, put his hands behind his head and said, "Forty-thousand."

"Done," I said.

"What?"

"I'd have taken thirty-five, but seeing as you are offering forty, I'll take that."

Charles feigned disappointment but soon had a grin on his smug chops.

"It'll look great on that wall, don't you think?"

He was pointing to a vacant patch above a long set of maple antique drawers.

I nodded, pouting my lower lip.

My friend was resting his chin on a thumb. "Is that all you've come for, old boy, to fleece me out of house and home for that old raffle prize?"

"Err, no, actually…" I locked my fingers together on my lap and inhaled a large one, before launching into the whole saga of what had transpired this last couple of weeks.

Charles listened intently, nodding now and again, occasionally sipping at his coffee, absorbed in my tale, soaking up every word.

My good friend will probably be one of the richest people in Britain someday; his passion and drive to succeed were second to none. I'd witnessed it many times, and I was about to witness it again.

Upon me finishing laying out my predicament, he was aghast. "Putin's got cancer?"

"So we believe."

"So, is he dying then?"

"Evidently not soon enough."

"These two activists, the Fyodorovs, are not eligible to front a political party?"

"No, you have to reside in Russia; they're over here in exile."

"But they know the right people who might?"

"They indicated as much, yes."

With that, Charles buzzed through to Helen. He asked her to do six things: Find out how much of a lease was left on the coffee shop. Bring two brochures of the coffee shop into his office. Ask George to bring the car around in half an hour. Find the caretaker of the coffee shop. Arrange a meeting with the three wise men for this afternoon, and lastly, when she came in, to take down my personal details.

I sat there blatantly bewildered.

"Let me explain," he said. "We help to manage, lease, rent, and look after, more than three hundred properties, mostly in London, but some around the country. We also help to sell them for clients, of course, but I think I've got the perfect headquarters for your new venture, and best of all, won't cost you a penny for at least a year."

My head was swimming, "Eh?"

Charles drove on at rally speed. "Money won't be a problem anyway from now on... I'll get to that in a minute... The Coffee House, to give it its official title, was leased to a consortium of African coffee growers for three years, whilst their offices in the city were being renovated. The work finished early, so they handed back the keys, a year before the lease was up. They paid for the full term naturally..."

"Hold on a minute, Charles. You're losing me. Are you saying you want to be a part of the White Rose party?"

"Not on your life, old boy. I'm no politician, but, what I gather from what you have told me makes perfect sense. Putin's gotta go; otherwise, this war's going to drag on for years. And a new party with modern, fresh ideals is just what that country needs. I'd like to help get it up and running, and I have the means to do it."

"It's a very dangerous game, Charles. Are you sure you want to get involved?"

"Oh, I'm not going to put my name on anything, just connect the dots. I've been itching to do something to help Ukraine ever since this thing began. God, we could be changing history here."

I nodded pensively. "You mentioned money not being a problem?"

"Yes, I did. The coffee shop is one thing, you'll see. It'll make an excellent headquarters for the time being…This all has to be done in secret, right?"

I nodded.

Charles smiled. "How exciting. Now, and this is the fortunate bit, we look after the properties of forty-seven Russian oligarchs, spread around the capital, Londongrad as it's affectionately known. The British government has brought sanctions upon these businessmen and impounded their houses. Luckily, they have entrusted the properties to us, to maintain until the war is resolved, and the dust settled."

"Okay." The word stretched from my lips like elastic.

"Well, we receive a small amount of money from the treasury, to hold the keys, but, and even though all their assets are supposed to be frozen, we still get maintenance money from the oligarchs. It comes from off-shore accounts, mostly in the Cayman islands."

"Charles, you're not doing anything illegal are you?"

"Not at all. Everything goes through the books. So far, the government hasn't been able to shut down those avenues of revenue because they don't belong to the people they have sanctioned. It's all very protracted. But guess what? What do you think all of these oligarchs have in common?"

"They're all loaded?"

"Absolutely they are, yes, but what else?"

I shrugged.

"They all fucking hate Putin!"

I screwed up my eyes. "What? All of them? Haven't they had their assets frozen because they are affiliated with the bloke?"

"That's the assumption of the British government because these guys have to keep cosy with the Kremlin to maintain their businesses. They have to be seen to support Putin. Otherwise, they cannot exist, and they certainly can't stand up to him. But in reality, they hate what he is doing to their country and the terrorization they have to endure. The idea you have just brokered to me will be like music to their ears. I reckon you'll get the backing of every one of them."

"Can they be trusted? Aren't they all gangsters, ruthless people, only in it for themselves?"

"Noooo, I mean, some of them might be, but they'll all want to get their assets back and their businesses operating again as soon as possible. They are losing fortunes every day this war carries on. So, if we can come up with a proposal to put to the government where each of the oligarchs donates anonymously, say, two million pounds to The Russian White Rose party, a party intent on deposing President Putin at the next general election, then I think it'll prove to our government whose side the businessmen are really on."

"Ninety-four million quid!?" I was gobsmacked.

"Well, minus our usual fifteen per cent conveyance fee, of course, so that'll be, err…"

Charles tapped onto his calculator, "…Eighty-one million, seven-hundred and thirty-nine thousand, plus change."

I was flabbergasted.

"You'll get over twelve million just for sorting this out? No wonder you're smiling."

"Well, the company will, but we've got bills to pay, rates, staff, you know."

"Bloody hell!" was all I could muster.

Helen came back into the office carrying the brochures Charles had asked for, and her iPad. "The caretaker's name at The Coffee House is James Knight, or Jim as he likes to be called."

"Ah, yes, Jim, I recall, a cheeky chappy," Charles declared.

"So I hear," responded Helen. "Quick with a witty comeback, apparently."

She took my full details down, along with two other names to act as signatories; I gave her Victoria's, who usually dealt with our house's finances and Beau's because he was the senior medical student. Helen would obtain their details later; I hoped they wouldn't mind me agreeing to this without consulting them first.

This infant of an idea was evolving fast and felt slightly like it was slipping out of my hands.

"The three wise men have all been informed of your need for their presence this afternoon, Charles. I said three o'clock. Does that suit your plans?"

"Perfectly, Helen. That'll be all for now."

She left the office.

"Who are these three wise blokes then Charles, mysterious gurus who pull all the strings?"

"Hardly. My accountant, my company director and my bank manager. They're all ex-Oxford boys and integral parts of our machine."

"I see. I look forward to meeting them."

Helen buzzed through. "George is out front waiting for you, Charles."

"Thank you; tell him we'll be down in a minute."

I'd known George for a long time. He was a proper gent who had rescued Charles and me on numerous occasions from parties or adrenalin-fuelled weekends, where we had been in a variety of states.

One parachute jump experience weekend, we shall never forget and neither will George, who still ribs me about it to this day.

Charles' Bentley Flying Spur was the epitome of a status symbol. Silver grey, with linen-coloured soft leather interior, it ran as smooth as silk and almost noiseless inside the hermetically sealed casing. A car doesn't make the man, but it sure made me feel special, sunk into the luxurious rear seat, afraid to touch anything without spoiling it, as we cruised the streets of London into the city and our destination, Haymarket.

Charles wanted to know a little more about the Fyodorovs, if they were the genuine article, if they could be trusted, and what their ambitions were.

All I could say was that Nikolay had recommended them and, as Charles knew, Nikolay did not suffer fools gladly. If he thought they were the right people for the job, he was probably right, but we can all be fooled.

Obviously, Charles wanted to be introduced to the pair, before any procedures were put into place and asked me to see if I could arrange a meeting for this coming Friday. I said I would find out.

The Haymarket is a one-way street and double yellow-lined on both sides of the road, but there is a loading bay outside the cinema, so George dropped us off there and then drove off to find a parking bay.

We hopped across the street and, after a short walk, came to the entrance to the Coffee House offices. They were above a restaurant which occupied the ground floor of a four-storey, cream-coloured Georgian building, that at one time may have been a townhouse.

Charles fingered the intercom button on the wall, which was swiftly answered by Jim Knight somewhere on the other side. Jim buzzed us in.

Immediately in front of us was the reception area, alabaster white and chrome, comfortable-looking black leather sofas and a chrome coffee table, but not much else.

There was a polished steel elevator door on the right-hand wall, a glass-panelled staircase on the left, and, I was told, toilets to the rear.

Jim, ambled down the stairs towards us in his blue security uniform, with a crooked smile and remnants of old acne scars that once pitted his cheery round face and neck.

My mind wandered back to a friend at school who had terrible acne. Bulbous pus-filled boils, which overwhelmed his appearance. The poor lad must have gone through hell every day.

But that affliction was definitely past tense for Jim, who appeared to be as happy as Larry.

"Morning, chaps. Better in than out!" he quipped, effortlessly bouncing down the treads.

"It is this morning, Jim, a bit sharp out there," answered Charles. He indicated towards me with his left arm. "This is Abel Llewellyn, a good friend of mine; he's come to view the premises."

"Right you are," said the caretaker. "Where do you want to start?"

This was all alien to me,

"Umm, all of it, I suppose."

"Well, nothing much more to see down here apart from the bogs. Do you wanna see those?"

"No, that's all right. We'll skip them."

"Follow me then; he chirped, turned on his heels and headed back up the way he had come.

The stairs terminated on the first floor with a large white marble square landing and more steel elevator doors on the opposite wall. A conference room spanned the front of the building and hosted a long smoked glass table and thirty chairs. Three small offices ran down the hall to our left, opposite a spacious staffroom and more toilets. All of the offices were walled with glass, partially screened halfway down with a silvery etched effect.

At the rear end of this floor, there were bi-folding doors which opened up onto a wide paved balcony and a polished timber staircase that angled down gently to a formal mature walled garden, ideal for lawn parties.

The second floor, accessible via the lift or emergency stairwell and decorated exactly the same as downstairs, had four larger offices and yet more toilets.

The third floor was one big room, with twenty workstations, partitioned off with portable screens, and yes, more toilets.

The penthouse, however, had two self-contained flats. A two-bedroom and a three-bedroom both fully furnished and decorated to a high standard, mostly in alabaster white but with beige carpets. White drape curtains and billowing nets encased the windows, giving the apartments a very colonial appearance. A pair of crossed elephant tusks on the wall wouldn't have seemed out of place in here.

Jim then took us back to the lift and down to the basement, where a fully fitted commercial kitchen lay dormant, a stainless-steel sleeping creature, dreaming of crepes Suzette and cheese soufflés.

At the end, tucked away in a corner, was the caretaker's little apartment, a one-bedroom affair. We didn't need to go in there. It was private, Jim's sanctuary.

There was also an emergency exit down here, leading to the garden, which in turn had another emergency exit to a side street.

It was Charles' policy to install a live-in caretaker on all of his big sites. Usually, ex-military people acted as security and maintenance men, and were a good deterrent for squatters should the building become vacant, such as this.

"What do you think?" asked Charles as we ventured out onto the Haymarket after the tour.

"Perfect." I smirked. "Any organisation would be chuffed to bits to have that handed to them on a plate. It's modern, luxurious, self-contained and smack bang in the middle of town, close to all the foreign embassies. I'm almost embarrassed to say yes, we'll take it."

"Well it's there for the taking, but we better see if these Fyodorovs are the real McCoy first. I'll get some people on it, and run some checks. I have faith in Nikolay, but it's best to be certain; we don't want to waste everyone's time."

"No, no, of course, this needs to be done right."

My mind was now ambiguous, was I racing ahead too fast and just grabbing the first Russians that came along shouting death to Putin. We needed assurances.

Charles got on his phone and called George back, and then Helen, who he asked to transfer fifty thousand pounds into my bank from his personal account.

When came off the phone I said, "You don't have to do that now. The White Rose party doesn't need my money if these oligarchs are going to cough up."

"It's not for the party. It's for the painting. You deserve it, old boy."

Charles also reminded me that we wouldn't be training this weekend. He had a wedding to go to in Scotland, a fine occasion to shake the dust off his old kilt.

With his knobbly knees, that wasn't going to be a pretty sight.

5

It was arranged to meet Milana and Andrei at Piccadilly underground station, at 6 p.m. Milana would come straight from work at Lidl in Harrow on the Bakerloo line. Andrei worked as a carpenter on stage sets in the West End, so he'd just get a cab.

Beau and I travelled in my car down the M40 into Uxbridge, parked up and then caught the tube directly into Piccadilly. Nikolay wanted to come, but we all agreed that the Fyodorovs were probably under observation, and therefore zero contact with Dr Plotnikov's son should be maintained, given the present circumstances.

It felt a little like being on some kind of espionage caper.

Milana looked resplendent in her full-length, mid-brown faux fur coat and matching Cossack hat, but it totally blew out of the water her alter ego of a typical British supermarket shelf stacker. She was undeniably Russian.

Andrei was the less overtly eastern block in appearance, donning a pair of patch pocket work-wear trousers and safety trainers. But his tan leather, Goose-down quilted jacket, however, was a dead giveaway.

Once we had acknowledged each other with a short nod, the Fyodorovs walked out of the station twenty metres ahead of us, down Haymarket to the restaurant below the Coffee House and went inside, as if they were having a meal there. Then, as had been prearranged with the management, were shown out the back door into the garden, met by Jim Knight and then escorted upstairs to the conference room, where Charles and his company director, Nigel Brookes, were waiting for us.

Beau and I used the front door.

With the introductions over, Milana lunged straight in. "So, Mr Pettifer, why are we here?"

I'd kept them in the dark about the entire purpose of our meeting this evening; I wanted it hidden under wraps as much as possible. Only saying that I had some mutually beneficial people that I wanted them to meet. Neither did I want it to appear like an interview for the job, just a mere meet and greet, with a meal thrown in, to test the waters and see what transpired. The restaurant was bringing up some food at seven o'clock.

"Please be seated," said Charles. An array of nibbles, wine and Vodka had already been spread down the centre of the big glass table at the near end.

I for one couldn't wait to dive in. I was starving.

Charles continued, "My good friend Abel and I go way back. We went to University together. We are like brothers…"

Milana's cobalt eyes flicked between us, measuring the situation.

"…On Monday, he came to my office in Hampstead with an audacious plan and a probing question. Did I possibly know any Russian billionaires who might be sympathetic to your cause and willing to back a new political party?"

Andrei's eyes rolled around the room. "This is not your office?"

"Oh, no, old boy. This is just a property we manage on behalf of its owner."

"Who is?"

"Anonymous."

Andrei shrugged, unfazed.

"And do you?" asked Milana.

"What, know a sympathetic oligarch?" Charles paused, rendered temporarily senseless by her beautiful face. "Yes, my dear, quite a few in fact, but I'll get to that in a moment."

Charles looked at his director. "Nigel?"

The director was in his fifties and had a round, ruddy face, a mop of curly salt and pepper hair and a busy walrus moustache. He placed both hands on the table in front of himself and swallowed hard.

"Let's be very clear from the start. We are a prestigious firm of solicitors. We handle transactions, conveyancing, brokerage and management of very exclusive properties, nothing else. And we are definitely not involved with politics, or political parties in any way, shape or form."

The Fyodorovs looked confused.

Nigel continued, "Having said that, we are in the business of making money, and when an opportunity presents itself, we are open to entertaining it if it falls within our specialised parameters."

Milana studied him intently. "Do you suppose to monetize the activities of our little group?"

"No, no, something altogether different. Tell me, how much support do have back home in Russia? Theoretically, if a new political party, a moderate, green party, the centre of the field and open to international cooperation, should arise in your country right now, with you two involved, how many people would support that?"

The brother and sister team exchanged disbelieving looks.

"Theoretically, it could be done," said Andrei. "But Putin will never let that happen. He snuffs out any inkling of opposition the moment it raises its head. The so-called opposition parties that exist in the lower house are a shame and all under his thumb. They're just there for show, to make believe the Kremlin is observing the constitution."

Nigel squinted. "But what if I tell you we have several clients, super-rich Oligarchs who are currently under sanction by the British government and totally pissed off with Putin and his ludicrous campaign, who are quite willing to fund a new political party that will oust the autocratic dwarf and bring some stability back to their country, along with the release of their fortunes?"

"We have been through this with Abel," said the Russian. "Neither of us can form nor head a new party. We do not reside in Russia."

Charles stepped in. "No, but you can structure a new party over here, procure party members in Russia, appoint a leader, someone who is of your mindset, who is right to premier your country. You probably have an ideal candidate in mind. We can get you the funding if you do the leg work. It can all be done in secret for the time being, but it'll be your names above the door. Our company will have nothing to do with that."

Milana frowned. "You do realise, to register a new party, we'd need at least fifty-thousand members, with at least five-hundred representatives in half of our country's regions and two-hundred and fifty in the remaining areas?"

Charles was wide-eyed. "I did not."

"Also," she continued, "prospective candidates from political parties that are not represented in the Duma must collect more than two-million signatures from supporters throughout the country, to be registered to run for president."

Nigel blew through his lips. "Doesn't make it easy, does he?"

"This is what we know," said Andrei.

By the look on Milana's face, she was obviously contemplating the cards on the table. There was a pregnant pause before she inhaled, and spoke again. "We have about two hundred and sixty sleeping agents in Russia, waiting for a call to action, good people, loyal to our cause. With their associates and some relatives, I believe we could muster up about a thousand representatives, who would go on the campaign trail, stirring up support. We think that the youth are on our side, students and the tech-savvy, people who have accessed the world's media…"

Andrei interrupted. "We also have three high-ranking ex-military personnel, who defected and are now living in the UK in exile. They come to our meetings twice a week. They know other officers still serving in the military who are sympathetic to our rhetoric, but they are scared to speak out against the regime for obvious reasons."

"This is true," said Milana, "If those serving officers had some reassurances, a political force with the power to challenge those bastards in the council of ministers, then they would join us as well."

"Don't forget the Rainbow vote," said Beau. "Nikolay assures us that the gay fraternity would back the White Rose party wholeheartedly."

"Absolutely. Homosexuality is being oppressed even more. By current estimations, there are around eight million gay people in Russia. That's a lot of votes."

Charles stood up. "Drink, anyone? I know I will."

"Da, about time." Andrei joked.

The Russian pair both took a large splash of vodka. Beau, Nigel and Charles each had a glass of red wine, whereas I opted for a dram of single malt, just the one though, a winter warmer. I had to drive back to Oxford later.

"Tell me," inquired Charles, "has anyone ever threatened Putin's position as president since he last took over?"

"Sergei Furgal," said Andrei, "once the leader of the LDPR, the liberal democrats. He's currently in jail on false murder charges. If convicted, he could face life in prison."

"Why do you say they are false charges?"

"Everyone knows Furgal is not a murderer. He has a medical degree. He's into saving people not killing them. He was proving too popular. In 2018 he was elected Governor of Khabarovsk Krai in a landslide victory. Putin had backed Furgal's opponent, Vyacheslav Shport, who didn't stand a chance. From then on, his party won some state-wide and local elections, gaining two seats in the State Duma. Putin got twitchy and had him arrested in July 2020. Tens of thousands of people protested in the streets, but little happened as a result. His arrest had nothing to do with murders; it was purely political, wiping out the opposition. Mikhail Degtyarev runs the LDPR now; he is an anti-American imperialist nationalist, who is pro-war in Ukraine, and an asshole."

I wondered when the food was arriving; I hadn't eaten anything in seven hours. I grabbed a handful of ready-salted crisps, popped a butterfly shrimp in my mouth and sat back down. It only served to make me hungrier.

Nigel went on. "Before we proceed any further, can we be clear on your policies?"

He looked at both Russians, shifting his eyes from one to another.

Milana spoke first. "We consider ourselves democratic environmentalists. We advocate free and fair elections, an open independent media, an end to human rights violations and endemic corruption."

"Yes," said Andrei. "Animal rights too. We want a greener, more sustainable ecology, an end to fossil fuel dependency and a turn towards carbon-zero emissions. We want more open borders, less secrecy and friendlier international trade deals."

"Quite frankly," added Milana, "the opposite of what Putin has today."

My attention was drawn to the elevator doors on the landing. They slid open noiselessly and out popped Jim, followed by three waiters, two girls and a boy, dressed in white shirts and black trousers. They each carried a silver tray containing two covered silver terrines.

Charles was enthused. "Ah, starters," he announced. "I hope you don't mind, but I took the liberty of ordering for everyone."

As long as it was edible, I didn't mind in the slightest. I was ravenous.

It turned out to be delightful. The restaurant downstairs was Italian and one with superb chefs it seemed. For starters we had a Caprese salad, some classic Bruschetta, half a dozen chicken and parmesan stuffed Portobello mushrooms, and a plate of roasted red pepper and caramelized onion Focaccia.

The mains were a simple choice. Charles had opted for just two dishes, Ragu Bolognese with Lasagne noodles, and a Porcini mushroom and white wine risotto. The garlic cheese bread that came with it was delicious, a meal in itself.

After the plates were cleared away, the question of accommodation was addressed.

Milana laughed, probably to mask her embarrassment; she and Andrei shared a one-bedroom flat above a Laundromat in Wealdstone. They'd been there for five years. It was cramped and poorly heated, but it was all they could afford. She made a pun, "If only Andrei would let me have the bed, I'd get a decent night's sleep."

I wasn't sure if she was actually joking.

Charles stood up again and filled everyone's glass, apart from mine; I abstained, with a large glug of Vodka.

"I believe," he said, "we believe, I think I'm right in saying, and I know it's early days, but, we think that you two, Milana and Andrei, are the best people to move the White Rose party towards fruition. But before I ask you to make a decision, I think that a tour is in order."

Milana puckered her face. "A tour?"

"Yes, of this auspicious building. You see, if you were to take on the responsibility of creating a new political party, one that would stop this war in Ukraine and fundamentally change history, then this property, including the two penthouse flats in the attic, would be yours to use rent-free for a year, essentially your new headquarters."

"*Ot'yebis'*," blurted Andrei, wryly astonished.

Milana shook her head disappointedly. "You can take the man out of Moscow…"

Charles smirked. "You would give us this building?"

"Well, the use of it for a year, by the end of which, we should hope, that you have set up your own facilities in your motherland."

Milana was astounded, she raised her hand in acceptance. "Lead on," she implored.

When the tour had finished and we were all back in the lobby, Andrei and Milana were both in tears. Undoubtedly in shock, this gift was way beyond their imagining yesterday, an opportunity they could not refuse.

Milana composed herself. "These businessmen that you represent, how much of a donation will they amount to?"

"Just shy of eighty-two million... Sterling," confirmed Nigel.

I don't think their eyes could have gotten any wider.

"It's in the White Rose bank account already," I added.

Milana's eyes actually got bigger. "There's a bank account?"

"Oh, yes. Beau, Victoria and I are all signatories. You and Andrei will be as well, of course. That way, none of us individually can run off with the money. Not that we'd want to run off with Russian oligarch money anyway, you know. I'm rather fond of my kneecaps and such..."

I paused mid-ramble; the Fyodorovs were questioning me with their eyebrows.

"...Anyway, it's all sorted. All you have to do is provide the bank with your details and sign a few papers."

Nigel interrupted, "Actually, there's quite a lot of paperwork to do. Our associates require a modicum of assurances, conditions, terms, that sort of thing. But, be assured, our company is here to guide you both through it all and make certain everything is legal and above board."

The brother and sister were obviously overwhelmed. They were lost for words. Eventually, Milana spoke, "Of course, we want to accept this fantastic opportunity, *spasibo*. We would be fools not to. It's just that it's a lot to take in, and I feel that Andrei and I need to talk about it privately."

"Absolutely," said Charles. "Go home, have a chat, take your time, and let us know after the weekend."

The Fyodorovs left the way they'd come in, via the back door. We gave them a twenty-minute head-start and then left by the front.

"Need a lift, lads?" Charles asked.

I gave it a stab. "If you are going anywhere near Uxbridge, then yeah, that'll be nice."

"Could do, I suppose. I'll call George. He's just around the corner."

***

Driving through Jericho on Monday evening, I passed a florist shop. It was just before five, and a lady was bringing in her front. It presented me with an idea.

Charles had called me earlier in the day, telling me that the Fyodorovs had accepted his generous offer and were moving into the two-bed apartment this week. They had both quit their jobs, but because it was short notice, we only thought it fair that the White Rose party should compensate their bosses with a donation of five hundred pounds each to help find replacements. This seemed to work adequately.

I parked my Volvo and hurried through the drizzle to the shop. It was dark and the suddenness of my approach made the unsuspecting florist jump out of her skin when I blurted, "Hello," from the shadows.

"Oh, my life," she responded, both hands on her chest.

"Sorry to startle you. I know you are packing up, but do you happen to have any white roses left?"

"No, sorry, we don't stock them as an everyday item. But I can get some for you. When would you want them for?"

I thought for a second. "Can they be delivered?"

"Yes, of course. Where to?"

"London."

"Oh, have to be Interflora for that. I can arrange it for you if you like?"

So she did. I asked for a dozen white roses to be delivered to the Coffee House on Friday. On the message card I wrote, "To Milana, Andrei and The White Rose Party, from the Oxford eight, God bless xxx."

It had been a while since I had bought flowers and the eighty-five pounds cost rather startled me. But still, I told myself it was the perfect gesture.

Because the owner of the shop had been so hospitable, and beyond her usual closing time, I took a couple of her business cards away with me, suggesting that there may be more business coming her way soon. You never know when you might need a florist.

Back at Lemon Grove, after another sumptuous meal expertly cooked by Safira, we converged in the Raft, as was now convention, to discuss our next moves.

My housemates were all still putting in twelve-hour shifts at the hospital and cramming in all the studying they could. So they each didn't have the spare time they'd like to put into the White Rose Party.

But for now, Beau and Victoria would handle the initial oversight of the finances, until an accounts department could be employed at headquarters. Charles' people would handle HMRC and Companies House.

Arouna, Lukas, Safira, Jack and his girlfriend, Agatha, were respectively going to set up websites in Ukrainian, German, Spanish and Swedish, for ex-pat Russians who want to see a change in the motherland, clandestinely join the party and, crucially, vote for The White Rose when the time was right.

As for Nikolay, he would be helping Milana and Andrei closely with policy writing and organising the leaflet content, the printing of it, and their distribution.

That left me to help with recruitment at Coffee House. I had more spare time than the others and was due some holiday anyway, so I couldn't see it as being a problem.

The following Friday, I took a trip up to London to see how the Fyodorovs were settling in. To my amazement, the place was a hive of activity.

Delivery guys were hauling in all manner of office equipment, boxes on sack-barrows, under their arms, in hands, an army of uniformed van drivers, taking stuff from the street into the building like soldier ants moving the colony.

Nobody questioned my entrance through the open doors, although, it seemed, a receptionist had been installed behind the front desk. She was too busy ushering couriers towards the elevator to even notice me.

I took the stairs to the lobby and found Andrei directing people like a traffic cop. The offices on this level were awash with people, tech guys installing computers and such, like BT Open Reach people upgrading the phone system. A chef in his whites shouted something in Russian along the hall near the kitchen.

Andrei spotted me. "Ah, Abel my friend, welcome to asylum."

"Kicked off already, have we?" I suddenly felt quite redundant.

"We are Russian. We like to rush in." A big smile creased his unshaven cheeks.

"Where did you find all these people?" I was referring to the apparent 'staff' that was occupying the various rooms, some glued to their phones, some rushing from office to office with bits of paper in their hands.

"They are my fellow countrymen, the future of Russia, but above all, they are our friends!" he bellowed.

I inhaled and looked about, nodding at the frantic scene. "Okay, okay." I smirked. I couldn't stop smiling. These guys weren't wasting any time.

"Where's Milana?" I said above the hubbub.

"She's upstairs, sorting her own office out. Go up," he urged.

I needed no encouragement and, seeing that the elevator was fully engaged, waded through the stockade of people towards the rear staircase.

The installation maelstrom hadn't reached the second floor yet. It was peaceful up here, in stark contrast to the tumult below.

Milana stood in one of the larger offices, her back to me, studying a large framed colour photograph of a young man dressed in black on a city street, brandishing a pole attached to a rippling white and blue flag above his head.

I thought she hadn't heard my approach, but surprised me by saying, "Does that look straight to you?"

I stopped mid-track and stared at it, trying to place the nation it represented. Nothing came to mind.

"Spot on. What country is it from?"

"Ours hopefully. It's a symbol of resistance. The current Russian tricolour is stained with blood, and it violates the principles of vexiollogy. Protesters around the world against the invasion of Ukraine are flying this flag in unity and presenting change."

"And the principles of vexiollogy are?"

She turned towards me, her gorgeous face compassionate to my ignorance, like a kind teacher to a very small child.

"When it comes to flags, there are two types of colours. Group one includes gold, yellow, silver, and white, while group two includes colours like red, blue, black, and green. On a well-designed flag, no two colours from the same group should touch; they should be separated by a colour from the other group. In Russia's flag, the blue and red stripes touch. We shall do away with that."

I melted into a blue and white puddle on the cream looped Berber carpet.

"Good, yes," was all I could muster.

Her grey velvet eyes temporarily shut me down, the briefest intrusion reached in and touched my soul. I was sampled. She blinked and broke the connection.

"The flowers, Abel, what a thoughtful gift. They are beautiful. You must thank everyone on my behalf."

"The least we could do," I said, coming to my senses. "Where did you put them?"

"Oh, they're up in my room. Jim Knight found me a vase from somewhere."

"I understand he is very resourceful."

"Yes, we're glad he is here."

"So," I said, "I've actually come down to help with recruitment, but I see you have that all in hand. Is there anything else I can do? I have all day."

"How are your designer skills?"

"Well, I'm not bad at drawing."

"Good," she said tersely. "Eventually, a white rose will be our symbol, of course, but for now, as you know, we are posing as an environmental group. Until the time is right and we have enough support that Putin and his tired old men won't crush our movement before it has begun."

"Right."

"So, I'd like you to make an emblem that would be, how do you say, right up your street, a Silver Birch tree, a magnificent tree, the national tree of Mother Russia."

"I could doodle up a draft, I suppose, but we'd need a professional image drawn by a graphic designer if we are going to use it as an emblem."

"Of course, of course," she said offhandedly. "And what about our manifesto, could you help me with that? I have some ideas, but maybe you can elaborate."

By the end of the afternoon, as people moved in and set up equipment around us, we had come up with an initial ten proposed mandates, should the White Rose Party win an election.

They were thus:

1. The immediate ceasefire of all hostilities in Ukraine.

2. The immediate withdrawal of all occupying forces from Ukraine, including Crimea and Transnistria.

3. Consideration for a long-term solution for all parties in the disputed areas of the Donbas region.

4. Immediate inquiry into the possible release of all political prisoners.

5. The immediate re-connection of all gas and oil pipelines supplying the West.

6. Re-instituting all previous international trade links before the Ukraine invasion, plus instigating talks with all foreign powers to embark on new trade deals.

7. A clear manifesto to show the Russian people how the White Rose Party intends to tackle climate change and reach net-zero greenhouse gas emissions by 2050.

8. To have clear and honest communication with the mothers of dead and missing soldiers from the Ukraine war.

9. Equal rights for all Russian citizens and an intolerance of discrimination, homophobia, racism, sexism and all other forms of bigotry.

10. An unreserved apology to Ukraine and its entire population, with financial packages and assistance to rebuild entirely the devastated villages, towns and cities.

It was a satisfying, if somewhat optimistic, document to help write. Yet, it was wholeheartedly Milana's resolution; to bring this policy to fruition should the party succeed.

So, I was in it now, a fully-fledged, committed participant. There was no turning away. I felt like a revolutionary.

"Do you want dinner?" she said when we had finished.

For a brief moment, I imagined she was going to knock up a Stroganov upstairs, a candle-lit meal for two perhaps, but what she meant was for us, and Andrei, to nip down to the Italian restaurant and grab a table. It was still a great idea. I was famished.

On the way out, we passed the Coffee House's white stone pillars on either side of the front door.

"We should have brass plaques made for both of these," I said, "with the Birch tree emblem on, and White Rose engraved beneath. That'll fool 'em."

"It fools me," remarked Andrei.

6

During the entirety of March, major cities in the north, east and south of Ukraine were under constant attack. We watched the news nightly, as horrific stories of death, siege and destruction spilt from the TV into the Raft, often in real-time, from intrepid reporters, from all the news channels, on the front lines and in key locations.

Hundreds of thousands of evacuees were heading west into Poland, Germany, Slovakia and Hungary, anywhere away from the killing. Heartbreaking stories of families being ripped apart as the women, children and the old sought refuge in safe countries, whilst the men and many young women stayed behind and took up arms to defend their homeland.

Civil defence units sprang up in all major cities and video footage of scores of people making thousands of Molotov cocktails abounded. It was the only weapon available to them at the time, but fight the aggressor they would, to the death if need be, and their resolute determination to repel the invaders was way beyond impressive.

With limited resources, the Ukrainian armed forces were fighting back and were having some success. A sixty-kilometre column of Russian vehicles, including tanks, armoured vehicles, artillery and some fifteen thousand troops heading for Kyiv, had stalled thirty kilometres from the capital, repelled by makeshift roadblocks, attacks from small hit-and-run units and Turkish-made drones. Also, there were reports of fuel and food shortages, bad planning and disorganisation.

In some areas, the concentration of vehicles was as thick as three abreast on the road but, thankfully, they were going nowhere. And a Major General, Andrei Sukhovetsky, was shot dead by a sniper as he ventured to the front to see what had stalled his convoy.

On the 21st of March during the battle of Sumy, a Russian airstrike damaged one of the ammonia tanks at the Sumykhimprom plant, contaminating land within a two-and-a-half kilometre radius, including the villages of Novoselytsya and Verkhnya Syrovatka. Due to the direction of the wind, the city of Sumy was largely unaffected despite its proximity to the leak.

Two days before the leak, Mikhail Mizintsev, the Chief of Russia's National Defence Management Centre, claimed that Ukrainian nationalists were plotting a false flag chemical attack in Sumy. Mizintsev alleged on the 19th of March that mines had been placed in chemical storage facilities at the plant to poison residents in case of Russian troop advancement into the city. He also alleged that a secondary school was similarly sabotaged in Kotlyarovo, Mykolaiv Oblast.

All bullshit and toxic propaganda, to blame the Ukrainians for Russia's appalling acts of terrorism. And the west was having none of it.

On that very day, Nikolay received a message from Sergei, saying that The Scalpel had made contact with Dmitri, Nikolay's brother. Who for some reason wasn't as guarded as his father.

The day before, The Scalpel had managed to slip a very small mobile phone to Dmitri. They'd had a conversation that night, and Nikolay was now relaying that discussion to us in the Raft.

On Saturday 18th December 2021, members of The Federal Protective Service arrived simultaneously at both Dmitri and Maxim's family homes, whereupon the families were put under house arrest and all communication devices to the outside world confiscated.

For what purpose, they had no idea at the time. However, the two oncologists were allowed to carry on with their regular work at the Federal hospital and the Blokhin cancer research centre in Moscow, albeit under heavy guard.

It soon became apparent to the doctors why the incarceration of their families and the stringent security had been forced upon them when Putin was brought into their care and theirs alone. His diagnosis was above top secret, for the sake of a successful military campaign, and the unity of the nation. If his condition became world news, it would end him.

The Scalpel would not elaborate anymore on the state of Putin's health but said that Nikolay's family were all well and safe at present time. He would be back in touch when he had more news.

***

Saturday, April 2nd. Yakhroma, Dmitroysky district, Moscow.

Veronika Sokolova, a delivery girl from a nearby bakery, squelched through the dirty sludge-strewn drive of Dr Plotnikov's country house, encumbered with a large cake box and twenty, inflated pink helium balloons, emblazoned with a number five.

It was little Mischa's birthday, Maxim's granddaughter. Ordinarily, the grandparents would have travelled to Dmitri's house to see their offspring, but today was a special day, a day that needed a garden and a lot more space than the younger doctor's cramped townhouse could offer.

It may have been just shy of eleven degrees Celsius outside, but the two FSO men hunkered in the front of their black Mercedes sedan may as well have been in a fridge. Despite being wrapped up in their thick woollen uniforms and quilted jackets, the men would shiver all night long.

The temperature was going to drop to minus five or six tonight, pretty cold for the time of year, and both of them were hating every boring minute of it.

The night shift was twelve intolerable hours of frozen torture. Forbidden to fall asleep, and only having each other for company, with overused anecdotes, old jokes and mundane gripes to listen to.

Yuri hated his fucking job, and after ten years in the service, Grigor was getting there too.

Their eyes followed the bakery girl and flinched as she slid on the snow melt and nearly dropped the cake.

"That wouldn't have been pretty," remarked Yuri.

"Nope, pretty funny though."

"You're a sadist; it could have ruined the little girl's birthday surprise."

Grigor squinted. "Why are they having the party here anyway? They normally drive into town on a Saturday."

"Nina's gout, it's got really bad apparently. Maxim has brought home a wheelchair from the hospital, just to move her around the house. They don't want to be travelling while she's like this."

"Humph," grunted Grigor. "Too much rich fucking food. That'll teach the overpaid arseholes."

"Now, now, the Plotnikovs do a fine fucking job, keeping our illustrious leader alive. They deserve a decent wage."

"Yeah, well fuck him as well; sticking us out here all fucking night. It's inhuman."

Yuri shook his head. If this car was bugged, his partner wouldn't have to endure many more nights in his comfy leather seat. He'd be thrown in a Gulag, or worse.

Anna arrived at half past five. Wheeling in a pink child's bicycle and a large bag-for-life, loaded with presents. It seemed little Mischa, was going to be thoroughly spoilt today.

A Kia Sportage drove in just before six, and parked close to the house. Out jumped the over-exuberant Mischa and her little brother Lev from the back seats, leisurely followed by their parents, Dmitri and his wife, Orina.

Yuri made a note of their arrival in his pocketbook, but it was nothing to get excited about.

Around seven, Maxim brought out two slices of cake for his security detail and a bottle of, top-quality, Beluga Gold Line Vodka.

The two FSO men nodded in surprised approval.

"Expensive stuff," affirmed Yuri.

"Well, it is a party after all," said the doctor. "And it's bloody freezing out here tonight. To your health, boys."

They raised their cake to him before he turned and walked back into the house. The sleeping pills he'd crushed into the cream filling would take effect within half an hour. Doubled with the vodka, they'd be out for the count all night.

Somewhere near the city morgue, Moscow region. Taldomskiy City District, Rabochiy Posyolok Zaprudnya, 24 kilometres away.

One of The Scalpel's contacts, who worked at the morgue, had 'borrowed' a van for the weekend on the pretence of using it to move some furniture.

It was common practice amongst the staff, better than hiring an expensive box wagon from Rentmotors. So nobody batted an eyelid.

The van was parked in a dark corner of a supermarket car park as requested, away from security cameras. The keys were on top of a rear tyre, under the wheel arch.

The Scalpel opened the back doors for a quick scan of its contents. The lad had done well, five new body bags on the deck, empty.

He'd have no trouble from the police driving the mortuary van around, even at this late hour. The insignia-written vehicles were used at all times of the day. It wouldn't raise any red flags.

One kilometre away, in the lot of a DIY store, The Fox was waiting for The Scalpel inside his estate car. Again, he'd been diligent that there were no CCTV cameras overlooking his position, and no street lights to highlight his activities.

As a ruse, his car was filled with painting and decorating tools and materials. On the roof rack, he had secured a pair of recently purchased Transforma ladders, which he had sprayed matt black two days ago. He'd also purchased a large dark green canvas ground sheet. This was still in its packaging on the passenger seat.

The Fox wasn't taking any chances in case he was filmed. He wore a builder's dust mask, a baseball cap and sunglasses. With Covid fears still prevalent, it wouldn't be unusual for someone to be taking precautions, especially ambulance drivers.

The pair had met on a few occasions before, but tonight wasn't a time for informal greetings and small talk. Tonight they were on a mission, a dangerous, ultra-secret one, and if they were caught it would be the end of their liberty, maybe even their lives.

Little was said; the ladders and the groundsheet went in the back of the van and were then covered over by the body bags.

Both men got in the van, The Scalpel at the wheel, and then departed towards Yakhroma.

The closest they could get to their target, without raising suspicion, was an open-sided hay barn, in a field a kilometre and a half away from the Plotnikov's house. Which meant a laborious trek across frozen rutted fields, bridging a muddy dyke, and cutting through a thick hedgerow, there and back again. But it was the only way they wouldn't be spotted by a nosy neighbour or a passing car.

The Fox and Scalpel changed into black army fatigues and applied black cam cream to their faces. This felt like a proper Special Forces type of gig, although neither of them had ever been in the military.

With just a slight crescent moon, offering the faintest of illumination, the pair followed the hedgerow south, keeping to it tight and as silently as they possibly could, encumbered with the ladders and the canvas sheet.

The Fox cursed the cold night air for exposing their laboured breath with ghostly vapour plumes. This could give away their position, should someone be out on this bitter night and look their way. But there was nothing they could do about it, just push on.

The Plotnikov home was fairly isolated, on the edge of town and it backed onto the farmland. When it was built in the eighties, the then owners had erected a three-metre wire fence around the perimeter, topped with V-shaped double brackets and barbed wire. They certainly took their security very seriously; it looked more like a prison fence than a garden boundary.

"Devil's rope," whispered The Scalpel.

"Huh?"

"That's what some people call barbed wire."

"Nasty stuff. That's why I bought the ground sheet. Someone is bound to get caught up in it."

The fence on this side was woven with brambles and ivy, and on the other, screened by a cropped conifer hedge. So the barrier was quite wide.

They both adjusted their ladders to form inverted L-shapes, then they placed one on either side of the fence, covering the bridging section with the ground sheet.

When it was secure, The Scalpel texted Dmitri on a burner phone he'd bought for the job. Dmitri had a similar phone.

If the security guards had been immobilised, Maxim was to bring the entire family to the fence where they would be helped over by The Fox, straddling the top.

They were all instructed to wear dark clothing and bring nothing with them, except their passports and their wallets.

The two children had been given sedatives and were being carried by the adults. The slightest noise from them would travel a distance in the still of the night, and they couldn't take any chances.

Dr Plotnikov's two Doberman Pinchers were also given sedatives to knock them out. It broke his heart having to leave them behind, but knew they could never be smuggled out of the country undetected. He hoped that they would go to a sanctuary and that some kind soul would take them on eventually. They were lovely dogs.

Dmitri held back, keeping an eye on the sleeping beauties out front from a bedroom window, until all the family had successfully scaled the perimeter, and then joined them in the field.

As quiet as ants, the adults took turns in carrying the children across the uneven open terrain, slipping, stumbling, and tripping at times.

A five- and a three-year-old can get mighty heavy after a short while and their rapid exit was proving to be an exhausting, nerve-wracking experience.

Maxim hated to be leaving the wonderful life he'd built over the past fifty-five years. His fulfilling job, their lovely house, their friends, their brilliant social life, they were running from oppressed tyranny into uncertainty. But they could no longer live under a gun. Here they were scared, paranoid and incarcerated, so it felt like they had no choice but to flee.

The thing that was crippling them the most about this desertion was the certain interrogation of their immediate family members left behind, here in Russia. They would, without a doubt, be picked up and questioned, which was wholly unfair.

Hopefully, as none of them knew anything at all about this escape, no harm would come to any of them.

At the van, the adult family members got into the body bags, the children went in with Orina and Nina. They were zipped up with just a small gap at the top of the bag for a breathing hole, and the bags were arranged together near the bulkhead to lessen the risk of being thrown around.

Truck stop, A108, outskirts of Klin, Klinsky District, Moscow Oblast. Ninety minutes later.

Sergei Stevens may have been a most respected ophthalmologist, but he was also a farmer's son and could drive anything you put in front of him since the age of fourteen. Including the vehicle he was stretched out in, snuggled up in a sleeping bag, in the compartment above the cab of his very own articulated lorry.

Seeing an artic parked up with a trailer full of livestock in this part of the world wasn't unusual. Neither was the name Stevens, emblazoned on the side of the truck.

Sergei's dad had been exporting cattle to Gorbatov, two hundred kilometres east of Moscow, for decades. They loved the White Parks for their robust nature and the ability to eat a very poor diet.

Earlier today, Sergei had transported twenty, two-year-old bullocks to a farm close to Nizhny Novgorod and replaced them with twenty, eight months old, Red Tambov's. These animals were good for both beef and milk production, and Stevens' farm would fatten them up for the market.

The cab swayed with every passing vehicle, like an adult in a cradle, he was being rocked to sleep.

Two hoots on a horn wrenched him from slumber. It was ten seventeen. They had arrived.

Sergei climbed out of the passenger door and walked halfway to the rear of his trailer, where he met for the first time his charges in this clandestine extradition. It was people smuggling, but for the good of the people.

They shook each other's eager hands and spoke rapidly in Russian. It was good to put faces to the telephone voices and the authors of so much covert text

Sergei suggested bringing them out of the side door of the van and along the near side. So they were less likely to be seen by passers-by.

It was dark, of course, but bright oncoming headlights might catch the unusual scene and alert the authorities.

The two partisans unzipped the body bags, talking gently all the while. Thankfully, the kids were still both asleep, but the adults were mightily pleased to be getting out of the immensely claustrophobic, uncomfortable bin liners. It was anyone's worst nightmare, lying prostrate on that cold metal floor, unable to shift position or comfort one another. Plus, most of them needed a pee.

Still, it had to be done, and now another cramped and stifling containment was to follow, but at least they would all be together in one space.

In the back of the trailer, the front third had been partitioned off with steel rails, to stop the cattle munching on a stack of fresh hay bales. They had plenty enough to eat and drink in troughs along the sides of the trailer.

Underneath the hay bales, Sergei had hidden a 6x4 ft garden shed, in which he'd stashed a supply of food, drinks, sleeping bags and blankets. There were also two bench seats and a chemical toilet behind a curtain. Things were going to get very impersonal and stuffy, so he'd also inserted a length of stench pipe through the roof of the shed ad hoc, and hidden that with further hay bales.

Whilst Sergei was in the process of removing concealing bales from the shed door, the Plotnikovs piled up at the curb and huddled together like a bleak rack of bowling pins, shivering uncontrollably, and keen to get in from the cold.

This was also the first moment Sergei had met his partner's family, which was not the way he had envisaged it to be. This was painful, unorthodox and full of constraining secrecy. For one, Nikolay had not informed them of his relationship with Sergei, only that he was a friend from university. He was not ready to come out to his parents yet. And now was not the right time.

A spot of improvisation was called for.

"Hi, hi, hi," Sergei feigned enthusiastically, "Come on up."

He helped the children and the ladies first. The men climbed on board themselves, and Sergei showed them their quarters.

"In the boxes under the seats, there is hot chocolate and coffee in thermos flasks, it should still be warm. There's juice, water and a little Vodka too."

Maxim shook Sergei firmly with both his hands. For a surgeon, his grip was phenomenal.

"It is beyond words, what you are doing for us, Sergei. I realise the consequences if we are caught. And I can't thank you enough."

Sergei was doing it, not just because it was the right thing to do, but for love. And although he could not reveal that reason at the moment, one day, it would all become clear.

Suddenly, The Scalpel appeared outside.

"I'm coming with you," he blurted.

"That's not part of the plan," relayed Sergei.

"I know. I apologise, but I can't go back to the hospital. It's too risky. The FSO will soon link me to Dmitri, and I'm too young to go to prison."

"What about the van?"

"The Fox will drop it back where I found it and get a friend to pick him up and take him to his car. He has work in the morning, at the café near Red Square."

Sergei sighed; it was more baggage than he'd bargained for. And he was unsure if the British would grant him asylum as well as the Plotnikovs. But he'd take him to Latvia and then see what could be done.

"Get in," he said tersely.

It was going to be an uncomfortable ten-hour trip to the border crossing at Terehova, but at least it wasn't cold inside the shed. The hay bales proved to be excellent insulation.

Anna, who was sitting on the floor, and using a blanket for a cushion, stared at The Scalpel. "Now you are part of the family," she said. "What do we call you? The Scalpel is a bit of a mouthful."

He smiled lopsidedly. "Scal'. You can call me Scal'." He was giving nothing away.

Maxim chuckled; he respected The Scalpel's bravery.

Sergei had given Dmitri a walkie-talkie so that he could update the family on their position from time to time and make sure they were okay. A long and stressful night lay ahead, and sleep was the best possible thing they could do, but try as they might, it just would not come to the men.

Importing livestock into Latvia from Russia was a regular occurrence. Stevens' farm had been doing it for decades, but the paperwork had to be correct. Each animal had its passport and would be individually inspected by a member of the State Border Guard.

Sergei only had twenty young bullocks on board, so normally this wouldn't take long. But as of 17th March, Latvia had banned private transport crossing its borders from all countries. Goods vehicles, however, were exempt, especially those carrying food. Seeing that this livestock had come from Russia meant that a more stringent than normal approach was being adhered to.

Sergei radioed Dmitri, "Approaching border."

"Roger," he replied. "Will it take long?"

"There is a queue of trucks waiting to get through, maybe fourteen in total. It could be a while, yes. They all have to be checked. Over."

"Roger. Only the kids are getting restless. I don't know how long I can keep them quiet. Over."

"Roger. Do you have any more sedatives? Over."

"Yes, but I don't want to give them any more. It could be dangerous. Over."

"Okay, just try and occupy them as best you can. We need complete silence once a border guard gets on board. And don't use the radio anymore until we are through, okay? Over."

"Roger, over and out."

It was now eight twenty-nine. Two carriageways of stacked-up lorries edged their way forward with the engines ticking over, as one at a time they were ushered to one side of the gated, six-lane border crossing, for inspection.

It was taking around twenty minutes per truck, and Sergei was getting listless and edgy through the lack of sleep. As he neared the front of the queue, the blood drained from his head. They were checking the interior of the trailers with sniffer dogs!

Looking for refugees no doubt.

Bollocks, he thought. The game's up. He could see himself being arrested and the Plotnikovs, after all the stress they'd been through last night, being denied entry.

The only hope they had was the cows. If they had defecated sufficiently, it might be enough to mask the smell of seven humans shitting themselves in the hay.

Sergei pulled up to the designated spot, where a guard beckoned him out of the cab. He climbed down and arched his back. It was good to get out of that tin can for a while.

"Greetings," he said to the guard. Who just nodded upwards in reply. He blatantly wasn't in a very good mood.

"Papers?" bid the guard.

Sergei reached back into the cab and retrieved the documents.

"They're all in order," he said, trying to remain cheerful.

The Misery flicked through the certification and then marched to the tail-end of the trailer, and ordered the tailgate to be lowered.

Sergei complied. The stench of the cow-pat splattered interior was overwhelming. The official climbed the ramp to where the stainless steel inner gate was holding back the wary young bullocks, whilst another guard circled the truck with a brown and white Springer Spaniel, on amphetamines apparently, neurotically sniffing the underside of the truck. The dog's tail wagged extraordinarily fast, threatening to make the animal airborne.

Inside the shed, the tension was corporeal. The adults were barely breathing, waiting for the sounds of discovery to crack their silence.

Mischa suddenly spoke, "Can we get out now, mummy? It's horrible in here."

Orina put a finger to her mouth and faintly shushed. "Remember our little game," she whispered. "If you keep quiet, you will get to fly in an aeroplane."

"I don't want to go in an aeroplane. I want my bike," complained the little girl.

"Shushhh," appealed both Dmitri and Maxim.

"I wanna go in a plane!" blurted Lev.

"Shush, little one, shush," pleaded Orina, wrapping the toddler in her arms to smother the noise.

Maxim raised and extended both arms; palms flat, he pushed the air down. "Everyone, quiet," he demanded in a whisper.

Again, they waited, ears on high alert for the expected sound of bales being removed from the door. All that could be heard was the faint throb of the engine and the rear doors being lowered.

Maxim closed his eyes and prayed. They must get through. To be sent back now would be deemed treason and certain imprisonment for all of them. He could not bear the thought of it.

"You've brought hay back with you? Don't you have hay on your farm?" enquired the sceptical guard.

"Novgorod grass, it's what these animals are raised on. It's better to wean them off it slowly than to just put them out to pasture on Latvian meadow. It's too rich and will give them colic," Sergei lied.

The guard eyed him suspiciously.

The cows were getting anxious, they began mooing and rearing up onto one another.

A truck pulled alongside Sergei's, brandishing a fertilizer company logo.

The sniffer dog raced over to it, followed unwittingly by his handler.

The guard on Sergei's truck squinted as if in pain, this next inspection was not going to be a pleasant one.

He handed Sergei back his papers and waved him on with a flick of his hand. They were in the clear.

Once in the cab and through the border gate, Sergei was straight on the radio to Dmitri.

"Latvia," he crackled on the other end.

The sound of cheering distorted the little speaker in Sergei's hand.

"When do we reach the farm?" asked Dmitri.

"Not too long, about an hour."

It was sweet relief to hear. Nina snuggled against her husband and smiled lightly. Things were going to be okay.

Instead of driving directly to the farm, Sergei branched off from the main road and headed down a single track, through a forest, to open land, where they had a huge covered silage store and some sheds where they kept farm vehicles.

There to meet him was his sister Pipene and her husband, Karol, with two cars.

Although it was Sunday, the farm still had workers on it, and you never could be too sure. The sight of a bunch of people exiting from the rear of the animal transporter would surely pique some interest and maybe arouse a Russian sympathiser.

But a couple of carloads of friends could just mean a gathering for Sunday lunch.

After warm greetings and a stretch of cramped limbs, the cars headed off to the farmhouse whilst Sergei, exhausted as he was, hauled the truck off to the cow sheds and deposited his jittery new herd into a pen strewn with fresh straw, food, water and a bit of tranquillity at last.

Inside the ancient stone farmhouse, the Plotnikovs and Scal' were introduced to Sergei's other sister, Stasya, her husband, Rurik, and a gaggle of small children.

Both of the Russian men were vehemently against the invasion of Ukraine and despised Putin with a passion, labelling him as an idiot who dwelled in the last century.

The entire household of adults knew of the escape plan in advance, but they were a tight unit and pledged to the cause. Nothing would slip from within these walls.

When Sergei arrived, all he wanted was to sleep, but Stasya made him eat with all the family, hot beetroot soup, Pelmeni dumplings in broth, and mountains of dark rye bread with homemade butter. After which, her brother sloped off to his room and collapsed unconscious on his bed.

During some deep conversation, one by one the Plotnikov family took it in turn to shower, or bath, and change into some new clothes that Pipene had bought for them. Not to the Moscow women's taste, of course, more farmer's daughter than a city dweller, but they were grateful all the same. They'd blend in better with their surroundings, and it was only temporary.

The travellers were deadbeat and in much need of a good night's sleep. Tomorrow was going to be intense, but that was another day.

They were shown to their rooms, apart from the unexpected Scal', who had to rough it on the couch.

Monday 4th April 8:33 a.m.

Sergei came in from the cold, entering the farmhouse kitchen via the back door and immediately appreciating the roaring fire in the hearth. It chased the chills from his bones like a shuddering spectre fleeing his spine.

He'd been to a nearby village, to pick up groceries and make a call on his burner phone to the British embassy in Riga.

The adult Plotnikovs and Scal' sat around the battered, hefty oak table, finishing a breakfast of porridge topped with berries, rye bread, hams and cheeses.

Pipene was entertaining the school of children on the couch and floor in front of the TV, broadcasting Dora the explorer, dubbed in Latvian. Most of them, including Mischa and Lev, had jam-smeared faces, which was heartwarming to see.

"How did you get on?" asked Maxim soberly.

"I was put through to a Third Secretary. After I told him I had Putin's private surgeons and their families with me, who want to seek asylum in the UK, he put me on hold while he spoke to his superior…"

"And?"

"The counsellor, Jerome Croft, came back himself. They are very anxious to meet you all as soon as possible." Sergei smiled. "They'll take you all in."

The husbands hugged their wives with glee. Those words brought tremendous relief.

"Even me?" inquired Scal' timidly.

"Even you."

"Does he speak Russian?" asked Dmitri.

"I don't know, but there's certain to be interpreters, I'm sure."

Maxim was nodding. "And what time are we to meet?"

"Ten o'clock today. The embassy is sending two unmarked cars to a rendezvous by the fishing lake at Cirma. It's about thirty-five kilometres from here. There is a bait shop on the shoreline, with a large car park. It's out of the season, of course, so it's unlikely anyone else will be there."

"Will you take us there?" asked Orina.

"Pipene and Karol have offered. I want to remain unknown for now."

Vaguely unsure of how this was going to pan out, Nina asked, "Will we ever see you again, Sergei?"

"I'll make damn sure of it," he affirmed.

The lake would be a beautiful spot in the summer and probably very busy, but right now it was desolate, windswept and partially frozen. The family huddled on a couple of benches, trying to stave off the cold. Wrapped in colourful padded jackets, bobble hats, scarves and mittens, they looked like tourists who had picked the wrong destination.

Bang on 10 o'clock, an Audi estate car and a VW SUV rolled onto the hard-standing in front of them and came to a halt.

A young woman in her mid-twenties got out of the Audi, wearing jeans and a three-quarter-length white cashmere coat.

She approached the teeth-chattering family. "Dr Plotnikov?"

Both Dmitri and Maxim nodded.

She smiled. "This way, please." She indicated towards the cars with a sideways nod.

Without any more prompts, the frozen family launched themselves at the waiting warm cars. Dmitri and his lot went in the SUV, the rest in the Audi.

It was a three-hour trip to Riga; little was said along the way. Each adult stared out the windows, as an unfamiliar landscape rolled by, lost in their thoughts, hoping they had done the right thing, wondering what was to become of them.

Both surgeons had moved their savings into Swiss bank accounts some time ago in anticipation of something like this. They each had a little cash with them, not too much, just enough to get by for a couple of weeks.

They knew all of their assets were lost, material things that could be regained, but all of that stuff was easily worth the exchange for freedom.

The Ambassador, Andrew Pillsbury, an unassuming, white-haired man in his early sixties, received them in his office, accompanied by Jerome Croft, a guy who looked like he'd lived a charmed life, not a sign of stress whatsoever. They came in via the back door and were ushered straight upstairs.

The building was typically grandiose, internally ornate and plush. And for all that was going on in the world, the atmosphere inside was paradoxically tranquil and reserved.

The woman in the white coat led them in.

"Ah, welcome, welcome," said Pillsbury. "Do any of you speak English?"

"A little," replied Maxim.

"Well, it's a good job we have Anja here to interpret because my Russian stinks. She speaks nine languages, you know."

"Impressive," said Maxim, nodding at the woman boasting a sweet smile.

"Would you all like something to drink, tea, coffee, squash? You must all be parched?"

The drinks order was given and brought through by another member of staff. It was certainly needed.

The conversation continued in both languages.

"I had a conversation with the Home Secretary this morning," said Pillsbury. "It seems that H.M. Government is perfectly willing to accept you all in without exception. Might be a few questions fired your way though. I expect that given your close association with Mr Putin, the chaps at Thames House think they could benefit from a little intel'."

"No doubt," said Maxim. "And we would be happy to assist in any way we can."

As long as the women and children were excused from any drilling by MI5, then Maxim, Dmitri and The Scalpel would be pleased to divulge anything they wanted to know. They had already accepted that the British security services would be extremely interested in their involvement with the President. And anything that could help to bring Putin down would be in their favour.

Pillsbury looked content with that answer. "We have a plane waiting on the tarmac at Lidosta for you; it's scheduled to leave four-thirty. There's plenty of time to get you on it. No need to go through the front door. It's all been arranged. There's even a meal on board, I believe."

"We are overwhelmed, truly, Ambassador," said Maxim, "but I wonder if it is at all possible, could I get a message through to my son, saying that we are coming to England? He lives in Oxford and has no idea that we have escaped."

"By all means, you can call him directly from here. This is a secure line. We'll also send a car to pick him up and bring him to meet you at Brize Norton. It's not that far from Oxford."

And so it was arranged. Nikolay was ecstatic, but not surprised to hear from his father. Sergei had already let him know via the chat line, albeit in code, 'Operation Bag, a complete success'.

The plane landed at RAF Brize Norton at five thirty-three GMT. Nikolay was waiting in the arrivals lounge of the main terminal. He'd arrived there a short time before, having been picked up by two airmen in an unmarked Vauxhall Insignia.

I was still at work when he departed, but Safira and Victoria waved him off from our porch doorway. They said he was anxious, excited, yet strangely stoic, like a sleeping beehive, as Safira put it.

With their passes, the RAF guys were let straight through the main gate and up to the terminal building, where one of them accompanied Nikolay into arrivals.

There he was met by an MI5 operative, who briefed him on the current situation.

His family were due to arrive imminently. The women and children were to be taken to an area where they could freshen up, settle the children, rest and later be interviewed, whilst the men would be questioned straight away by home office personnel.

The Home Secretary, Estelle Silverman, had rescheduled her afternoon to welcome the Plotnikovs into the British asylum system in person, flanked by several home office employees and besuited security staff.

The interview itself was an abridged version, a formality in essence.

By now, the British government knew all too well who the Plotnikovs were, and what high value.

They wouldn't be denied refugee status; their application would be fast-tracked and done in secret. They would be given a safe house to live in, complete with security service protection in exchange for some juicy titbits, of course.

As for The Scalpel, he would be rewarded with a new identity, a place to stay and a job if he wanted it, perhaps for the new political party being set up in the capital.

Eventually, after a two-hour wait on a big brown leather chair, Nikolay was ushered into a smaller lounge, where his entire family were waiting.

The outpouring of emotion was heart-wrenching for those who witnessed it. The relief in Nikolay's body was visible.

He went first to his father and mother hugging each of them in turn like he would break their backs, kissing them on both cheeks. Then Dmitri and his sister, Anna, followed by Orina and lastly The Scalpel, whom he grabbed by the hand and then drew him in close for a tight man-hug. "Thank you, my friend," he said, "you have saved their lives."

The children, who did not know him, were still in a state of confusion, subdued and wary. Their uncle crouched down in front of them and spoke softly, introducing himself and adding, welcome to Britain. They continued to look bewildered.

To his father, Nikolay simply said, "Is it true?"

Maxim said nothing, but the slight twitch of his head gave Nikolay all he needed to know.

The family were left to their own devices for a further hour, after which the same MI5 agent who met Nikolay in the terminal came to get him. It was time to go home.

He would see them again in a matter of days, after they had settled into their new surroundings. There were more questions to be asked by the British intelligence service, but that was only to be expected.

For now, Nikolay was just content to have them here on English soil, in safe hands.

We threw a party, of course. With all the abject horror going on in the world, the success of Operation Bag was the only good news story to come out of Russia in years.

The Kremlin would have known about the Plotnikov's disappearance within twelve hours of their escape, but as yet, had not released any acknowledgement of the defection, or that anyone had gone missing at all, let alone Putin's oncologists.

It was Friday 8th of April; we were all in the Raft, beers in hand, expectantly waiting for the six o'clock news to start on the TV.

Maxim and Dmitri were due to make an appearance, live on the show, from a secret location. The BBC was making a massive thing of it.

By now the whole world knew of the Plotnikovs daring escape from the grips of tyranny, but nobody knew how they'd done it, or who had aided them across the border. Their whereabouts were an unknown factor. Most guesses were the USA, but in actuality, they were in a safe house in Surrey.

The CIA was desperate to get their hands on the doctors, but they were being kept at bay by protocol until MI5 had gleaned all that was knowable from them.

Even Nikolay didn't know what his father and brother were going to say on air, but he figured it wouldn't be too incriminating.

As it happened, a solicitor read out a statement, whilst the two doctors sat on either side of him, behind a desk in a brightly lit hall, impassive and unreadable.

The statement read: First and foremost, we would like to thank the British government for granting us asylum. Without this, our family would be stateless people.

We are also indebted to the countries and people who aided in our escape from internment and oppression in the country of our birth, a situation that we could never have imagined would ever be conceivable.

The people who have helped us are, in our opinion, superheroes and we will forever be in their debt.

The solicitor went on to say that it was now common knowledge that both doctors Plotnikov were President Putin's exclusive physicians, but are bound by doctor-patient confidentiality, and therefore cannot comment on the welfare or the condition of their charge.

He finished by saying that the Plotnikovs will stay in England until it is safe to return to Russia with impunity.

Once the statement was over, the programme returned to the studio, where the presenter asked the resident TV doctor her opinion on the broadcast. She simply said, "You don't have two of the finest oncologists in Russia to take care of an ingrown toenail."

Nods from several other medical professionals in the studio registered their agreement.

***

Whilst Operation Bag was in progress, the White Rose party had been busy.

Activating their sleeping agents, who, together with their network of supporters, had managed to distribute one million of the first leaflets from the new party.

Printed in secret and at enormous risk to the small press which carried out the print run, they read:

Putin is destroying your country, stealing your freedom and returning Russia to the dark ages of imperialistic oppression and subjugation.

Your sons, brothers and fathers are being killed in a senseless war waged on familiar Slavic soil, our kin murdered by a ruthless, selfish regime.

Your country is now the most hated failed state in the world, the economy is spiralling into the dirt, international trade has ceased, foreign investment retreated, and global franchises have gone.

The shops will soon be empty, and hunger and famine will follow.

On top of this, Putin is terminally ill with cancer, a corrupt weak leader, hell bent on a legacy of rubble, ash and burning embers.
Rise, citizens of Russia. It is time for a change.
The White Rose Party.
Democratic, Environmental, and Ethical are coming.

7

By the 7th of April, Russian troops deployed to the northern front by the Eastern Military District, pulled back from the Kyiv offensive, apparently to resupply and then redeploy to the Donbas region, in order to reinforce the renewed invasion of south-eastern Ukraine.

The Kyiv, Chernihiv and Sumy regions were now free of the Russian invaders and in the wake of the retreating divisions, atrocities were being revealed in village after village.

At least twenty dead Ukrainian civilians were seen in the streets by news reporters in the hamlet of Bucha and, according to the village's mayor, two hundred and eighty bodies were found buried in mass graves. Human Rights Watch reported war crimes all over the occupied areas of Ukraine, including executions, rape, torture, and looting.

Kharkiv was under Russian control, as was the southern city of Kherson.

The strategically important port city of Mariupol was under siege, bombarded by the Black Sea Fleet and attacked by thousands of Marines; it was rapidly becoming a city of rubble.

Only three pockets of resistance were left in the city and they were completely encircled. What units remained of the 36th Separate Marine Brigade, and the ragtag Azov regiment, who were mostly made up of volunteers, foreign fighters and local militia, retreated to the underground, nuclear bombproof, tunnel complex of the Azovstal Steel Works.

A third pocket was centred in the Illich steel plant in the north.

Long-range bombers and advancing tank and artillery rounds were pummelling Azovstal to powder yet still, the Ukrainian resistance held out, led by Lieutenant Colonel Denys Prokopenko. An estimated eight-hundred embattled troops vowed to fight to the death to hold this important land bridge, from falling into Russian hands.

Military experts estimated their chances of survival to be not more than three days.

Putin's war of attrition escalated on civilian targets. Hospitals, schools, playgrounds and residential buildings were all, in his eyes, legitimate targets. On the 8th of April, a train station at Kramatorsk was hit by a Russian rocket strike, killing at least fifty-seven people and wounding a hundred and nine others. The governor of the Donetsk region said thousands of people had been at the station at the time.

New graves with dozens of Ukrainian civilians were found in the village of Buzova, near Kyiv, that for weeks had been occupied by Russian forces. And on the 10th of April, it was reported that Dnipro Airport, as well as the infrastructure around it, had completely destroyed by Russian shelling.

I had been listening to the news in my ear pods as I travelled in the back of a black London cab. It was another deplorable war story, one of countless many that I was worryingly getting desensitized to.

I pulled out my ear pods; I'd had enough gloom for a Sunday morning.

Being in the back of a black cab, for me, has a timeless, nostalgic feel to it, no matter how much the cars are modernised. And, I have found, has its benefits too. A big city black-cab driver always knows what is going on, and when asked, will give you chapter and verse about it.

I questioned the cabby on whether he'd taken any passengers to the Russian White Rose party headquarters before.

His eyes flicked at me in the rearview mirror.

"You're the first," he chirped. "I've been past it a few times and wondered what was going on. Them blue and white flags fluttering outside are a bit of a mystery. And what's with all the flowers outside? Someone die there?"

I smiled. "No, not at all. They're white roses. It's an outpouring of sympathy from supporters of the party. It has been formed to counter President Putin, oust him from power if possible, and end this terrible war."

"Oh, I see, an anti-war mob. That's alright with me then. Me an' the boys were only talking about it this morning on the rank, the suffering them poor Ukraine people are going through. I wish I could do more, only I'm too old and fat to be any use on the front line."

"You could hand out a few leaflets."

I went on to explain what we were doing with the leaflet drop.

"You got some on ya?" he asked.

"Yes, I always carry a few with me, just in case someone's interested."

I retrieved a handful from my man-bag and placed them on the seat beside me.

"There you go. I'll leave them there."

"Smashing. I'll 'and 'em out."

We'd arrived in Haymarket. I pulled out a twenty-pound note to pay him, but he refused it, saying that I should put it to good use with the party. But I assured him we had plenty of money and pushed the twenty into his hand, saying have a cup of tea with the boys on me. He surrendered, nodded and said, "Alright, have a great day, mate."

I intended to.

I stood on the pavement facing HQ, astounded by the sheer number of flowers that had been laid there recently, right next to the front door.

White roses, as I had discovered for myself, weren't cheap, and the pile of them left here had grown substantially since I was last in the Haymarket.

It was a justifying and humbling experience, to feel the solidarity.

I also noted that the brass plaques had been fitted to the porch pillars, bearing the party name and the Silver Birch emblem. It was good to see that Andrei had chosen a decent engraver to make and install them.

With an air of pride at being a part of this rapidly growing movement, I entered the building high on life and with spring on my mind.

Strangely, there wasn't anybody in reception. In fact, it was mausoleum quiet, but then again it was a Sunday.

I tentatively ventured up the stairs, straining my ears for the least bit of sound. There was nothing, just the labour of my own breathing.

I was now on tenterhooks. Had assassins been in and wiped everybody out?

My imagination grew, and I stepped as quietly as I could, just in case the gunmen were still in the building, men in black fatigues, silenced guns at the ready, waiting for me to appear around the corner, followed by a sledgehammer thud to the chest and then blackness.

Reaching the last step before the foyer, I stopped and listened again. There it was, a faint rumble of unintelligible audio. Somewhere a TV was broadcasting.

Gingerly stepping up and into the foyer, I fully expected to see bodies strewn across the furniture and blood splattered up the walls, but again nothing. The room was clean as a whistle.

As I progressed into the hall, the TV volume increased. It was coming from the floor above.

Still cautious, but bolstered by the lack of corpses, I wandered down the hall and up the rear staircase, the news channel getting louder all the while. When I reached the landing, all became clear; everyone was crammed into Andrei's office watching a live stream on a sixty-inch screen on his wall.

Jim Knight, The Scalpel, six members of staff, plus the two new security guys, had joined Andrei and Milana and were all transfixed by the telly.

If I had been an assassin stealthily ascending the back stairs, I'd have had carte blanche.

The channel was showing people being dragged from a parked car, handcuffed and frogmarched to a waiting Russian black police van.

Even without the scrolling dialogue, I knew what I was witnessing. And to be honest, I was a bit pissed off, having predicted a few days ago that this would happen.

Standing in the doorway, I caught Milana's attention. She noticed my annoyance and beckoned me in.

"They've arrested Oleg, Grisha and Nadia at the Georgian border."

I silently nodded, keeping my eyes on the TV.

"It broke first on Telegram, then CCN got a hold of it, and now it's everywhere."

I turned to face her. "What's the Kremlin saying?"

"Usual bullshit, that three leading activists were caught trying to smuggle secret government information out of the country. Utter crap!"

Andrei joined in, "They said it would endanger the Russian State, ha! They had no such thing with them."

"We knew it had gone wrong yesterday evening," continued Milana, "when we lost contact with them. The private jet we had chartered in Kutaisi airport waited six hours on the tarmac before it had to leave."

Everyone in the room knew how devastating to the party these arrests were. And if Putin gets his way, three more innocent politicians would be spending the next fifteen years in prison.

Without trying to sound smug, I said softly, "We should have waited until they were here before we announced the merger."

Milana sighed and gave me a thin-lipped response.

Oleg Stepanov was fifty-two, married with two children, a lawyer and ecologist, who, along with Grisha Tarasova and Nadia Guseva, founded The Green Russia party in 2012. With just four seats in the State parliament, the party are ranked a lowly ninth out of all the Russian parties.

But, because of the White Rose's status of being a non-registered party and since the Fyodorovs know the green party members from their activist days, very well, they were the obvious candidates to consider for a merger and keeping Oleg at the helm.

The two parties' ideologies were almost the same, so it made perfect sense. They had an established party with a charismatic, likeable leader. Were already campaigning for environmental rights in opposition to Putin's regime, aligned with new wealthy backers and had a force of young, eager activists, hell-bent on routing out the canker that was bringing the country to its knees.

The party leaders had spoken several times in the past week via Zoom calls and had agreed on all points that the two parties should become one, retaining The Russian White Rose Party as its name and Oleg as its leader. The paperwork just had to be autographed for the merger to take place and that's why the three Greens were on their way over.

A press release and a celebration had been arranged for tomorrow, in the garden at the rear of the house. Everything was in place; the invites had gone out, and the TV stations due to arrive first thing in the morning.

With their arrest, the whole shebang was now null and void. I could see Milana and Andrei were physically deflated.

"Why don't we take a break from the TV," I suggested. "Go relax in the conference room, have a drink, and think about our next moves?"

Two weary heads nodded in agreement.

The staff all had jobs to be getting with anyway. Scal', who had been recruited into the IT department, always had something to do.

Jim left with his two security guards to man the front desk and patrol the perimeter. I couldn't help but admire their smart new black uniforms; they almost looked like the Met police.

"Coffee, anyone?" I enquired.

"Vakaka for me," grunted Andrei. "I don't want to stay awake."

"Same for me," said Milana, "but you have whatever you want, darling. The kitchen staff are in."

I ventured down to the kitchen. They were busy preparing lunch. I didn't want to bother them, so went into the staffroom and used the coffee machine in there. It made a decent cappuccino.

My mind was backtracking over the might-have-been's. If only we could have got Oleg Stepanov over here.

The last Russian Presidential General Election in 2018 had eight candidates in the running. Only one incumbent remains in office, Boris Titov, from the Party of Growth. His party came 6th in the election with just 0.76 per cent of the vote, so he is of no significant threat to Putin. Of the rest, one has died under mysterious circumstances, and one has fled the country, exiled to Israel.

In retrospect, and obviously since this morning's arrests, we should have kept the merger a secret until it was formalised. I had argued the fact, but Oleg, being a man of intense morality, wanted no surreptitious activity to undermine his integrity. He liked everything to be above board and transparent. And look where that has got him.

The cattle truck method through Latvia was suggested but categorically turned down.

Milana received a call from reception; a delivery had arrived at the front door. She and Andrei came and found me. She knew what it was and wanted me to see it being unwrapped. She was more than excited; I wondered what it could be.

Jim was also down in reception; he helped the delivery guy bring it in on a sack barrow and then gave him a tenner tip.

Cutting through the cardboard with a penknife and then ripping off the bubble wrap, Jim revealed a spanking new, solid, light oak lectern.

It was a beautiful piece of craftsmanship, with a quatrefoil base, a slender cross-section stem and an angled rectangular book-rest, with a raised lip to stop papers falling off.

All we needed now was someone to stand behind it.

"Could you put it in the basement for now please, Jim?" asked Milana.

"Sure," he said. "Vanya here can give me a hand."

The two security men got one end each of the lectern and hauled it towards the elevator.

Milana, Andrei and I sauntered back up to the conference room.

We sat there swaying in our seats, each of us pondering the future, none of us talking, when in popped Jim with a tray of coffee and pastries.

"Elevenses," he proclaimed.

I for one was grateful for it; I hadn't eaten anything since six this morning.

He also placed four Sunday papers on the table, all of which had a front page which covered Oleg, Grisha and Nadia's arrests.

None of us felt like re-experiencing the tragedy just yet.

"They've arrested Oleg's wife as well, you know," mentioned Andrei. "Nobody can reach any of his family members."

I sighed. "Good God, this bloke leaves no stone unturned, does he?"

"Any threat…" said Milana, "then, thut!" She made the sound and the visual of a throat being cut.

Jim was tidying a display of roses in the window. Some of the blooms had gone over, and he was hooking them out.

"I'll get some fresh ones from downstairs and liven this lot up," he muttered.

No one paid him much attention. We were too consumed with our predicament.

I spoke first. "I think we should vote on it."

"On what, darling?" Milana seemed confused.

"Whether to go ahead with the press release tomorrow. Without the merger, what is the point?"

She took a breath to speak, but Jim interrupted.

"Sorry for earwigging, and I know it's none of my business, but, why don't one of you become like me, a caretaker, just until you can find a new leader, that is? Then at least you'll have something to announce to the press tomorrow."

I arched my eyebrows. "That's a perfectly good idea, Jim. What do you two think?"

The Fyodorovs spoke in their native tongue for some time. Crescendoing at one point with what sounded like an argument, before calming down and ending with a disgruntled Andrei.

"I will do it," announced Milana. "I am the eldest, fluent in six languages and a better speaker than him. I'm the obvious choice."

She had weaponized her conceit and Andrei had come out wounded.

However, three obstacles had to be overcome.

All of the party members, both here and in Russia, had to be in agreement with Milana's caretaker position.

Secondly, I now had an acceptance speech to write in less than twenty-seven hours. And thirdly, as Milana had just informed us, she didn't even own a decent dress, let alone a skirt, and her hair was a complete mess.

She looked alright to me.

I pondered the problem.

"Have you ever seen the film *Pretty Woman*? You know with Richard Gere and Julia Roberts?"

She gave me a withering look. "Of course, I have, Abel. Every girl has seen *Pretty Woman*. And every girl wants to be treated like Julia Roberts."

"Well, why don't you take one of the girls and one of the security guys and go shopping? I mean, this ain't Rodeo Drive, but there's plenty of decent clothes shops round here."

She smiled wickedly. "Are you going to be my Richard Gere?"

"Depends how you scrub up," I quipped.

Milana gave Jim and me a double take.

"Are all Englishmen as cheeky as this?"

Jim chuckled. "Not all of us, no. You've lucked out here."

Within a few hours, Milana had received the green light from party representatives in Russia and those still at liberty in the Green party. She was now unofficially the caretaker leader of both parties.

The atmosphere here, back at HQ, was electric. The staff were frantically making calls to let all who were attending tomorrow aware of the new circumstances.

Whilst Milana went shopping, Jim and I busied ourselves putting up posters for the event outside the building. And bunting and Russian flags out in the garden.

All was in order; the press release would take place at two o'clock Monday afternoon, 11th of April.

***

Tulips of every hue illuminated the flower beds of the Coffee House garden; great shiny blocks of wax-like colour had emerged in recent days, a sweetshop for the bees. Trees sporting white and pink blossoms arced above borders, fancy parasols soaking up the morning sun, and dappling the brick walls with floral silhouettes.

Some of the mature deciduous trees were already in leaf, whilst others still had tightly packed vibrant green buds. The early pollinators were busy at work, gathering a golden harvest, much needed for the emerging hives and colonies.

I adored this time of year, the awakening, life in the making. It energized me.

We'd had no rain for a few days, so the grass, recently cropped by the ever-attentive Jim, was perfect for hundreds of feet to trample over.

There were a few clouds in the sky, but nothing much to threaten an otherwise beautiful morning.

I'd taken another day off. My boss wasn't too pleased with me, but I couldn't miss this event. It was all-encompassing for me and my fellow housemates, several of whom would also be here.

Around a hundred media people were in attendance. A crescent of cameras edged the lawn and three hundred well-wishers, including politicians, and members of staff from various embassies, particularly the Russian embassy, filled the lawn.

MI5 most definitely had a presence, as did Homeland Security and the CIA.

Standing beside the vacant lectern, looking down from the patio, I could see Nikolay, Victoria and Beau in the crowd. The Plotnikov family wanted to come, but it was deemed too dangerous. They could watch the broadcast live on TV anyway.

With just minutes to go before Milana was due to make her speech, I returned to the house.

Our staff members were lining the walls and would follow their new caretaker leader outside, once she passed through.

Jim, Andrei and I waited in the lobby for Milana to pop out of the elevator in all her splendour.

The doors pinged and she emerged, chatting furiously with Ksenia, who'd been helping with her hair and makeup.

She was wearing a tight-fitting electric blue dress, with a plunging neckline and matching high-healed stilettos. Her blonde curls cascaded over her shoulders, and her makeup was subtle, just enough to accentuate her steel grey eyes and full lips.

The butterflies inside me took flight and left me breathless.

She stopped in front of me.

"Scrubbed up okay?" She teased.

"You look incredible," was all I could muster.

She leaned in and whispered a quote from Pretty Woman, "I appreciate this whole seduction thing you've got going on, but let me give you a tip: I'm a sure thing."

I nearly dissolved.

She sashayed off with us boys in her wake, carried along by her aroma.

"Is it warm out?" she said without looking back.

"About fourteen degrees," replied Jim.

"Practically summer in Moscow," she quipped.

As she passed each member of staff, they touched her lightly on the shoulder, letting her know they were all with her out there.

Milana Fyodorova, a supermarket shelf stacker, stepped out into temperate sunshine and the world's stage, having undergone the biggest career change in history.

8

Milana composed herself behind the lectern.

The crowd noise subsided to a hush.

She began. "I would first like to thank you all for being here today. Today is a momentous occasion. As you are fully aware, the leader of our party and two other party members were illegally detained on Saturday by the FSO, as they legally tried to cross the Georgian border.

"They are accused of trying to smuggle classified documents out of the country for subversive use.

"I can categorically state that those accusations are fictitious and a complete fabrication intended to nullify our party and bring to it our demise.

"Oleg Stepanov, Grisha Tarasova and Nadia Guseva are three of the most forthright people I know. They were not smuggling any documents out of the country. The only papers they had with them were from their own manifesto and their passports.

"They were due to catch a plane, to bring them here to London, where it had been arranged for our two parties to unite, coming together officially as The White Rose Party.

"Oleg himself should have been behind this lectern making his own speech. Instead, he is frustratingly imprisoned, along with his wife, I might add, for no other reason than being a man of honesty and integrity."

Even though it was broad daylight, the brilliance from the camera lights was intense. But it didn't faze Milana, she continued.

"This detainment is an absolute disgrace and will be challenged by our lawyers in Russia to the highest degree.

"Putin is scared of people, scared of a real challenger. This abominable war against our brothers in Ukraine is failing. It will fail. He is a disgrace to our nation and a fool, an embarrassment, and the cracks in his imperialistic armour are starting to appear. His army is failing on the battlefront, and he is failing at home, so all he can do is lash out at real statesmen, men like Oleg Stepanov, who can make an absolute difference."

She paused for a few moments. I caught my breath, thinking that the occasion had overwhelmed her, but it hadn't. She was just going for effect.

"Our party members have come together and decided that for the interim, until we can find a new legitimate leader for The White Rose Party, I shall be the caretaker leader. This is a position I am honoured to accept and will carry out to the best of my abilities.

"We sent a letter to President Putin on the 5th of April, declaring our intent to merge our two parties and to run for the presidency in 2024. This is what has got him riled. He has not replied with words, only with a pathetic, drastic action.

"I know you are watching, President Putin, and I have this to say to you. There are a hundred and nine million registered voters in Russia. If Oleg Stepanov was here today and a Presidential election was held tomorrow, then he would receive eighty per cent of those votes, and you would be arrested and tried for crimes against the nation."

A collective cheer reverberated around the garden wall, from the crowd of mostly ex-pat Russians and those in exile.

Jim whispered to me, "Where did she get that figure from?"

I shrugged. "Born with it, I think."

Jim chuckled. He knew I knew what he meant.

As the cheers petered out, she resumed her speech.

"Mr Putin, you have made many mistakes; the war with our neighbour is just one of them. Continuing to treat your own people as disposable pawns in your vile chess game is as despicable as you are delusional, and our country will pay the price for many decades to come.

"Putin, I implore you, no I beg you. Step down now, end this senseless war, put your people first, or else we're coming for you, Mr Putin, WE ARE COMING!"

The applause was deafening. Milana was humbled by its ferocity. She was just about to step aside, when a girl of around eight years old strode up to her clasping a small bouquet of white and yellow roses. They were a gift from the Ukraine embassy.

Milana bent down to accept the flowers. She spoke to the girl in Ukrainian, saying that The White Rose Party doors were always open. She kissed the girl on the forehead, waved to the crowd and then turned and went back inside.

Another volley of applause greeted her as she walked down the hall. A selection of drinks and canapés littered the conference room table, and various invited dignitaries were filtering inside for a meet and greet.

Milana was accosted immediately by a posse of staff members, congratulating her on her speech. I made for the drinks table, poured a glass of chilled white wine for the boss, and grabbed myself a bottle of cold beer.

Interrupting the gaggle of well-wishers, I stretched an arm in between them, handing Milana the wine.

She must have been as dry as a polystyrene crisp on a bed of sawdust, because she downed half the contents of the glass in one gulp. It was impressive.

She asked me what I thought of her speech. I said that I wished I'd been out front to see her make it. I mean, her rearview was something to behold but, in this instance, I would have preferred to have watched her face.

She suggested that we go to her office and re-watch the coverage. She'd recorded it.

Making her apologies, she said she'd be back in a few minutes, and together with Andrei, we headed upstairs for her office.

Just before her speech started, Andrei's phone went off. He said sorry and slipped out of the office to take the call.

We watched the re-run in silence, Milana sipping on her wine, me taking the occasional swig of beer.

I was in awe of the woman. Her persona on and off screen was mesmerising. If anyone could rouse a nation to collectively change its mindset, it would definitely be her.

"Can I ask you a question?" I said when the speech was over.

"Of course, darling. What is it?"

"Where did you get that figure of eighty per cent of the votes going Oleg's way?"

She smiled a crooked smile. "I made it up. In our business, I think it's called propaganda."

This troubled me. I crinkled my brow.

"Isn't it our policy to be honest and totally transparent?"

She smiled again, that teacher-to-a-child smile she used to such calming effect.

"That wasn't for our people; it was for Putin, to put him on edge. But look, I do have some basis for that number."

Milana put her glass down on her desk and walked over to a whiteboard on an easel which had a blue satin cloth draped over it.

She pulled the cloth and let it fall to the floor.

The board was headed with the title 'Forecast of potential votes for the next Presidential election', beneath which was a list of figures.

"In the last election," she pointed out, "Putin got a very dubious, fifty-six million, four hundred and thirty thousand votes, right, more than seventy-seven per cent of the vote."

"Mmm," I concurred.

"The Communists got twelve per cent, the Liberals, six, and all rest combined around five per cent."

"Uh-huh." I had no idea of the figures, so just went along with her analogy.

"So, we need to take more than seventy-seven per cent to win the election, right?"

"Err?"

She ploughed on.

"We know from our network that we have at least five million supporters in Russia. Oleg's party has a loyal one million who will come across to us. The Rainbow vote will definitely get us at least six million."

"Right," I said cautiously.

"Students. There are 8.2 million students in Russia. We believe we could secure two-thirds of them. That's 6.15 million.

"For the mothers of dead or wounded soldiers, we're looking at, at least fifty thousand there.

"Political Prisoners and supporters from the lower ranked parties, who'll probably join our cause, another five hundred and fifty thousand.

"Motorcycle clubs, and those who lost their jobs within the media, entertainment and the arts, another eighty thousand.

"Sportsmen and women who've been banned from participating anywhere in the world, fifty thousand.

"And people who have relations in Ukraine, we think it's probably about eight million.

"That all adds up to twenty-six million, eight hundred and seventy-five thousand votes. Not enough, right?"

"Umm?"

"But, when you consider the strain and constriction he is putting on his people, the disillusioned and the devastated, then I think we could get another fifty million, easy."

"Milana?"

"Yes?"

"We don't need that many."

"What do you mean?"

"We only need to get a little over half of what Putin got last time around. Even if all the other political parties kept their loyal supporters, we only need to secure twenty-nine million votes to topple his regime, around 45 per cent of the turnout."

It was a light bulb moment. She stopped in her tracks. "Of course, of course, what was I thinking? Abel, you are brilliant... But what if there is a bigger turnout? What if more people vote?

"If more people are stirred into voting, it'll be because they want change, and they feel they have something worth voting for. We have to show them that it's the White Rose Party and nothing else."

She smiled once more, and then swayed towards me in that intoxicating blue dress. Put her hands on each side of my face and kissed me. The softest, warmest kiss I'd ever experienced. There were no tongues, just a passionate five seconds of incapacitating, soul-sundering bliss. I didn't know how to react; I just stood there and let it happen.

She captured me with her eyes and said, "I think I should get back to our guests now," then she let me go, turned and wiggled out of her office, leaving me bedazzled.

I sat on the edge of a desk, flummoxed, before Jim came in with a message. My housemates were wondering where I was.

"Ah, right," I said. "I'll be down in a minute."

He plucked a tissue from a box on Milana's desk and handed it to me. "Here," he said, grinning, "You need to get rid of the evidence, Mr Gere."

I studied the lipstick smear on the tissue. It really wasn't my colour.

***

I spent the whole of Tuesday with Matvei Drozdov. He was the new head of the environmental department. His enthusiasm for making Russia carbon neutral by 2050 was invigorating.

His commitment to those goals hadn't unnoticed by the Russian authorities. Hence, his exile and living in Britain.

Matvei used to be an adviser to Oleg's green party, three years ago, but after unbearable pressure, and too many warnings from the FSO, he was forced to leave the country he loved so much and seek out a safe haven from which to conduct his lobbying for change.

It was obvious to him that Putin couldn't give two shits about protecting the environment, and this war was exasperating, escalating carbon emission manyfold, destroying fragile habitats and obliterating mature woodlands. He was incensed.

It was going to take decades to rebuild the environments the bombs had destroyed, but Matvei had an ambitious plan, to plant three billion trees across the vast sub-continent, making Russia the lungs of Europe.

We were kindred spirits and I was honoured to work with him. He was dynamic, forthright and relentless, a proper nuisance to the dogmatic, imperious, protocol-adhering nationalist at the Kremlin.

He was an asset to the party and when the White Rose took over, he would be at the forefront of policy making, I was sure of it.

It was getting late; I had to head back to Oxford. I was wanted in Norfolk tomorrow for a very important meeting and needed to freshen up, change the clothes I'd been wearing since Sunday and put a different head on.

But, I wanted to say goodbye to Milana before I left. And perhaps another one of those Russian thank you's.

She looked perplexed, behind her desk, troubled, in fact.

"Are you okay?" I probed.

"Yes, Abel, I'm fine," she replied despondently.

She didn't look fine; she looked like Atlas was sitting on her shoulders.

Being the most talked about person in the whole world right now, and having her face on the front page of nearly every newspaper there is, must have been quite stifling for her. And if you're not used to such media attention, then it must feel like a huge responsibility to suddenly have to deal with, an enormous persona to uphold.

Plus, she'd just publically excluded herself from Putin's Christmas card list. But it wasn't any of that which had saddened her.

"I have something for you to read on the train ride home," she said, sliding an A4 brown envelope across her desk.

She stared at me silently for what seemed like thirty seconds but was probably only five. And then said something that made the hairs stand up on the back of my neck.

"Abel, the White Rose Party will be in the Kremlin within a year."

It was a provocative statement. I let it sink in.

I thought she was being a tad optimistic seeing that the election wasn't until 2024. But the power of positive thinking and all that…

"For the sake of the world, Milana, I hope you are right."

With that, she rounded her desk and gave me what I was hoping for. It was a powerful embrace, our energy fields entwined in our own private little harmonic convergence, a pink luminescence that both surprised and engulfed the pair of us.

"Does that mean we're engaged now," I joked.

Her smoky eyes devoured me again. Her smile was wry.

She pushed me away abruptly. "In my country, we date first."

The chemistry between us was undeniable. She was the instigator, so who was I to stand in her way.

"Okay," I said. "How about the weekend? I can be back next Saturday."

Milana bounced her head from side to side with a 'maybe' written on her face.

"If time allows for it, I'll call you," she said. "Now go, or you'll have to spend the night here again."

That sounded like an excellent idea, but not in with The Scalpel again. I'd much prefer the caretaker leader's bedroom.

Once on the tube, I extracted the contents of the envelope. It was two letters, sent originally via e-mail and translated from Russian into English.

The first letter was from a young lady called Kira Smirnova. It read as follows:

Dear Miss Fyodorova,

On Monday 11th of April, around five o'clock in the afternoon, my two friends and I watched your speech in London on our mobile phones, whilst we sat in the park next to the housing complex where we all live, in the Maryina Roshcha district, a suburb of Moscow.

The housing blocks around the park are all very similar, the perimeter is lined with maple and birch trees. There is a central fountain, a children's play area and kiosks selling beer, coffee, sweets and sandwiches.

There is always plenty of seating and tables, where usually old men meet to play chess or put the world to right.

Mothers and grandmothers watch over their loved ones, and teenagers like me and my friends, are usually glued to our phones and tablets.

It's always a peaceful, safe place to be.

In the late afternoon of the 11th, people gathered in great numbers in the park, far more than I have ever seen before. People from all occupations, street cleaners, accountants and factory workers, all kinds of people, most of whom live here in the complex.

They gathered for one reason, to listen to your speech. It was all you could hear and one word that stood out above the rest, 'Caretaker'. It moved us all.

You said that if an election was held tomorrow, then your party would receive eighty per cent of the vote. Well, I'm here to tell you, that judging from the reaction of the crowd in our little park on that day, then you are probably right.

My friends and I turn eighteen very soon, and you can count on our vote.

Best regards,
Kira, Natalia and Yulia.

The second letter read:

Dear Milana,

On the very first day of the special military operation in Ukraine, my eldest brother, Ivan, who is twenty-three, lost both of his legs above the knees from a mortar round explosion at Antonov airport.

He now lives with us in our cramped apartment, on the seventh floor of a state-owned block in Volgograd. He is waiting for an appointment to be measured for prosthetic legs, but this may be some time. He is in a great deal of pain and suffering badly from post-traumatic stress.

My younger brother, Kostya, has just turned eighteen and has been conscripted into the army. We are not permitted any contact with him for the foreseeable future, which has put an enormous strain on my mother's mental well-being.

I have only been spared military duty because of my poor eyesight; I am blind in one eye from a bicycle accident several years ago.

The war in Ukraine has destroyed my family. My father, who works for a government department, could not decide if it was right or not, for us to attack our neighbours. Whereas, the rest of my family, including my grandparents, all were in agreement that it is a war purely waged to enlarge one person's ego.

The amount of arguing that has raged within our walls over the past two weeks has eventually taken its toll. My father has suffered a massive stroke and is now on a life support machine in the hospital.

I love my father wholeheartedly, but I pray that he doesn't survive this miserable tragedy because he will never be the same man again.

As you can imagine, my mother is at a loss for what to do and is out of her mind with grief.

Putin's decision to invade Ukraine has had devastating results on not just the battlefield, and in the towns and villages in Ukraine, but in many thousands of homes here in Russia also. We are very much also collateral damage and an insignificant loss to the war machine. Putin would not shed a tear for us.

My brothers, my mother and I are in no doubt. If the White Rose is allowed to become a party here in Russia and you put up a candidate in the next presidential election, then you can count on us four to vote for you.

Best wishes,
Polina.

I returned the letters to the envelope, sat back a starred out of the window, watching the London suburbs recede, sucked into the past by time's Hoover, each moment marked by the clack of a sleeper, visited, gone, never to be seen again.

Lost moments, reams of regret, things, alas, you can never replay. Putin must be reeling with self-reproach right now.

What a prat, I thought. In such a high-profile way, blatantly removing the major competition, only to have it immediately replaced by a far greater threat, someone who has clearly been accepted into the hearts of the Russian people, and in such a short space of time.

It was only two letters, no need to get carried away, but reading between the lines, it's undeniable that these people do not want to live under a cloud of uncertainty for the rest of their lives.

With a favourable wind, the day will come when the Russian people will thank the Ukrainians for standing up to bully-boy Putin and his thugs, repelling everything that the tyrant is throwing at them, denying his expansionist rhetoric.

When we first entertained the idea of wanting to do something to help end the war, it was quickly agreed that the best scenario would be for Putin's reign to be expunged by his own people. I haven't wavered from that but, as time has progressed, I have seen that even if The White Rose Party proved beyond doubt that ninety-nine per cent of the populace wanted him out, this narcissistic sociopath could not bring himself to relinquish the reins whilst he still drew breath.

Milana, Andrei, The Scalpel and I had discussed this yesterday, and we decided to change tack for the next leaflet distribution, focussing not on Putin directly, but on his inner circle.

The Scalpel, I was surprised to learn, was fifty-five years old. He was very well educated and, as a bonus, had sources within the Kremlin.

He told us that Putin had around two thousand die-hard supporters at his command. However, when the question of how many of them would actually take a bullet for their boss was raised, he pouted and replied that it would perhaps be just the lower end of double figures.

Putin was a lost cause. No words or reasoning were going to change his agenda. We all knew that.

So, a brave and brilliant, bloodless war of information, facts, figures and revelation was called for. We needed to give his people the truth, something they have been and are being denied.

Our next propaganda promotion was going to be staggering. One hundred and twenty million leaflets distributed in every major city throughout Russia, alongside three million posters, put up by a network of fifteen thousand White Rose supporters, over seven days in May.

The revelations we will provide will definitely hit home, especially to those who surround the president.

We may not be able to hit his jugular, but we can perhaps cut off some of his life support.

9

It was fast approaching seven in the evening on Saturday the 16th of April. I had been loitering around headquarters all day, doing nothing much in particular, desperate to spend some precious moments alone with my heart's desire. But she was way too busy for a suitor's cavalier triviality; she had the world to save.

The Fyodorovs were on the cusp of unleashing the formidable plan they had been moulding all week, secretly, behind closed doors. And at last, I'd gained an audience with the most popular person in the press today, only to be presented with a shocker.

"The war in Ukraine will be over, and The White Rose party firmly installed within the Kremlin by September."

Milana's provocative statement struck me instantly as profoundly over-confident, more wishful thinking than certainty.

But she was overtly sincere and alabaster cold in her delivery.

Jim, The Scalpel and I, sat in a row in her office with six raised eyebrows, comically resembling a viaduct of incredulous concern.

"And... This will happen how?" I ventured to ask.

"I will explain in a minute, but first, who wants pizza?"

We all did. I, for one, was dog-hungry and downstairs they made arguably the most authentic Italian pizza in town. It was superb.

Andrei rang through and ordered the food, whilst Jim fetched some ice-cold lagers and a bottle of Frascati from the chiller cabinet in the kitchen.

Whilst we waited for the deliciousness to arrive, Milana began to unveil their decisive mandates.

"Firstly, I need to impress the pivotal importance of the upcoming leaflet distribution. We have considered delivering our manifesto electronically, but our experts assure us that this will fail. Our messages will be blocked, and even on the dark web, we will not reach anywhere near the number of ordinary people to make a difference."

All three of us nodded in agreement.

"Putin has everything locked down so tight that only an old-fashioned leaflet drop is going to get through. Dangerous as it is for our brave agents in the motherland, everybody above the age of sixteen must learn the truth of what is really happening beyond Russia's borders, and know that there is an alternative to the Machiavellian despot who is herding them like sheep towards an apocalyptic end."

"Yes!" growled The Scalpel, clenching his fist.

I drew breath. "And what is the content of the leaflet?"

Milana reached for a notepad on her desk.

"We are offering the Russian people a one-off, life-changing decision. The most critical choice, they will ever have to make.

"It will state that one minute after The White Rose Party is elected and Oleg Stepanov is declared president, The Crimea and the Donbas regions of Ukraine will be handed back to the country and all occupying forces and pseudo governments will be withdrawn. And then talks will begin to bring about peaceful agreements between the Ukrainian government and the people's republics of Donetsk and Luhansk."

Waves of incredulity rippled through me. Had Milana and Andrei gone power crazy? Surely the matter of the Donbas was for Ukraine and the United Nations to broker.

Andrei caught my concern and urged his sister on with an encouraging nod.

She continued, "The conflicts in the Crimea and the Donbas have been raging for eight years. These regions do not belong to Russia and have been illegally occupied since 2014.

"Once we have withdrawn our troops and all Russian influence from these regions, the separatists will have little choice but to sit around the negotiating table with the Ukraine government and work something out.

"We can help with this by offering patronage to anyone who wants to remain Russian, and re-settle them on Russian soil."

We nodded in silence. Milana went on.

"We have consulted warfare analysts and military experts. Putin cannot possibly win this war with the military strength that he has. Much of his equipment is Soviet era and although he has plenty of it, it is outmatched by modern-day ordinance which is slowly being filtered into the Ukraine forces by the West…"

"Yes," said Andrei, "and, Putin would need at least a million men, not the two-hundred thousand he initially sent in, to have any hope of ever taking the entire country. It was a futile plan to begin with."

"On top of this," extended Milana, "a defending soldier fighting on home soil, fighting for his neighbourhood, his family, is worth the equivalent of three foreign invaders. This is what the experts say, examining two thousand years of warfare. And we have seen it already. The casualty rate of our young men, according to UN observers, is far greater than the Ukraine numbers. They have halted the advances of a much larger army, repelled them from the Kyiv region and have started to push further to the east."

"The Ukrainian soldier also has the knowledge of the familiar ground, the support of the local civilian population, and an uninterrupted supply chain of ammunition and equipment coming from more than forty countries worldwide. This is not so for the Russian soldier," added Andrei.

I interjected, "But there are rogue states out there, sympathetic to Putin's regime, that would resupply him if he requested it."

"Yes," replied Milana. "Most worryingly, China, but so far, thank God, they are, how do you say it? Sitting on the fence?"

I rocked in my seat pensively, slowly nodding.

"Is all this going in the leaflet?" asked Jim.

"Yes," barked Andrei. "The bullet points anyway."

"Plus more," acknowledged Milana. Her gaze drifted towards the floor as she considered delivering the next bite of intel'.

"Igor, one of our analysts, who has a master's degree in war studies from King's College, here in London, has estimated the casualty count if this war continues for two more years."

She paused, looked down at the floor again and blew through her lips. It was obviously hard reading.

"Russian soldiers killed, injured or missing in action, four-hundred thousand. Ukraine soldiers killed, injured or missing in action, two-hundred thousand. Ukraine civilians killed or wounded, including children and unborn babies, eighty thousand."

Milana appeared absolutely shattered by these numbers. Andrei took up the mantel.

"To add to this, it is calculated that if the enormous stockpile of grain is blockaded permanently from leaving Ukrainian ports, then famine will result in parts of the world that absolutely rely on it, such as certain countries in Africa. Then millions more people could die from starvation."

The Scalpel joined in. "The regular army is being depleted of trained, professional men. Each time a Russian soldier is killed, he is replaced by a conscript, hurried through basic training and thrown into battle with scant knowledge of what he is doing there, or why he is fighting his neighbour. We are also hearing of the Wagner group, the private military company, founded by that arsehole chef, Yevgeny Prigozhin, who are now operating in the Donbas and recruiting convicted murderers into their ranks with a promise of a pardon if they survive."

"We'll see how strong their loyalty is when the first bullet cracks past their head," remarked Jim.

"We've seen it already," informed The Scalpel. "These guys are surrendering at the first opportunity."

"It's clear," continued Milana, "human life is two a Kopeck to Putin. The young men he is shovelling into the war are just coals onto a fire, of which he thinks he has a limitless supply. But this isn't the siege of Stalingrad all over again. You can't just hurtle thousands of new recruits, drawn from the far reaches of the continent, towards the shrapnel and flying lead and hope that the overwhelming numbers will be enough. Besides, we are the aggressor here, and the Ukrainians are going to fight tooth and nail to defend their country."

"The people need to know the rate at which our young men are dying," said Andrei. "As is typical in our culture, the true figures are kept secret, hidden from the masses, so as not to pour disdain upon Russia's glorious and noble rout of Neo-Nazism and pseudo-fascist cleansing. The real figures will be published in our leaflet."

"Moving on..." Milana was keen to get away from the upsetting details of the mortality rates in this conflict, and on to more of what The White Rose Party could do for the country.

"We all know of the devastating impact burning fossil fuels is having on the planet. Even with all the sanctions being placed on our country, its oligarchs and Putin in particular, we still export millions of gallons of oil and gas, with income estimates in the region of an eye-watering six-hundred and forty million Euros per day! A colossal amount of money to fund the country's war machine.

"Yet we are missing an opportunity. Economists believe that in seven years, a barrel of oil will only be worth half as much as it is today because green energy is being realised as the only way forward to prevent a climate catastrophe. Perhaps not to reverse the damage we have already done, but to stop any further destruction and halt global warming.

"Every day this war continues, Russia gets put further towards the back of the queue of the green initiative, further behind with renewable energy technologies and critical installations."

Andrei took over, "Currently, renewable energy sources equate to only 3.6 per cent of our national energy mix. This is feeble; we plan to increase that output tenfold, spending one trillion rubles on the infrastructure by 2035."

That sounded like a staggering amount of money. "What's that in pound notes?" I asked.

"A little over eleven billion," he replied.

Compared to the quadrillions Russia was taking in fossil fuel revenue, this seemed like a rather small investment. Yet, I reasoned that a huge country like Russia would cost a colossal amount of money to run, and when the war is over, they are going to be forced to rebuild Ukraine at a formidable sum.

Here we were, people who only a few weeks ago were struggling to pay their energy bills at home, now talking off handily about spending billions as if it were nothing. It was a bizarre moment for me.

Milana took a sip of wine before resuming with her manifesto.

"One reason Putin and his cronies would have us believe he invaded Ukraine is that he felt threatened by the advancement of NATO and would soon be bordered by not one, but four NATO members, with Finland, Sweden and possibly Ukraine joining the alliance.

"But we all know the real reason he has started this war is to deflect attention away from his illicit gains and extremely lavish lifestyle. What with his super-yachts and his luxurious villas scattered around the world. Statisticians believe he is secretly the richest man on the planet, amassing a two-hundred billion-dollar fortune, gleaned from threatening our country's wealthiest oligarchs with persecution if they didn't hand over fifty per cent of their income directly to him.

"He has brainwashed a nation, but if the true facts came out about the depth of his corruption and his ill-gotten amassed fortune, then he would be ousted immediately, put in prison and all his wealth confiscated."

"We cannot blame Finland for wanting to join NATO," said The Scalpel. "They believe they are next in line to be invaded."

Milana nodded pensively. You could see on her face she was playing the outcome of that scenario in her mind.

She inhaled sharply. "We want to address the issue of re-settlement," she said. "When we relinquish our hold on the Crimea and the Donbas, we estimate there will be a figure of around one million people who will not want to be known as Ukrainian, and who will not want to carry on living in that country.

"They are all welcome to relocate on Russian soil, or wherever they wish to go, and we as a government will help them financially and logistically with that move."

"Yes," continued Andrei. "There will also be financial packages to act as compensation for those who have had to give up businesses and property. And for those who were in rented accommodation, we will offer two years of rent money, so they can re-establish themselves in a new environment."

Jim posed a question. "What about the old folks, the retired?"

"Those as well, Jim. All will receive compensation," replied Milana, "But, to dissuade any tricksters or profiteers, anyone wanting to return to Ukraine after they have received compensation will be denied. All money will be paid in Rubles, and those who may be considering the offer will have a year in which to do so."

It was my turn to ask a question. I had been thinking about this for some minutes.

"How are we to observe the reaction to this leaflet drop? I know this will be a massive litmus test to see who is on our side, but how will we analyse its effect? We can't very well do a poll."

"Here's the exciting part, darling." Milana was aglow with impending information. "On the 23rd of May, we are asking for everyone who is supporting our cause, and not in critical employment, to strike for the day, and wear something white, a dress a shirt, a hat, something in their hair or lapel, a white flower, preferably a rose, in their window, or a white balloon, anything to show their allegiance to The White Rose Party.

"But, we will implore all of the bars, cafes and parks to stay open, so that people can be seen to be talking to one another, in solidarity, an open rebellion en masse."

That brought a smile to my face, but also a massive pang of concern. "The regime is not going to put up with this, thousands will be arrested!"

"Some will, for sure," she agreed, "but if hundreds of thousands of people join in, the police won't be able to arrest everyone or have places to incarcerate them. And the army, well we know where they are."

"Are you certain that enough people are going to go for this? Risk their liberty?"

"We're counting on it, Abel. Otherwise, we are sunk," said Andrei.

I screwed up my face, perturbed.

Milana absorbed my anguish. "Look," she said, "Putin's never going to end this war around the negotiating table. He'll see that as being weak, the Kremlin will see it as weak and so will the country. No, he'll keep on pounding Ukraine for years, like he's still doing in Syria, a war of attrition, breaking down the people's spirits and reducing the towns and villages to rubble. As long as he's got the bombs and raw recruits to throw at it, he will. He doesn't care for human life, and a withdrawal will only prove him to be a loser, a position from which he could not survive.

"So, it's down to us to convince the country that they have the wrong man in power and that there is a much better way to run a country; our way, a freer and fairer society, with green credentials and more open policies.

"After the leaflet distribution, I will stand outside this building on the 23rd of May, and broadcast live to my people, the people of Russia, and they will hear me."

It was a powerful proclamation, and I believed in her sincerity wholeheartedly. The facts in their manifesto were all true as far as we could discern, and the Russian people deserved to know the truth. But, whether they believed the document, or took it to their hearts, was unknown.

It made sense to me, with my western upbringing and mentality, but I'm not Russian, neither have I ever been there, and so cannot possibly begin to perceive their way of thinking, or predict their response.

The Scalpel, on the other hand, was jubilant.

"*Otlichno, dorogaya, u nas yest' eto v sumke*" (Superb, darling, we have this in the bag), he blurted, before hugging both his countrymen and kissing them on their cheeks.

I took it as being a positive affirmation.

"Someone's happy," ribbed Jim. "Listen, Milana, I'm only a caretaker, but in my humble opinion, it sounds like a plan."

"Sometimes, Jim, it's left to the caretaker to put the house in order, don't you think?"

She winked at the ex-soldier, who was grinning like a sanctimonious cat from Cheshire.

At that moment, a call came up from reception. The pizzas had arrived.

As we ate, Milana divulged a couple of things which required immediate attention.

Firstly, a draft of the leaflet needed to be knocked up. Nikolay had done a reasonable job of the last flier. So I was charged with asking him to do likewise with this one, albeit a much larger document.

She wanted to include all of the mandates they had just laid out to us, but she wanted Nikolay to go heavy on the green issues, rubber-stamping ours as an ecological party.

Secondly, she wanted the consensus of a broader audience, my housemates in particular and the party's fixer, my dear friend Charles. Before the release date, she needed to know if it could be tweaked, edited, re-written, or made perfect.

It was at this point that a name for the operation should be suggested. The Scalpel thought that the word pizza would be apt, seeing that the leaflets would be flat and delivered. But everyone else thought that didn't sit right.

"What's the name of those little fishes you often have on your pizza, Abel?" asked Andrei.

"Anchovies?" I queried.

"Ah, yes, anchovies. It is a strong message we are sending."

"Operation Anchovy, I like it," said Milana. "Scal', inform our agents in the motherland that the leaflet drop will take place on Friday the 20th and Saturday the 21st of May. They will not go to print until four days before then and security will as usual be watertight."

A pyramid scheme had been implemented. One hundred and twenty million leaflets would be distributed between a thousand and four agents, each of whom would divvy their load up between four sub-agents, who will then divide their quota between twenty associates. Which meant each individual was responsible for less than fifteen-hundred leaflets.

If those people could enlist even more help to hand them out, even better.

By far, the most difficult part of this operation was logistics. We were talking about lorry loads of paper, bearing illicit, criminalised material, travelling undetected across thousands of miles, to all corners of Russia, in just four days.

If any one of those drivers or agents turned tail, or got caught, then it was all over and a lot of people would go to jail.

I had tremendous respect for those brave souls involved, and guilty to be terribly privileged on this side of the English Channel.

I was lost in my own thoughts but came to realise that the three Russians were talking and laughing in their own tongue.

"What's so funny?" I ventured to ask.

"Scal' just made a joke," answered Milana smiling. "He said that this was going to fuck Putin in the arse."

It wasn't the first time I'd heard Milana swear, and I doubt it would be the last. I returned a thin smile, wishing I could be as confident as my compatriots.

10

I was transported back to Lemon Grove, Sunday afternoon, on the sweetest of air. Last night had been incredible, and half of me felt like it was in fact actually a dream. Opaque, untouchable imagery, I could barely recall. But it had been real alright. I'd spent the night in the arms of an amazing woman.

I was hoping it would be a recurring dream, for although we had well and truly cemented our relationship, it couldn't be official, not just yet anyway. Milana had a persona to protect; a lovesick puppy in tow would weaken her prestige.

I had the mandates with me and had requested for all my housemates to be in attendance tonight in the Raft, so that I might relate the bullet points to my friends.

The only one who couldn't make it was Nikolay. He was still on shift, but he would read through them in his own time when he returned.

Even though I was just reciting someone else's typed text, I still felt anxious about doing it justice. This could turn out to be a historical document and I wanted to deliver it in the manner in which it was intended.

My housemates had been glued to the TV, watching a news article covering the opening of The White Rose Party office in Paris.

It was small in comparison to the London headquarters, a converted retail outlet on the corner of two streets, but it was in sight of the Russian embassy, which would rub salt into Putin's wound.

Our offices were popping up in capital cities all over Europe and getting plenty of media attention. So much so, they were being dubbed Russia's second embassy, which must be absolutely infuriating the Kremlin bods.

"This is gaining momentum, I see."

My friends all turned their heads.

"Oh, hi, Abel. Didn't hear you come in," said Safira. "Paris today, Madrid tomorrow."

"Good 'o."

Our oligarchs were certainly putting their money where their mouths were, and this enterprise sure needed bottomless pockets.

Although I was smiling on the outside, deep down I had genuine concerns about the safety of our remote office staff. It would be so easy for Russian agents to cause severe carnage if Putin felt his tenure was seriously threatened.

"So, I've got the mandates here, which I'd like to read to you all. Milana and Andrei would appreciate your opinions, and input if you feel that some amendments need to be made.

"We have a little while before it goes to print."

They listened intently as I ran through the policy's doctrine, heads nodding occasionally. When I had finished, there was silence, and then Jack raised a point which everyone had been considering, the very question that I had asked Milana this morning.

"What if nobody strikes, or wears white on the 23rd of May?"

"I can only repeat what Milana told me earlier today. If the Russian people do not join us, then they have carved out their own destiny, and war and deprivation will be the only things they have to look forward to."

More nodding and pensive brooding ensued. I could tell what they were all thinking. This all depended on how daring the citizens of Russia were willing to be, and how much they wanted to change.

"So!" I clapped my hands together. "What's for dinner?"

"Whatever you are making yourself, Abe," said Victoria wryly. "We've all had ours."

"Charming," I said. "Any beans in the cupboard?"

I telephoned Milana later that night, to let her know that everyone here was thoroughly enthusiastic about the contents of the leaflet. I left out the tiny morsel of concern we all felt. She didn't need any negativity right now.

I'd yet to show it to Charles, of course, but he was a positive thinker and would have absolute faith in the Russian public, I'm sure.

I felt some fatigue in her voice.

"What's wrong?"

"Oh, nothing really. I'm just keen to see the finished article and have it sent on its way. It's frustrating having to wait, but this is our game. So much depends on that piece of paper."

"Indeed, it does. Well look, Nikolay said he'll have the draft ready by Saturday, so I'll bring it over to you on Sunday. Then, if you are happy with it, it's down to the printers to get it out on time for dispatch."

"Yes, but do you think it'll work, Abel? Do you truly believe that it will work?"

I wasn't one hundred per cent convinced, so had to be diplomatic.

"Let's put it this way, The White Rose Party is Russia's best chance for peace and world stability. The people would be fools to ignore us."

***

Wednesday 20th April

I had a meeting with the top brass at Acorn, a government-backed commission whose job it was to oversee woodland regeneration and forestry development throughout Great Britain. They covered all aspects of the chain, from seed propagation to sapling planting, land allocation, material distribution and arboreal management.

One of our green-minded Oligarchs wanted to invest three hundred and sixty million pounds into the acquisition and planting of three billion native hardwood trees in his homeland. This superbly fitted in with Matvei's plans, and I had been tasked with finding the suppliers.

The revenue stream would flow through The White Rose Party and on to Acorn, who would allocate the funds to the nurseries, a very lucrative, tidy deal for those growers.

Shipping would be handled at this end all the way to Poland, where the trees would be transferred into Russian freight, and the planting done at a local level.

The planting, of course, would only take place when the war was over and The White Rose Party were in office.

I was up at five o'clock and in the kitchen, on auto-pilot, rustling up my breakfast. As is protocol in our house, being first up, I had brewed a couple of pots of coffee for the late risers.

Having slipped two slices of thick-cut white bread into the toaster, I was leant against the worktop, waiting for them to pop up and be liberally spread with an exuberant amount of butter and a knife's width of Marmite.

Arouna lumbered in, wrapped up tight in her pink velour dressing gown, dragging her slippered feet, still half asleep.

"Morning, Dozy," I ribbed.

"Mmm," was all she could muster.

Instantly, I knew something wasn't right with our Ukrainian.

"Can I get you a mug of coffee?"

"I'll do it," she said wearily.

I was vexed; this should have been one of the happiest days of her life. Her mum and sister were finally arriving this afternoon. She should be effervescing.

"What's wrong, Arouna?"

"Urgh," she said, pouring out the coffee. "I've put myself under a lot of pressure today. I have to meet my mum and sister in London, then get back here, buy all the stuff for the meal tonight, prepare and cook it whilst settling them in, and all they'll want to do is talk my arse off. Ukh, there isn't enough time…"

Hoping to impress her mum and sister with a big welcome, feed the rest of us, work at the hospital, and help with the opening of the Ukrainian office, on top of this, having the constant worry about what was happening with the rest of her family back home, obviously, the pressure was getting too much.

She plonked herself down at the table.

I had an idea.

"Listen," I said, "why don't you just give Sid Squid a call and ask them for ten cod and chips to be picked up tonight at six forty-five? We have plenty of booze here, and for pudding, there's a tub of Raspberry Ripple in the freezer and a box of Magnums.

"No washing up. We can eat straight out of the paper on our laps, the old-fashioned way, in the Raft. The only thing you'll have to lay on is the salt and vinegar and the sauces."

She stared at me with a blank expression.

I didn't know if she was going to call me a twat or thank me.

Instead, she rose from her chair, wandered towards me and planted a kiss on my right cheek.

"The British people never cease to amaze me," she said. "You are the loveliest, most giving people I have ever met. Ukraine will never forget how you stood by us in our hour of need. But you do eat the strangest of things."

She looked down at my plate.

I guffawed. "You never know, your mum and sister might like a drop of the old favourite."

Arouna screwed up her face. "This I doubt very much." She assured me, "Statistics say that fifty per cent of people love it."

"Alright," she said, holding out a hand, "I bet you they both hate it."

"Two pints at The Otter?"

"Two pints at The Otter."

We sealed the deal.

***

I'd had a good day, securing two nurseries, one in Somerset and one in Devon. Each could supply broadleaf saplings, native to Russia, at an annual rate of one million trees for twenty years. Funding would be given up front, providing security and long-term employment for all of their staff.

I just needed to find forty-eight more growers.

Arriving back at Lemon Grove timely, as Beau and Lukas were pulling in with the fish and chips, I could smell the aroma of a much-anticipated supper as soon as they exited the Ka.

"Evening, chaps. I've been dreaming of this all day."

"Me also," said Lukas. "I have eaten so much of this stuff now, I could be considered British."

Beau smirked at the German's flippancy.

"Are they here?"

"Yes, they arrived a few hours ago. They seemed a bit overwhelmed," replied Beau.

Understandable, I thought, seeing the ordeal they've been through.

In the kitchen I was introduced to Ksenia, Arouna's mum, and encouraged to kiss both her rosy plump cheeks. She had a round, jolly face, which shrouded a deep well of pain. The worry was thinly disguised, seared in her deep ocean-blue eyes.

Lena, Arouna's sister, was nothing like her. She was stick-thin, dyed raven hair, heavily tattooed and adorned with a multitude of body piercings. Apparently, she was into death metal and cigarettes, not really the kissy, kissy kind.

We all filed into the Raft and sat where there was space, food on laps. I perched next to Arouna, who must have said about three times what a good idea this was, to get the fish and chips.

War is appalling, in any language. It cannot be anything other than annihilating, destructive, horrific, painful and desolate. It brings out the worst in people, cruelty, murder, torture, vandalism, vengeance and immorality. Yet amongst all that chaos, terror and fervent slaughter, a flicker of irony can still be found.

Arouna told us of one such story involving her brother, Olek.

With greasy, sticky fingers she held up a photograph of him proudly standing with his two mates, Igor and Albert, in their freshly acquired ill-fitting combat gear.

The story had to be told in both English and Ukrainian, so it was a staggered delivery, but that didn't matter.

"*Vyrodky!*" she said. "Geeks, all three of them. They've been friends since primary school, and all of them are addicted to their PlayStations, remote-controlled cars, any gadgets really.

"They were good at the games, though. They have even won competitions with prize money and stuff.

"Well, when they got a little older, they all had part-time jobs, which meant a little money. So what did they spend it on? More games."

Arouna threw her arms up like it was the most stupid thing in the world for a teenage boy who liked gaming, to spend his money on.

"I thought he was never going to grow up," she continued, "and my father had countless arguments with him about wasting his hard-earned cash on things of such little importance, but it fell on deaf ears.

"Well, two weeks after Olek left school and found a full-time job in a tech store, those bastards invaded our country. So the call went out to all men over the age of eighteen to be conscripted into the army. The poor boy was terrified, but he stood up and did his duty."

"Your father as well, Arouna?" asked Safira.

"Yes, all fit men between the ages of eighteen and sixty. I mean who wouldn't want to fight for their country? A lot of women have joined up too."

"Does your dad have any previous military experience?" asked Jack.

"Yes, when we were still a part of the Soviet Union. He was in the army for four years, which meant that, because he is a veteran, his training was separate from the raw recruits like Olek and his friends. They are in very different regiments now."

Ksenia spoke to her daughter briefly.

"Oh, yes, the letter," she said. "So, we received a letter from Olek, some weeks after they had been enlisted. He was heavily restricted on what he could say, but what basically happened was that the three boys turned up at training camp, and straight away were ruled out as fighting men. Both the staff sergeant and the commanding officer agreed that these three weren't the right sort of material for the front line, too weak, too puny..." Arouna laughed.

"...But these are desperate times and the army couldn't turn people away, or discriminate. Also, there are many roles to play in a modern army, and a five-minute chat with their commanding officer had them sent on a very different path."

"Oh, and what was that?" My interest was piqued.

"Well, his letter finished by saying that all three of them were fast-tracked through basic training and then given the rank of lieutenant, three skinny eighteen-year-old geeks! That's some accolade! They are now all teaching other recruits how to operate and fly drones; it's something they did before the war for fun and are experts at it."

"Fly drones?" said Jack. "What, for reconnaissance?"

Arouna shrugged. "I don't know. I suppose so. Anyway, he signed off by saying, 'Tell dad to practice his salute. I'll be expecting one from him in the future.' "

A few subdued laughs bobbed about the room.

"That's amazing, Arouna," said Victoria. "You must feel very proud."

"Well," she raised one shoulder, "at least he's not on, well, he wasn't on the front line at that time."

"And your father?" said, Beau.

"I don't know where he is."

I imagined that they were somewhere near the front line, where the drones could be deployed, but thought better of letting Arouna into my head.

Ksenia, just sat there slightly rocking in her seat and contently smiling, with oily chip fat on her chin.

***

I spent Friday in Herefordshire and west Wales, locking in three more nurseries to supply us with saplings for the next twenty years.

I arrived back home just after seven and went to see Nikolay in his room, who was still working on the leaflet.

"Any progress, mate?"

"I still have a little more to do, but it will be finished before tomorrow."

"Cool. Are you doing a draft in English, so I can show Charles?"

"Yes, do not worry, Abel. I will leave them on the kitchen table in an envelope."

I was meeting up with Charles for our regular training session on the water in the morning and was keen to get his opinion on the wording in the leaflet.

***

The conditions for training were perfect now. Temperatures in the mid-teens, with warm sunshine, Britain was definitely bursting into bloom, a chlorophyll explosion, nature burgeoning with vim and vigour.

The water was as flat as a billiard table, green-grey, its surface reflecting the perfect sky and the blousy river banks in an upturned image.

The blades of our oars cut through the liquid with beautifully timed symmetry as we pulled ourselves robustly towards the boathouse and the end of our two-hour session.

It felt great to be alive, but felonious to be so fortunate.

After we had cleaned and stowed away the scull, we sat on a bench with a cup of coffee, courtesy of the clubhouse, and had a quick Q&A about The White Rose Party. It was the apt moment to present Charles with the draft leaflet.

He studied it for a while, reading it entirely, whilst I studied a ladybird that had settled on the back of my hand. Red with seven black spots, its tiny steps tickled as it walked across my skin, stopping temporarily to sunbathe, before raising its sugar-shell wings and cumbersomely taking to the air, departing on an undetermined flight path.

Charles rested the paper on his thigh and looked towards the water.

"What do you think?" I asked.

He answered with a question. "Do you like the cards I send you for Christmas?"

Charles had studied graphic design in sixth form. He was rather good at it and had it not been for a career in law, this would have been his chosen vocation.

Every year, he makes hand-drawn cards, tailored towards the individuals that receive them. My parents and I get one without fail.

I chuckled. "You know I like them. They're unique, better than anything you can buy off the shelf."

"Damn right," he assured me.

"You know, my mum has kept every single one you've ever sent her. She's even framed a couple, and hangs them on the wall at Christmas."

Charles smiled with pride. "Well then, you've just answered your own question."

My confusion crinkled my face.

"The content of the leaflet is good, but its presentation is… uninspiring."

"Oh, right."

"Do you have any paper, a pen and something to lean on in that bag of yours?"

"Er, yeah, I think I do."

I reached around to my man-bag and rummaged through the pile of documentation I had in there, retrieving a virgin piece of white A4, a Biro and a clipboard.

"What else you got in there, a spade, and some tree stakes?"

I laughed.

Charles folded the paper in half, so that it was a pamphlet, and pondered it for thirty seconds, before roughly sketching on the front cover and then something on the back.

The front was headed with 'Vote for the Russian White Rose Party' in large lettering, under which was a square space for a picture of Oleg Stepanov, beneath that he'd written the words 'Leader', and 'In Prison'.

Under this were two more squares, one for Grisha Tarasova, 'Deputy Leader', 'In Prison', and one for Milana, 'Caretaker Leader'.

At the bottom, he had written in bold, 'The green party for peace, prosperity and progress'.

Inside he left blank, but at the bottom of the back page, it read, 'Don't wake up on the 24th of May with a head full of regret. Go on strike. Wear something white. The Russian White Rose Party needs your vote'.

Before I had a chance to react, Charles said, "Think not of this as a leaflet, nor a flyer. This is an invitation, and it must be presented so, in the best possible way. The printers must use the finest paper available, and it must be perfect in every detail.

"Because, Abel, this is a great idea, but you'll only get one shot at it. Putin won't allow you to get away with this again."

He was right, of course; we might not even get away with it this time.

"Oh, and another thing..." He grabbed back the paper and doodled a birch tree in the top left-hand corner and a rose in the right. "This should be on every corner, including the inside. Symbolism is a key ingredient."

"Something to hold on to, something to follow."

"That's right, and the more basic the better."

Charles asked me to pass on his apologies to Nikolay; he wasn't trying to take over the design, just adding his experience and training to the mix.

If we were going to get this 'invitation' to a hundred and twenty million Russians, it had to be of the finest quality we could produce, and be impressive, so it wasn't discarded like the junk mail that comes through the letterbox, but acknowledged as important, and read thoroughly.

Charles suggested I pick up a ream of top-grade copy paper on the way home so that Nikolay had something to work with.

"By the way," he added, "I think I've found the perfect unit for The White Rose US office."

"Oh, yes?"

"It's a former art gallery on Wisconsin Avenue in Washington DC, and it's within sight of the Russian embassy."

Charles smirked; we both knew the psychology in the location.

"I'll talk to Milana mid-week. It's ours if we want it," he said.

We talked for a while longer. We were both going to miss these Saturday morning sessions after Henley was complete. I suggested we take up archery as a way of keeping our sporting prowess going. I'd always fancied giving the longbow a go.

"Archers?" he guffawed. "That'll officially sanction us to give two fingers to Putin."

I phoned Nikolay before I left the club, briefly giving him the lowdown on Charles' idea. He said he'd sort out the photographs we needed before I got back.

He was going to work on it tonight, so I'd have the finished article ready to take over to London in the morning.

When I got back to Lemon Grove, I called Milana; she was in a very upbeat mood. She was going to meet up with old friends from her home town who now lived in Amsterdam. Apparently, they were keen to join The White Rose Party, with the intent of opening a branch in the Netherlands.

She told me that forty-five thousand ex-pat Russians live in Holland, and most of them disagreed with the war in Ukraine, which was encouraging.

Milana asked what I was doing. The question seemed loaded. I had a distinct feeling that she was missing my company.

I told her that Jack, Victoria and I were watching Match of the Day and that I was having a beer, but going to bed real soon. I wanted to catch an early train in the morning and didn't want to be too tired.

Truth be told, I would have run all night to get to her, but I was trying to be cool.

11

Billowing clouds of cigarette smoke left their heads; it lingered in turmoil, then dissipated up into the crisp early London air. Vanya and Vladimir, the two V's, were on the street, propped against the building, evidently taking a break from guard duty and grabbing a critical nicotine fix.

As I approached, I expected the usual baiting about my beloved Fulham being slaughtered on Friday by Derby County. But nothing ventured forth; they just each gave me a glance and a sharp inclined nod.

"Boys," I acknowledged soberly, as I entered HQ.

Something was afoot at The White Rose Party.

Jim was inside, ahead of me, struggling with two loaded bread trays, stuffed to the gunnels with an assortment of fresh baked goods destined for the canteen.

He had the trays pinned between his belly and the elevator steel wall, waiting for the doors to open.

I hurried to lend him a hand, taking the handle on one side. He eased away from the wall, grateful for my assistance.

"Thanks, Abe," he said, solemnly.

"What's up, mate? Everyone seems a bit subdued this morning."

"Better let the boss explain. Let's just say, things aren't going quite according to plan."

I withdrew into myself, wondering what the hell had happened.

Milana and her brother had their backs to me as I eased into her office. They were fixating on a large map of Russia tacked to a cork board up on the rear wall.

The map was bristling with plastic-coated pins, hundreds of black ones, and a considerable number of yellow.

I walked over to Milana, kissed her on the cheek, tenderly bidding her good morning,

"Not a very good one, Abel, I'm afraid."

Her voice was weary and deflated.

Andrei's face was pale and saggy; he looked like he'd been up all night.

"What's happened?" I sombrely enquired.

Milana sharply inhaled. "Yesterday evening we received word from several of our agents in the motherland. The security services and the police are systematically raiding every printing press in the country, sweeping through the regions like a swarm of ink-hungry locusts. Confiscating some stock and making inventories for all that remained, so that they may be audited at any time, arresting anyone who resisted."

"He has us by balls," quoted Andrei. "We cannot print anything in Russia now."

I blew dejectedly through my lips. Bang goes Operation Anchovy, I thought.

"Do you think that we have an informer within the ranks?"

Milana appeared cross with me for even suggesting it. Andrei slowly shook his head, pouting. "Unlikely. He's probably just overreacting to the last paper drop. Typical Putin, he has to be in control of everything."

"What do all these pins represent?" I said, nodding towards the map.

Milana was frazzled but explained.

"The black pins show positions of our agents, the yellow ones…" She exhaled. "Are places where that bastard has raided, closed down, and confiscated material. Seven hundred and eighty-six printing works, all under twenty-four-hour surveillance."

I put an arm around Milana and pulled her in tight. My other hand rested on Andrei's shoulder. This was a devastating blow, totally scuttling all our plans.

In hindsight, it would have been a better idea to have done the bigger leaflet drop first. It would have had the element of surprise and the desired effect, but hindsight was useless to us now.

"Listen," I said, in an attempt to divert the despondency in the room, "obviously you are both very tired. Why don't you go grab a bite to eat, the breakfast things have arrived, and then go up and get some sleep? I'll be here all day; we can talk this over when you both have clearer heads."

They agreed, and sluggishly traipsed off in the direction of the rear stairwell.

I took off to find The Scalpel.

He was in his office on the floor below.

"What a fuck up," he said, dejectedly. "It could have worked."

"Yep," I said, despondently.

I handed him the envelope containing Nikolay's mock ups of the leaflet. He shook the contents onto his desk and then studied the Russian version.

"This is excellent," he assured me. "We can't waste this. We must find a way to make it work."

I raised my eyebrows to indicate that it was a tall order.

"Have Milana and Andrei seen it?"

"No, I didn't want to piss them off even more than there are already."

"And where are they now?"

"In the canteen, I think. I suggested they eat some breakfast before going off to bed."

"Right now, the motherland comes before Zavtrak."

And with that, he grasped the leaflet and rushed off to find his countrymen.

I followed him down in a state of subdued flux. I wanted to take care of the woman I was besotted by, but it was also imperative that the party succeed, yet I felt helpless to do either.

It seemed that all the staff were now down in the canteen. It was a hive of activity.

Apart from Jim, who was in the lobby, ham and cheese French stick in his hand, and indicating to me that he wanted a word.

Curious, I strolled over, despite the gravity-like urge to go and get a coffee and a croissant myself.

"Jim," I curtly invoked.

"Sit y'self down, mate. You'll wanna hear this."

I wondered what on earth it could be, that was so urgent it barred me from breakfast, and why he didn't have a plate for his sandwich.

I eased myself down onto the corner of the coffee table, whilst Jim perched on the edge of the couch.

He began, "When I joined the Para's, I signed up for fifteen years, and soon become best buddies with another grunt called Daniel Lane. He'd only signed up for a nine stretch, the reason being I'll get to in a minute…"

This was all very enlightening, but what did it have to do with anything?

"…We went through basic training together, got stationed at the same bases and went on several tours. Our love of Harley Davidson motorbikes made our bond even stronger." He chuckled. "I bet he's out on one now, disturbing the peace somewhere…"

I interrupted. I was hungry. "Sorry, Jim, your point is?"

"Ah, well the reason Dan only signed up for nine years, is that he'd promised his dad that he'd take over the family business when he got out."

"Which was?"

Jim chuckled again. "You're not gonna believe this…"

"Go on."

"Daniel Lane owns one of the oldest printing firms in Great Britain; they've been going nearly two hundred years."

"What?"

He had my full attention now.

"Yeah, and what's more, they're a bit unique."

"Whaddya mean?"

"Well, they do a lot of work for the government; the place is like Fort Knox. All the workers have to sign the official secrets act. It's all very hush, hush."

"And?"

"Well, I've been thinking about it, and I reckon Dan's business could take care of our little problem."

"What, print the leaflets over here? That many?"

"I think the firm's big enough; it's whether they've got the time. I'm sure the money would be appreciated."

"Are you still in touch with him?"

"Yeah, 'course. We meet up three or four times a year for a ride. I'll call him today if you like; see if we can set up a meeting."

"That would be marvellous, Jim. Please do that for me."

I'd picked up the English version of the leaflet, so pulled it out of my bag and handed it to Jim.

He read it intently and then said something righteous. "Bit posh, init?"

"Exactly, Jim. It's unlikely to be disregarded."

"Ah, right!" he said in a light bulb moment.

"Listen, mate," I said in hushed tones, "keep this to yourself for the moment. Make that call. I'm just going to grab a coffee. Be back in a sec."

Milana and Andrei had already retired to their respective apartments, so I had no distractions whilst obtaining some breakfast, also no guilty secret to hide. I wanted to be able to formulate something credible to present to our leader, not give her any more false hope.

When I returned to Jim, he was just finishing off his baguette, the evidence of which was scattered over his Buddha-style stomach.

"Did you get a hold of him, Jim?"

"No, but I left a message. He'll ring back."

"Good. So, if he were to take on the print run, have you any thoughts on how we might get the leaflets into the hands of our agents in Russia?"

"Got it all sussed, mate."

I smiled. This was a gargantuan task. "Really? Lay it on me then."

Jim finished his coffee with a slurp of froth.

"Four stages. The printing, which I will sort out. Distribution from here to Sergei, in Latvia, which someone like yourself could arrange. Getting it across the border, Sergei could do that. And four, The Scalpel could use his contacts inside Russia to get it to the agents."

I sat back deep into the couch and mulled over the thousands of things that could go wrong with a plan like that.

"Well, whaddya think?" prompted Jim after a short minute.

"What makes you think that Sergei would put his head on the block once more?"

"He's proved his worth already by getting Nikolay's family out."

"Yes, but that was personal, Jim. He has no reason to risk his life again."

"He doesn't have to risk his life. From what I understand, his farm borders Russia for fifteen miles, he just has to get our cargo across it."

"Hmm."

Before I took this plan to Milana, I had to have three people onboard, Daniel, Sergei and The Scalpel. It was going to take time, but I had all day.

I then said something that I wouldn't forget in a hurry. "I suppose I've drawn the longest straw, only having to find a lorry willing to take the leaflets to Latvia."

Jim gave me a condescending look.

"It'll take more than one lorry, Abe. I've already done the maths, a hundred and twenty million leaflets and three million posters, is going to need ten forty-foot artic's to transport it."

I suddenly felt rather foolish; I hadn't properly envisioned the quantity of paper needed for a task as big as this. It now dawned on me just how immense an operation this was, and how risky.

"Crikey, that's a bloody convoy. It'll stand out like a sore thumb. How would we disguise it?"

"We don't have to. They only need to go to Latvia, offload the cargo there, and then let The Scalpel's boys handle it through Russia."

"Right, and where would I hire ten, forty-foot artic's from?"

"A haulage company?"

"Of course, of course." My mind was racing with all the possibilities.

The Scalpel came out of the canteen and spied us down the hall. He made a B-line straight towards us. His stride was loping, and I wondered how he remained so energetic.

"What are you guys conspiring, tucked away in a corner?"

Was it that obvious? I thought.

"Sit down Scal'. Jim's had a brainwave."

Jim relayed his idea, thankfully, a shortened version of it.

Without hesitation, The Scalpel said he was in.

"Brilliant, Jim. We can do this. My network can handle the transport in Russia with no problem."

I was impressed at his confidence; he hadn't even asked anyone yet.

He did a quick bit of arithmetic out loud. "Twenty pallets on a forty-foot trailer, times ten, that's two hundred pallets…"

Jim and I both nodded passively.

"…I need a calculator."

He pulled out his phone and rapidly jabbed his thumbs at the screen, mumbling numbers to himself.

"Twenty-eight tonnes per truck," he announced. "Easily doable. An artic can take forty-four."

I didn't know how he worked that out, but I took his word for it.

He then began a rapid diatribe. "It would need twenty lorries inside Russia to take the divided pallets to the rendezvous points, where the agents can converge and distribute amongst themselves. We can disguise the contents of the pallets by placing a couple of flat-pack office desks on top and encasing the whole deal in reams of pallet wrap. The labels and the paperwork can be pre-done over there..."

He was either a really quick thinker, or he had thought about this already. I interrupted him. "Do you think that Sergei would be willing to help us once more?"

"Sure!" he affirmed. "He hates Putin with a passion. We'll have no problem there. I will call him this morning."

Before The Scalpel went back to his office, I asked him not to mention any of this to Milana or Andrei until we had formulated a firm plan, if indeed it was possible.

Our boss and her brother had been through enough upset recently. Having their parents imprisoned for the past five years was heartbreaking enough, and now this devastating blow with the print works. I could see little good in building up their hopes, only to have them dashed against the rocks once again.

I made a call to Nikolay, firstly to thank him for his excellent work on the leaflet, but then to give him the disastrous news about the clamp-down on the Russian printers.

He had no idea about Putin's latest repressive manoeuvres; he'd just this minute got out of bed.

Naturally, he was devastated. Not just because of the work he'd put into the leaflet, but for the future of the party and the effect it could have had on the war.

I then had to approach him about asking his partner to once again do something decisively dangerous. I put forward Jim's idea.

With a heavy heart, Nikolay agreed to call Sergei. The plan was feasible, but could send a lot of people to jail, or worse, if it all went wrong. We were only gonna get one stab at this. If the operation failed, the party would be rendered ineffective.

I eventually tracked down Jim again; he was in the back garden, raking up a raft of fallen magnolia petals.

"Are you the gardener as well now, mate?" I ribbed.

"It's not in the job description, Abe. But I like to keep the place tidy."

I smiled; in my experience, ex-soldiers tend to be that way inclined.

"Have you managed to talk with Daniel?"

"I was coming to find you when I'd cleared this lot up. Yeah, he was having a full English in a beach café down in Felpham. Sounds adorable."

"Ah yes, near Bognor Regis. I know it. Those sea fronts down there still exult with nostalgic charm. Is he able to help?"

"He thinks he can. The large pay packet was a deciding factor, but time is against us. If we want to get them into Russia by the 18th of May, that gives us just twenty-four days including weekends, to get the material to him, get it printed, approved, packaged, loaded and transported to Latvia. He reckons he'd have to impose a night shift to get it all done."

"Did you tell him what it was for?"

"Only the basic outline. I didn't go in too deep."

"Good, the fewer people know about it, the better."

"Dan's one hundred per cent discreet. You got no worries there."

"No, no, I wasn't discrediting him, Jim; it's just, well you know, this is life-changing stuff."

"Absolutely. You're in safe hands, Abe."

There was a pause whilst we stared at each other for five seconds.

"He'd like the memory stick in his hands by tomorrow morning. I said I'd run it over to him. It'll be nice to take the old girl for a spin. We haven't been out for a while."

"Where's he based?"

"Redhill in Surrey. Lovely part of the world."

"Yes, indeed."

"He said he'd make a proof, then courier it over for our approval, and if we like what we see, then he can order in the paper, which should arrive by the end of the week."

"Will he need anything else from us?"

"Just the transport. He reckons the trailers need to have side curtains. He'll obtain the pallets."

My phone trilled in my pocket. It was Nikolay. He hadn't dallied.

He told me that because Latvia was two hours ahead, he'd luckily caught Sergei, his two sisters and their husbands, all sitting around the kitchen table having their Sunday lunch.

They were discussing the future of the farm and had decided that they would be turning over to arable. There was little profit in the beef market any more, and crop production is more sustainable and certainly more eco-friendly.

They were going to employ a farm manager and more staff so that each of them could go back to their previous lives. Which meant Sergei would be coming back to England, much to Nikolay's satisfaction. It showed in his voice just how happy he was about this decision.

Sergei had put his phone on loudspeaker, so they all could be privy to the conversation. No farm workers were within earshot.

When Nikolay had finished outlining the plan, there was no hesitation. It was a resounding yes from the entire group. Not only that, Sergei said that he had a good idea of how to get the leaflets across the border.

Nikolay left it at that. He said he would call me later with Sergei's idea and probably some questions.

What started just over an hour ago as a wild concept was forming into something tangible.

So the heat was on, and I had to get myself into gear and start looking for a haulage company that could supply the artic's with drivers who could run the gauntlet and keep their mouths shut about the cargo onboard. Because undoubtedly, there were agents out there willing to kill for their country if necessary.

Also, I only had a short period in which to organise it, and it being Sunday, all the offices would be closed. Still, I could scour the internet and see what was potentially available.

I fancied getting out of the office for a while. I could take my laptop down to the nearest pub and have a quiet drink whilst searching. Jim was way too busy to come with me, so I went on my own.

The Gnat's Racker was heaving, and the smell of the carvery greeted me like a long-lost friend as I walked in through its doors.

After a five-minute wait, salivating at the bar, I managed to order a pint of bitter and a packet of pork scratchings, which I took outside to a pavement table. I could have easily demolished one of their Sunday roasts, but I was toying with the idea of maybe Jim and I knocking up something later for our Russian friends.

It was a warm and sunny day, but I sought the shade of the building in which to properly see my laptop screen.

I powered it up and within minutes was knee-deep in lists of haulage companies. I needed to refine my search, to European road hauliers. Still, there were dozens, so I tagged 'near Surrey', at the end of my search bar.

This narrowed it down considerably, but none of them seemed to have the amount of trucks we needed. I'd have to broaden my search once more.

Just then, a call came through on screen via Whatsapp. It was Sergei.

"Hi, Abel. Can we talk securely?"

I looked about me. There was only one other pavement table occupied by a young loved-up couple at the far end.

"Yes, Sergei. I'm quite alone. It's good to hear from you."

"Where are you?"

"Oh, I'm outside a pub, just down the street from HQ, having a crafty pint; it's a beautiful day today."

"You are making me jealous. Listen, can you record this conversation? You might find it helpful later on when you explain it to Milana and Andrei."

"Sure, just a moment." I tapped the red button. "Okay, go ahead."

"Okay. This operation you have proposed, has Nikolay told you we are all for it?"

"Oh, yes, he said that you may have an idea of how to get the cargo across the border."

"That's right; I am now convinced it is more than possible. I have spoken to my neighbour, a farmer on the other side. Our lands touch each other."

That sounded a bit agro-erotic. I let it slide.

"His name is Grigoriy Petrov. We had a chat this afternoon over a fence. He has three farms, but only one of them is occupied. The other two are worked, but no one lives there."

"Right."

"Well, he's agreed to let us use one of the unoccupied farms overnight, as a transfer station. As long as we can bring the goods through the fields and load them onto waiting trucks in the farmyard, and we can do it within eight hours, no one will know. Not his wife or family, nor any of our workers, will be privy to the exchange, and the cargo will be inside Russia without going through border control, and heading for its destination by dawn."

"Wow, that's amazing." Questions were popping up inside my head one after another. "Why is this Petrov willing to help? Has he been wronged by Putin?"

"His elder brother, Konstantin, was killed in the Afghan war back in '89. Grigoriy fucking hates him, would do anything to help depose him."

"Fair enough," I said. "Tell me, how are ten artic's going to drive across open fields?"

Sergei curled a crooked smile. "They're not; we have a plan for that."

He went on to reveal all of the details. In the end, he said it was imperative that at least one of our ten lorry drivers could manage a JCB Loadall Telehandler. Apparently, it was a type of forklift truck.

I said I'd see to it. He also suggested that a part of the load should be something to do with agriculture. It would give the trucks a legitimate reason for travelling to the farm. I thought about it for a second and said, "How about sixty thousand apple saplings, three hundred to a pallet, shrink-wrapped on top of the paper stacks?"

He was overjoyed.

We ended the conversation with me saying that I would call him back later, once I had had the chance to run through the plan with Milana and Andrei, who were at this point unaware that we were conniving to save the party, win an election and possibly end the war.

I finished my pint, folded down my laptop and headed straight back to party headquarters post haste.

The front entrance was locked. I used the keypad to gain entry. Nobody was in reception; the entire group of Sunday staff, five girls plus Vanya and Vladimir, were upstairs milling around in the offices.

Vanya and Ekaterina were studying the map in Milana's office.

Ekaterina, a studious brunette from Samara in southwest Russia, turned her head towards me as I entered. She gave me a resigned look.

"Putin and his henchmen are still at it," she revealed. "Sunday has no meaning to him; print works are still being raided."

I sighed. "Hell is empty, and all the Devils are here."

"What?" she quizzed.

"Shakespeare, Ekaterina. His wisdom reigns supreme even today."

I felt a sudden compulsion to collate everything I had on the new plan.

Taking my leave, I headed down one flight to the conference room, where I set up a large whiteboard on an easel.

With a marker pen, I wrote the heading Operation Anchovy.

If all goes to plan it was still on.

Beneath the heading, I split the board into five vertical sections and sub-headed them, Print (Jim), Artic's (Abel), Farm (Sergei), Pick up (Scalpel), and Delivery (agents).

Under each sub-heading, I added what had been achieved in each area so far. My section was pretty sparse, a worrying factor seeing that we only had twenty-four days to sort it out, and surely these things needed to be booked well in advance.

I slumped into a conference chair and wracked my brain. Who did I know with a fleet of lorries that would do me a favour?

The answer was staring me in the face; Milana's office window looked out onto the rear garden. A large oak tree in tight bud occupied a corner near the back wall.

Acorn used the same company to distribute all of their trees throughout the UK, a firm called Hart and Swan Haulage; they'd been doing it for decades, and they were massive.

There'd be no one at the office today, but tomorrow I could talk directly to the people who arranged logistics at the Commission, and they could introduce me to Hart and Swan.

I fired up my laptop once more and Googled the company.

Established in 1913, it was still owned by one of the founding families, the chairman, Julian Hart, and the directors, his two children, Alison and Dean.

They had a transport fleet of more than three hundred and fifty articulated lorries on the road at any one time, which covered the whole of Europe, the Middle East and North Africa, as well as a parcel delivery fleet of over a hundred vehicles that operated in mainland UK, and an export wing, delivering trucks and trailers to the entire African continent.

Interestingly enough, they also had an expansive collection of vintage, veteran and classical commercial vehicles, which they rented out to the film industry.

Surely this large corporation would have ten spare trucks to hire out in a few weeks.

I thought about the clandestine nature of the cargo. Whatever company we ended up using, the drivers would have to be made aware of the importance of secrecy. Even though the goods were not being transported illegally through any of the countries on the route, if the lorries were pulled over and inspected for any reason, the very nature of the leaflets might put the whole operation in jeopardy if it was spied upon by a Putin sympathizer, or if European police channels happen to be monitored by the Russian secret service.

A well-known brand like Hart and Swan might well be considered respectable enough not to be carrying any contraband, and therefore less likely to be searched on the roadside than some random unfamiliar trucks. But still, there was so much depending on this delivery; it would be prudent to be over-diligent.

I was buzzing now. I couldn't leave it until tomorrow. If I made a personal call to Wes Taylor, the coordinator at Acorn, he'd give me the number of the person I needed to talk to at Hart and Swan.

I rang him and semi-explained my predicament, emphasizing the sixty thousand Apple saplings being shipped to Latvia.

This was bait enough to get him to cough up the contact details, Glen Watson, European logistics manager and his mobile number.

Mr Watson wasn't best pleased to be bothered on a Sunday, especially during his round of golf. He was rather curt until I dangled a two million-pound carrot in his face. After which, he became more cordial.

Because I was an agent working on behalf of an as-yet undisclosed client, I would have to have a face-to-face with one of the directors. Unfortunately, Julian was in Spain, Dean in Scotland and Alison's diary was full.

I called the guy's bluff and insinuated that this was not going to be a one-off event and that a possible twenty-five more trips might be in the offing.

His thoughts of a pay increase were almost audible over the phone.

Mr Watson said that he would make some calls and be back in touch later that day.

This was progress, even if I had forced by somewhat devious means.

The bluff worked. Within fifteen minutes, Glen Watson called me back. I had an appointment with Alison Hart at two o'clock the following afternoon. She was looking forward to meeting me.

I bet she was.

The truth was, when we eventually start sending saplings to Russia weekly, we will need the transportation anyway, so it wasn't exactly a lie.

And now at least I had something to write on the whiteboard under my name. It felt good.

Rattling me from my vainglorious pat on the back, I heard the unmistakable sound of someone trying the locked door handle behind me. It was The Scalpel.

I strode over and let him in.

He eyed the whiteboard. "You've been busy, I see."

"Not a moment to lose, old chap. Time is of the essence."

"Indeed." He grinned. "And I'm sure Milana will be impressed."

"For the party." I smiled.

"Of course, of course." He crinkled the space between his eyebrows and nodded in approval.

Apparently, our thinly disguised affair was common knowledge amongst party members.

I brought The Scalpel up to date with the progress thus far and asked him if he wouldn't mind calling Sergei to cement the plan and exchange details.

He obliged immediately.

They spent half an hour on the phone, talking in Russian, during which I wandered down to the canteen, grabbed a filled baguette and a glass of apple juice, and devoured it out on the patio. In the afternoon sun, I was wasting away.

When I returned to the conference room, Scalpel asked me if I wanted to talk to Sergei, but I said I'd call him later after we had spoken to Milana and Andrei. They were at this moment unaware of the plans we were making at their behalf.

"Apart from our Russian drivers, we need men at the Petrov farm who can operate forklift trucks and others to act as lookouts. These will take time to find. Also, everybody involved will need two mobile phones, one as a backup. We don't want any dead batteries to jeopardise the whole operation."

"Good thinking. Money's no object," I assured him.

"And I've been thinking. Six of the twenty lorries have a two or three-day journey to make. These should be the ones loaded first in the Petrov yard, and each one also loaded with a couple of pallets of animal feed, in case they are stopped and searched.

The drivers can do what they like with the animal feed after the drops are made. Maybe it will be an incentive for them, some extra money."

I nodded pensively. "And should they get caught, can we rely on the drivers not to talk?"

"Depends on the torture. Nobody is made of iron." He shrugged. "This is a risky part of the operation. It's a long way to travel, and the police are super suspicious, especially now, during the war. I will be amazed if all leaflets get through, but we must try."

I was taken aback. "And your guys are willing to run that risk?"

"Of course, it is for freedom."

The Scalpel went to the whiteboard and wrote his achievements under his name.

Once more the door handle rattled the latch, resisting an attempt to be levered.

We peered out into the lobby to see Jim's questioning face beyond the glass.

I let him in.

"What the fuck?" he quizzed.

"Just keeping it on a need-to-know Jim," I told him.

We were midway through bringing him up to date when the door was tested for a third time.

I was about to show my annoyance when I realised it was Milana and Andrei, refreshed from their few hours of slumber.

"Why have you locked the door, Abel?"

This was the first time I'd seen her anywhere near aggravated.

"I'll explain," I replied as they filed in, eyes fixed on the whiteboard.

"You've both seen the leaflet that Nikolay has drawn up?"

"Yes, but what good is it sitting on my desk?" she said, sardonically.

"Ah, well, this is what we've been up to you see, while you were sleeping. Jim's plan really, but we didn't want to air it until we had some concrete foundations."

I went on to outline the details.

"…So, you see, Operation Anchovy can still go ahead as per the deadline."

Milana's incredible eyes became slit trenches.

"But you haven't procured the artic's yet, or the Russian drivers?"

I hesitated. "No, but I'm confident that I can secure the artic's by tomorrow, and, and, that Scal' can do likewise with the trucks in the motherland through his network."

I looked at The Scalpel for support; he declined his head in the affirmative.

"Brilliant!" she blurted. "You guys will be decorated for this."

That seemed like excessive merit, but this was a game-changer. At least we now believed that The White Rose Party was back in the game. Well done, Jim, I thought.

Milana was welling up. "Absolutely amazing, perfect," she gushed and reached out to hug me.

I took up her offer and squeezed her tight whilst Andrei was shaking the other two's hands.

"Who wrote the last line on the leaflet, about the people walking on eggshells?" she murmured.

"Err, Nikolay, I think. Yes, it must have been."

"It is very poignant and very apt. Our people are walking on eggshells right now, but they will have a choice come the 23rd of May to change their lives for the better. I hope for the entire world they make the right decision."

The adage about taking a horse to water came to mind, but I didn't want to bring any negatives to the table, so simply said, "How can they not?"

I suggested we give Sergei a FaceTime call. Milana and Andrei were yet to meet him and were keen to do so.

After I had told him that everybody here was one hundred per cent happy with the way things were progressing, I handed my phone over to Milana.

She introduced herself and her brother and then, in English, said that the Russian and Ukrainian people, and, the rest of the free world, owed him and his neighbour Mr Petrov, a huge debt of gratitude that was beyond words.

Their bravery and sacrifice will go down in tomes of history as being the acts of heroic men who altered the course of mankind.

I could see that Sergei was embarrassed by this. He modestly replied that if he could help to end the war, that would be reward enough for him.

"I have to say, though," he added, "that the gratitude should be extended to my mother and father…"

"For giving birth to you?" jibed Milana.

"No, no, nothing as conceited as that. It's just that when I was two days off from my tenth birthday, I woke around midnight feeling thirsty and hungry. So I got up and went down to the kitchen, hoping for a glass of milk and a biscuit.

"Before going back to bed, I saw my father through a crack in the door of the living room, sitting on the sofa by the roaring fire, watching TV, a glass of whisky in his hand.

"I crept in, hoping he wouldn't scold me for being out of bed, and climbed up onto the sofa beside him.

"He didn't berate me, not in the least; he put his arm around me and pulled me close, showing the love and support he always gave us, bonding us with a strength that many would envy.

"He was watching a documentary about a man called Simon Wiesenthal, a survivor of the Holocaust, who went on to hunt down fugitive Nazis."

Like the rest of the room, I wondered where this was going, and what it had to do with the operation. He carried on.

"The pictures and the film reels being broadcast will forever be ingrained in my mind. Men, and women, one after another being shot in the back of the head and dropped like sacks into a muddy trench, which they themselves had just completed digging.

"Families with young children, babies and the elderly, were being crammed into railway cattle trucks so tight they could barely breathe let alone move, and transported hundreds of miles, days on end without food, water or toilet facilities. It was horrific.

"Bulldozers pushing thousands of tangled naked bodies into mass graves, and bare-skinned skeletal people, mindlessly wandering about liberated camps, bereft of flesh, sensibility and hope, their dignity and spirit long since starved and beaten out of them.

"When the programme finished, my dad explained to my ten-year-old brain, in the best way he could, exactly what the Holocaust was and why we should never forget the horrors that men can do to each other.

"A year later, he took my two sisters and me to Auschwitz concentration camp in Poland. Pipene was sixteen at the time, Stasya fourteen.

"My mother didn't want to come; she had seen the abomination for herself before and couldn't stomach it a second time."

Sergei paused for reflection, reliving the experience all over again.

We waited in the stillness of our own, personal interpretation of Nazi Germany's abhorrent past.

He found the resolve to continue. "My mother, who recently passed, told me that what Putin and his henchmen are doing in the villages of Ukraine is not too dissimilar to Hitler's rampage through Europe. The damage and atrocities are appalling.

"But many of the despicable, evil Nazi bastards got away with their crimes for decades; some even took those crimes to their graves.

"We are not prepared to let this tyrannical regime do the same. They must be stopped."

Milana then spoke to him in Russian, "*Tam, gde puli i rakety terpyat neudachu, narod pobedit ikh.*"

Sergei held up an iron fist and shook it in affirmation.

Roughly translated, she had said, "Where bullets and missiles fail, the people will defeat them."

12

RAF Maddox Field, Northamptonshire, was decommissioned in 1991 and sold to private investment one year later. A large portion of which is owned by Swan and Hart Haulage, including the original second world war aircraft hangers, several outbuildings, a good deal of runway and, most impressively, the control tower, re-vamped to a high standard and presently the company's head office.

I had left London at six this morning and travelled back to Oxford, where I'd had a quick shower, put on fresh togs, and was on the road again by nine.

Fifty minutes later, I had driven through the entrance gates of the old airfield and marvelled at the staggering amount of vehicles lined up on the tarmac.

There was obviously a contingent of the current fleet, but also a vast array of veteran machines, stretched as far as the eye could see. Impressive was too small a word for it.

I parked in an outlined visitor-space and entered the control tower building. A friendly receptionist was expecting me and directed me to the stairwell. Alison's office was on the top floor.

The walls of the three flights were adorned with photographs of the company's lineage, monochrome snapshots of its humble beginnings, the smiling faces of the proud founders, the premises they owned along the way, and trucks through the ages, right up until the latest beasts of the road, an armada of new DAF XG+ trucks and trailers, fitted out in the red and white Swan and Hart livery.

I rounded the corner of the last half flight to be confronted by a goddess in a grey two-piece fitted suit, commanding the top step, hands on hips, mid-blue blouse unbuttoned to her cleavage and grinning at me.

Alison Hart, early forties, the image of Scarlet Johansson. It stopped me in my tracks.

"Mr Llewellyn?"

"Uh, yes," I stuttered. Scarlet had mastered the British accent perfectly.

"Nice to meet you. Come on up."

She turned and swayed through a glass doorway and into the modernised control room office space, taking her perfect bottom with her.

I followed a full two seconds later.

There was only one way to approach this meeting, I had told myself this morning, and that was to be completely honest and upfront about the goods to be transported and the nature of our cause.

They would not be carrying anything illegal through Europe, but the sensitivity of the printed material would create nervousness for whoever shipped it, and raise concerns for any officials that stopped and searched the wagons.

Plus, there was always a chance that if the existence of the cargo became common knowledge, Russian agents would without doubt, do their worst to derail the shipments.

The control room had retained its three hundred and sixty-degree, unobscured view of the airfield, and as I traversed the carpet towards Alison's partitioned office, the huge extent of their vehicle collection became wholly apparent. It was vast, and so I was led to believe, there were even more delicate machines inside the hangars as well.

She held the door open for me and I entered. I was more nervous now than I was when I had left the house this morning. Not knowing who to expect, her beauty had totally thrown me off balance.

The one thing I suppose I had in my favour was my association with Acorn, a customer of theirs for nigh on twenty years. It must surely give me some leverage. Plus, there was the contract-in-waiting for the Russian sapling transport, so I thought I'd use that as an introductory carrot, before coming to the real stick behind my short notice and rather demanding visit.

Alison gestured toward a two-seater sofa by a glass coffee table.

"How was your trip this morning, Mr Llewellyn? A pleasant one?"

"Very quick, actually. No hold-ups whatsoever."

"Wish I could say the same for all our consignments. The traffic Gods are in a playful mood today."

Alison sighed and perched herself on the cushioned edge of an adjacent armchair.

"Would you like a drink of some kind, Mr Llewellyn? Tea, coffee, something else?"

I was a tad parched.

"Just some water please, if that's okay?"

"Sure," she said, then went over to her intercom and buzzed through my requirements to her assistant.

"Now, how can we help you, Mr Llewellyn? I understand from Glen Watson that you were rather insistent that we meet today."

The tone of Alison's voice told me two things. Her time was precious and her patience was short. She wanted this over and done as quickly as possible, yet she was the epitome of cordiality.

I felt slightly intimidated, but there was too much riding on this meeting for it to be a concern. As a jug of water and a couple of glasses arrived, brought in by a thin girl with long white hair, I rushed straight in and babbled my way through a short version of my involvement with The White Rose party and the intentions of one of our funding oligarchs to plant a billion trees after the war had ended.

This was greeted with a listening ear and affirmative nods. It was a good deal for them. They would be happy to take it on when it occurred.

I then got to the meat and gravy.

"In the meantime, we need transport to take a cargo to Latvia, which absolutely has to be delivered by the 18th of May…"

Alison got up and retrieved a notepad and pen from her desk.

"No problem, Mr Llewellyn," she said, starting to jot the details down. "We have trucks constantly running to and from Latvia and Estonia. We also have a distribution centre on the outskirts of Riga, which is handy for the entire Baltic. What will we be transporting for you?"

She was staring straight into my eyes, pen and paper poised at the ready.

I was just about to launch into the sensitivity and the clandestine nature of the operation when the office door burst open without the precursor of a knock, and in stormed a burley chap in his sixties wearing blue jeans, a white T-shirt, red braces and Chelsea boots.

"Sorry, love, didn't know you had company," he bellowed upon seeing me.

"Dad!" she said, surprise in her voice. "I didn't think you were due back until tomorrow?"

She got up and hugged her old man.

The way he dressed, Julian Hart didn't give the impression of a multi-millionaire businessman; he looked more like a trucker, albeit a Hollywood version of one. I shouldn't have been surprised. This was his occupation.

"Pissing with rain in Spain, excuse my French, but you can't play golf in that shit, caught an early flight back home. Who do we have the pleasure of meeting today?" he said, beaming at me.

Alison introduced me. He knew Acorn, of course, and my employment with them, but until now we had never met.

He reached out a strong hand and thanked me for their custom over the years.

Alison's phone chimed. She looked at the screen and apologised. She had to take this call.

Whilst she ventured out of the office for some privacy, I told Julian that I was here to discuss the possibility of taking some freight to Latvia. He began to laugh, which was disconcerting, but then told me a story.

"In December 1979, me and old Tommy Almond, lovely guy, sadly no longer with us, got caught in a humungous snowstorm, the worst I've ever been in. The snow drift came up to our cab doors. Four days it took us to dig our way out. We were bleeding freezing. If it weren't for the help of the locals, we'd still be there. Lovely people, the Latvians. Took us another six days to get down to Calais, caught the last ferry back on Christmas Eve, and got home knackered at ten o'clock Christmas morning. Chloe, my wife, wasn't too impressed.

"Anyway, Dean was about one-and-a-half, and Alison had just been born. We opened our presents, before a wonderful dinner, and then, this is a true story, Mr Llewellyn, we sat down in the front-room to watch the Queen's speech, and the next thing I knew, I could smell bubble 'n squeak being cooked…"

I squinted, wondering who'd knock up bubble and squeak on Christmas afternoon, and just after they'd had dinner.

Julian paused for effect. "…It was lunchtime, Boxing Day!" He laughed. "I'd fallen asleep on the sofa and slept right through for twenty-four hours!"

He laughed some more, overjoyed with his anecdote. I smiled. It was funny.

"I made a promise to Chloe that day that I would never miss another Christmas, and I make sure none of my drivers do either. It's a family day, Mr Llewellyn, and we need to spend it with them."

"I couldn't agree more, Mr Hart. I do like Christmas at my family home."

Alison came back into the room, clutching her mobile phone like a weapon.

"Sorry about that," she said.

"I'll be going now," stated Julian, backing out of the room. "You must come down and take a look at our vintage collection while you're here, Mr Llewellyn. I'll be about downstairs if you need a guide…"

"Err…" I stopped him from retreating. "Actually, I think it would be more beneficial if we all sat in on this conversation, Mr Hart."

I felt more at ease talking to him than I did Alison, and I was trying to be diplomatic, but I'd failed miserably.

Alison knew she could handle this situation comfortably, without the assistance of her dad, and her annoyance showed on her face.

Julian looked a mite surprised and a little disturbed.

Before either of them could say another word, I quickly added, "Sorry, but once you have both heard what I'm about to say, I think you'll appreciate my request."

Julian's face wizened. He silently closed the door behind him and came and sat on an office chair which he'd pulled up beside Alison's armchair. She went to a drawer in her desk and retrieved an ashtray, then, walked over to a window and opened it.

Julian took out a thin cigar from a silver box in his pocket and lit it with an old-fashioned Ronson lighter.

"Don't mind if I smoke, do you?" he said to me between sucks on the thing to get it going.

"No, not at all," I replied.

He exhaled white exhaust and scrutinised me through the haze. "Now," he said, pointing his rolled tobacco leaf at me, "Why do you want us both here?"

"Well, first of all, let me say that the fewer people know about this transport, the more chance it has of success."

They were both clearly intrigued.

"As I explained earlier to Alison, apart from my job at the Forestry Commission, I also do voluntary work for The Russian White Rose Party, an ecological party who are deeply opposed to Putin's regime. Our immediate task is to have him voted out of office in the next general election, due to take place in 2024."

Both of them stared at me with blank expressions.

Julian interjected, "Surely, all opposition is repressed in Russia? All of the outspoken leaders and radicals are banged up, aren't they? Or bumped off?"

Alison joined in, "How come the White Rose Party is allowed to exist if it is in complete opposition to Putin?"

"It's true, the man who was due to lead our party, and both of his deputies are in prison. But the party itself, as yet, isn't represented in Russia at all. Our headquarters are in London, and we have many satellite offices around the globe, but until we have the backing of the Russian people, we can not operate in the country without being shut down."

There was a brief pause to digest the information revealed thus far before Julian spoke again.

"So, how do you plan to get the support of the Russian people, if they've never heard of you?"

"Ah, this is where Swan and Hart come in."

Inanimate expressions came back at me.

"Go on," prompted Julian, cautiously.

I went on to relate the idea taken from the German White Rose during the Second World War, and our initial leaflet drop having very limited effect, Putin's subsequent clampdown on all the printing works in Russia, and our resorting to having the new material printed here in the UK, shipped to Latvia, and then smuggled into Russia.

"Whereabouts in Latvia are you planning to offload these leaflets?" asked Alison, her tone implying that she hadn't warmed to the idea at all.

"At a farm on the border, about ten kilometres northeast of Ludza. Do you know Ludza?"

Julian nodded. "On the E22, east of Rēzekne."

"That's right. Our contacts there have organized, shall we say, a border crossing which is far from prying eyes, and…"

"We're not getting involved with any illicit smuggling operation, Mr Llewellyn. We are a legitimate company that prides itself in keeping everything above board," blurted Alison.

Julian shot her a questionable look.

"Err, no, no, I err, I do not intend to ask you to do anything illegal. The leaflets only need to be transported to the farm in Latvia and unloaded there. Our colleagues can do the rest from their end."

Alison simmered down. She sat on the edge of her desk and folded her arms.

"I don't understand," said her dad. "A load of leaflets don't take up that much room. Why don't you just rent a seven-ton box wagon and shift them yourselves? Or send 'em by air. It'll be far cheaper than hiring the likes of us."

"Because there are quite a few leaflets, Julian."

"Quite a few. How many?"

"A hundred and twenty million."

"Fuck me! That is a few!"

"Yes, we believe we will need two hundred pallets and ten, forty-foot artic's with curtain sides."

"Done ya homework, have ya?"

"Yes, quite meticulously. We would like every man, woman and child above the age of sixteen to read the leaflets, to give the population a realistic view of what's actually going on in the world, with the war and within their own country."

Alison was watching her dad, waiting for a reaction.

The clogs inside Julian's head were silently whirring, calculating, weighing up the risks.

He inhaled. "Well, Mr Llewellyn, you've certainly whetted my appetite…"

"Sorry, Julian, I don't wish to interrupt, but before we jump into any agreement, there are certain criteria we think need to be adhered to, if this operation is to run to fruition."

He puckered his face again. "Such as?"

"We think all of the lorries and trailers used in the transportation of the goods must be fully decorated in the company livery. This, with your impeccable reputation, we believe, will lessen the chances of being pulled over and searched en route.

"The fewer the officials know about the contents, the better."

Julian nodded.

"We think it prudent to take along a spare driver, as an insurance against anyone falling ill en route."

He continued to nod, contemplatively, unmoving in his chair.

"The convoy should leave no later than Saturday the 14th. This gives them four days, including Sunday, if that's acceptable, to make the one thousand four hundred and ninety-two-mile journey. This should be plenty of time, barring any hiccups."

Julian stepped in. "My drivers won't mind driving Sundays if they are on double time, but you're asking them to drive more than three hundred and fifty miles a day. That's a lot of tarmac to roll up. It's far better if they leave on the 13th. Give 'em some breathing room."

"Friday the 13th?"

"My wife was born on Friday the 13th. It hasn't done her any harm."

"Right." It was my turn to nod.

"It was only unlucky for the Knights Templar, Mr Llewellyn," added Alison.

"Indeed, it was," I agreed, before carrying on. "The rendezvous point for the convoy is at the 'Septini Pakaini' lorry park just outside Rezekne, on the A12. It's about forty-five miles from the farm.

"The drivers should be there no later than the 17th and proceed to the farm two at a time, with the Telehandler driver in the first truck…"

"Telehandler driver?" quizzed Alison.

"Oh, yes, I forgot to mention one of the drivers needs to be able to operate a JCB Loadall Telehandler. Is that a problem?"

"No," said Julian, biting his bottom lip. "I have someone in mind."

"Good," I said hurriedly. "The first two trucks will leave the park at five in the afternoon and drive to the farm where they will meet a lady called Stasya, at the entrance. She speaks perfect English and will be the liaison person for all the drivers that night.

"She will direct everyone where to go. I'll provide her mobile phone number to you and backup phones for all drivers, so there shouldn't be any issues with flat batteries, etc."

Julian screwed his face up with more concern.

"What sort of time scale are we talking about to get the trailers unloaded? Is it a big yard, can we turn around easily?"

"I'm assured it is plenty big enough to take three artic's at a time with room to swing around. There will be four people there to help with the offloading, but everything must be done, including the transfer across the border by five the next day, because the farm employees will be turning up for work around then, and they are not to know what is going on."

Julian blew through his lips. "Bit tight, init? Each trailer is gonna take an hour to get in, unload, and then get out again."

"Yes," I agreed earnestly. "Ten hours is enough."

"Well, it's your tail on the line. We can get your stuff there on time and unloaded, but if anything goes tits-up and your secret gets out, that's down to you, buddy."

"Fair enough," I accepted.

It was true, we were asking for quite a lot of connective parts to run flawlessly for this thing to work. But I had to have faith in the success of the plan, so much depended on it.

As the Harts digested the strategy so far, my next set of demands centred on the collection of the cargo.

"The process of printing has already been initiated, and because of the large amount of material, the printers only have so much storage capacity. So we need to start collecting the leaflets and housing them securely until they are ready to be transported.

"Therefore, we'd like two unmarked trucks and trailers to be at Lane's in Redhill in two days, to relieve them of the production so far. Do you have somewhere safe to store the pallets?"

"Yes," said Alison, "but it's not watertight security. Are the leaflets wrapped in anything?"

"Oh, yes, tightly bound in pallet wrap. They're unreadable through the film, plus they're in Russian anyway."

Alison scribbled away on her notepad.

"If any extra pallets are needed, they must all be plain, no writing on what-so-ever. It's best not to give the FSB any clues as to where these leaflets come from."

More scribbles.

"Besides the printed material, six thousand apple tree saplings on two hundred pallets and eighty flat pack office desks are going on the journey as well. The saplings will have to be retrieved from a grower in Norfolk beforehand and brought to your storage facility, and the desks can be picked up from an office furniture warehouse in Bedford."

The logistics of all this were starting to become dizzying.

"Hold on a minute, mate," interrupted Julian. "Supposing we have the time to do all this running around, and filling out all the bloody paperwork to get these things across Europe these days, and you have the money to pay for it all. Are you gonna be here to organise the loading of this cargo when the time comes for it to depart?

"I mean, you're gonna want it loaded in a specific manner I take it?"

"Yes, of course, leaflets and posters first, office desks on top, then the trees, all wrapped tightly in more pallet wrap. And don't worry, the party has sufficient funds for all this. We can pay you in advance if you like."

"That's a possibility. So, what are we going to put on the EU import declaration and the GMR forms? You gonna tell the truth, that we're carrying Russian propaganda leaflets, 'cause I can't see that being approved."

"We'll say it is Latvian advertising fliers and hope no one examines them in detail."

Julian twisted his mouth. "If you're gonna lie, it'll be your name on the forms."

Alison was puzzled. "What's with the apple saplings?"

"Ah, they are a gift to the farm, for helping us out."

She inclined her head slowly in comprehension.

"And the desks?"

"Just a ruse."

I paused before revealing the next instruction. Out of all the commodities to be shipped to Latvia, this one was going to cause the most concern.

"Oh, there's one other item that needs to be transported to the farm."

Alison raised her eyebrows. "Which is?"

"A hundred thousand pounds, in Russian Rubles."

"Cash!" she snapped. "What for?"

"Oh, it's to pay the Russian truck drivers on the other side."

"You can't take more than ten grand with you through Europe without filling out an endless online declaration form, which is so tedious, and they want to know the ins and outs of a cat's arse. Where it's come from, the intended recipient, what the money is going to be used for. It's a bureaucratic nightmare. So unless you are going to lie and transport it yourself, we can't do that for you."

"Hold on, hold on," said Julian, sensing my anxiety for the sudden spanner in the works. "I'll take it. I'll be the spare driver, but I want fifty grand as an extra, for risking my liberty."

"Dad!" protested Alison.

He held up a palm. "It's alright, love. I'm a big boy. I know all the risks, and I know a thing or two about moving money."

"We need to talk about this, Dad."

"Yes, we do, with Dean here also."

He meant without me in the room. Of cause, they needed a family confab; it was the right thing to do.

I continued, "If you do agree to take on this contract, Mr Hart, I will need to be introduced to all the drivers, to tell them in person what we expect of them, the risks involved and the importance of keeping this whole thing as secret as possible."

"Our drivers are all sound, Mr Llewellyn. Most of them have been with us for donkey's years. I can personally vouch for them," Julian assured me.

"Of course, I shall take your word for it. But for now, as a sweetener to clench this contract, we are willing to pay Hart and Swan four times the usual fee for this type of transport, and we will also give each of your drivers a five grand bonus, in cash. They can say they won it on a scratch card or something."

"Plus my fifty grand for taking the Rubles over?"

"Plus your fifty grand. Look, the reason I have come to you in the first place is because of the long-standing relationship you've had with Acorn. They know and trust you. Your reputation and excellent service record precede you. Everybody respects you.

And it's clear that most people who come into your employ stay forever, so I think that finding ten lorry drivers with integrity should not be a problem.

I would prefer to have drivers who regularly travel to Latvia and Estonia or even Ukrainian drivers. It will simplify things. But if this can't be so, I understand. I am asking a bit much."

"No, no," said Julian. "We have drivers of all nationalities, certainly a few from Ukraine."

"That's very encouraging. Listen, I know this is not a normal contract, and you need time to consider it. However, we do need to move fast on this, as time is not on our side."

Alison locked eyes on her father, waiting for him to respond.

After a very slow ten seconds of chin-stroking, he did. "Well, it's fair to say, Mr Llewellyn, you've certainly done your research. But, from my point of view, it seems there are a couple of oil slicks polluting the waters of disposition."

"And they are?"

"Suppose one of my rigs gets a routine pull, let's say in Lithuania. And the police officer decides to do a thorough check. Don't forget that curtain sides make it easy to access the cargo, and he finds that the paperwork doesn't match the goods being transported.

"Even though the Lithuanian authorities might be sympathetic to your cause, because we have broken EU laws, they will be forced to impound my artic's and lock up my drivers. Hart and Swan's reputation will be damaged, and the element of surprise would be lost for you."

"Yes, but…"

"Secondly, I think that what you are doing here is a courageous and morally apt thing to do, you have *my* respect.

"If what you are telling me is right, and The White Rose Party has a chance of booting Putin out, then I'm all for it.

"By denying you some of the tools you need to achieve that goal, well, I couldn't live with myself."

I was suddenly mute. I couldn't think of an answer to that.

Julian gave me more. "So this is what I suggest. Alison and I are gonna go next door into my office and ring Dean and have a chat about your needs. Then we'll come back in and give you a decision here and now. I can't be fairer than that."

"Yes, of course," I stammered. "Please take your time."

"Would you like something else to drink while you wait, Mr Llewellyn?" said Alison, forever courteous.

"I'll have a coffee now, if that's okay."

"Certainly," she said. "I'll have Lucy bring some in."

As is almost instinctive these days, when finding oneself alone with nothing in particular to do, I pulled out my phone and checked for messages. It was on silent mode for the meeting, but I swear I felt it vibrating in my jacket pocket earlier.

This turned out to be phantom vibes because not a single soul had contacted me the entire morning.

Billy-no-mates, I thought.

Alison's door swung open and in wafted a cafetiere of coffee, a petite jug of milk, a matching sugar bowl, and a cup and saucer carried on a tray by the trendy twenty-something with the long white hair.

I took more notice of her this time. She smelt like a tube of Refreshers and bubbled like one dropped into a bottle of Coke.

"Would you like a biscuit to go with your coffee, sir? We have some of those lovely Choco Leibniz in the cupboard. I've been waiting for an opportunity to crack the packet open."

"Ooh." I was suddenly peckish. "Go on then. You've sold them to me."

There was something incredibly lavish about these little German tablets from heaven, a guilty pleasure. I could easily demolish a whole packet with a cup of tea or coffee, dunking them in long enough to melt the chocolate so it liberally coated the corners of your mouth when you slid one in.

Fortunately for my waistline, Lucy only brought four of the plain chocolate delights back in on a saucer. It was enough, though, and I just about managed to devour them all before there was a tap on the office door.

A bloke with a mop of curly salt and pepper hair surrounding a chrome dome, and tortoise-shell glasses, poked his head through the door.

"Oh, hi," he said, surprised to see a stranger in the office. "Alison and Julian not here?"

"Next door." I indicated with my head.

"You must be Abel?"

"That's right," I replied, puzzled.

He walked in, carrying a green wallet file pressed between his bent forearm and belly.

"I'm Leon Holmes, General Dogsbody," he said, extending a hand. "Nice to meet you."

I reciprocated, just as the Harts filed in behind him.

"Ah, Leon," bellowed Julian, "did you get everything?"

"All here." Leon raised the green file and waggled it like floppy lettuce.

Alison spoke, "If we decide to take your contract on, Mr Llewellyn, Leon here will be playing an integral role."

"You haven't decided yet?"

"After speaking to Dean, we feel it's only right that the drivers be aware of the nature of the transport and of the risks they would be taking," said Julian. "Leon has pulled together a list of our blokes who he feels will be perfect for the job. If they all want to participate, Mr Llewellyn, then Hart and Swan are all in."

I almost fist-pumped the air with joy but reserved my excitement through fear of embarrassment. Alison caught my restrained elation, however, and acknowledged it with a wink and a warm smile, something up until now I thought was beyond her repertoire. I returned the gesture, my cheeks reddening.

Leon took the reins.

"I've picked out seven drivers whom I'm pretty sure will be up for this. Luck would have it they are all back at base tonight, so I'll arrange a meeting for tomorrow…"

I couldn't help but notice that Leon had only said seven drivers when we needed eleven. I decided not to interrupt, but to wait until he had finished before querying it.

"… Arkady Kravets, from Mykolaiv Ukraine, has been with us for more than thirty years, steady as a rock. His eldest son was working for us too, but he has gone back home to fight for his country. We miss him. He's a good lad.

"Danylo Melnyk, is also from Ukraine, somewhere near Lviv, I think. He's been here for ten years plus. He was once a regular to Estonia and Latvia and knows the route like the back of his hand.

"Kyrylo Bilenko, another Ukrainian, from Kremenchuck. He has been with the firm for eighteen years. His brother and eldest son were killed in the fighting three weeks ago. He's married with two grown-up daughters.

"Taras Holab, from Horlivka in the Donbas region, speaks fluent Russian. He used to do the Estonia/Latvia run all the time.

"Filip Jankowski, Polish. He's married to Yana, a Ukrainian, so speaks the language. Been with us for twenty years and is our most frequent driver to the Baltic States.

"Sam Hughes, English, twenty-eight. Came to us straight from school, started as a mechanic, did that for five years, and then went on the road. His girlfriend is a teacher; she often goes on trips with him during the school holidays. He only does the Baltic run. His dad works in the body shop.

"And lastly, another Brit, Jamie Holdsworth, forty-two. His wife is from Latvia. They have two children. He could probably drive to Riga with his eyes closed."

Julian slouched in the armchair. The massive grin on his face said he was proud of the team selection and of Leon for putting it together so quickly.

"Just one thing," I said, spoiling the pride fest. "But don't we need eleven drivers?"

"Yeah?" caroused Julian. "You don't think we're gonna miss this jolly, do ya?"

"We?" I asked, tentatively.

"Yeah," he boomed like I was missing the obvious. "Leon, Dean, Alison and me. This is a family business, Mr Llewellyn, and we love an adventure. I'll be in one of the first two trucks. I can handle a forklift."

I was taken aback. Not only did it sound like they'd already decided to take on the contract, but Alison, a driver? That had never crossed my mind.

"You have an HGV license, Alison?" I quizzed somewhat patronisingly, instantly wishing I'd kept my mouth shut.

She barked a sardonic laugh at me. "I was born with one." It was her turn to be condescending. "I've been driving trucks since the day I could reach the pedals."

"But this is no ordinary run."

"Piece of piss," she snapped and then laughed again.

It felt like I'd just been dragged into the twenty-first century by my ears.

"Besides," she continued, "I have my dad, my big brother and eight loyal friends to protect me, so I think I'll be okay, but if you're offering to chaperone me on the journey, you're welcome."

She was trying to embarrass me again, and it was working, but it didn't matter. I was now fairly certain they'd take on the job.

Julian guffawed at Alison's antics, before saying, "I'll tell you what, Mr Llewellyn. I'll have a couple of unmarked curtain trailers with twenty plain pallets dropped off at the printer's tomorrow. That'll take the strain off of your guy in Redhill."

"But I thought you wanted to get the approval of the drivers first before we go ahead?"

"I do, but whatever the outcome; it'll help you out, won't it? We can invoice you if it turns out it's just for the transportation and storage of these two loads. But actually, I know my drivers, and I'm pretty sure they're all gonna want to go, and not just for the money."

13

Tuesday 26th April.

On the day that UN Secretary-General António Guterres made a three-day trip to Russia and Ukraine amid criticism for the limited role played by the United Nations in the crisis, I headed back to Northamptonshire for the meeting with Hart & Swan's proposed truck drivers.

The news coming from Ukraine made grim viewing. Cataclysmic scenes of the heroic and dogged resistance of somewhere between five and eight hundred soldiers, who were making a last stand in the labyrinth of tunnels and bunkers under the besieged Azovstal Iron and Steel Works, in the port of Mariupol.

The town had been flattened by a barrage of Russian missiles and bombs coming from air, land and sea, and this was the last pocket of defiance, held up underground in nuclear-resistant shelters, drastically short of food, water, ammunition and medical supplies, yet determined to fight to the death for their country.

Ninety-five per cent of the city had been destroyed and the Russian forces were trying to strangle the final resistance with enormous costs to both sides.

There were also civilians hiding out with the soldiers in the tunnels, and a makeshift hospital trying to care for three hundred wounded, yet the airstrikes kept coming, as much as fifty separate strikes in one day.

Ukraine was claiming to have killed at least six thousand Russian soldiers, whilst Russia was saying that they in return had killed four thousand Ukrainian men and taken almost as many prisoners. Civilian casualty estimates were being put at two thousand, three hundred and fifty-seven dead, but some believed that number to be way, way higher.

I had to steel my reserve. All this hideous news of death and utter destruction made me even more determined to advance our plan and force an end to the nightmare.

The control tower of Maddox Field came into view, and my thoughts turned to the speech I had prepared overnight. A rousing Churchillian address that would clinch their hearts and minds, and put a fire in their bellies so earnestly they'd be convinced that what we are doing was a world-changing event and their part in it critical.

I was fifteen minutes late, not a great start.

"Morning, Mr Llewellyn," greeted the receptionist. "They're in the war room. They're expecting you."

"War room?" It struck an ominous chord.

"Through there." She pointed towards a pair of double doors to her left. "Our conference room, it used to be where they planned all the bombing runs during the war. It still has a lot of the old features inside."

"Oh." I smiled, thanked her, and scurried off towards the heavy-looking wooden swing doors.

"Ah, Mr Llewellyn, nice of you to join us," said Julian with a playful smile.

Alison sat there cross-legged on a swivel chair, a wry curl on her luscious lips and decked out like a model on the front cover of a glossy magazine.

She wore a cerise, figure-hugging short dress, with a matching wide-brimmed hat, pinned at a jaunty angle, and pink shoes with four-inch stiletto heels. Her forefoot was flexing impatiently.

She was flanked by someone who was obviously her brother; Dean looked very much like his dad, only four stone lighter and twice as dapper.

We shook hands; his grip was firmer than I had expected.

"Got held up?" he inquired.

"Ah, no, sorry. Sometimes it's bedlam in our house. Eight people all trying to use the facilities at once. It's a nightmare."

Dean nodded politely; he had no idea of my circumstances.

"You're here in one piece. That's the main thing."

"Shall we get on with it?" suggested Julian.

"Yes, of course."

I stiffened my resolve and turned to face seven new faces of various wear and tear, scattered around a lengthy vintage oak conference table. All eyes were fixed on me, the thoughts behind them hard to read.

"This is Abel Llewellyn, from the Russian White Rose Party," announced Julian Hart. "He has a few words for us all."

It occurred to me then, that the word Russian didn't sit well with the Ukrainian huddle.

Happy to give me the room, Julian joined his children and Leon Holmes behind me, to await my sermon.

I cleared my throat and began.

"First of all, thank you all for coming here today. I realise this is not a part of your normal working day, and you'd probably prefer to be out on the road, and who can blame you? It's a beautiful day." I smiled at my audience but received nothing in return.

"Erm, as Julian just said, I represent the Russian White Rose Party, an environmentally driven political party based here in the UK, but I am neither Russian nor do I have any Russian ancestry. My friends are, though, and together we started this party with two determined goals in mind, to oust that maniac despot Vladimir Putin and to end this catastrophic, senseless war in Ukraine."

What I presumed to be the Ukrainian contingent betrayed a faint acknowledgment with a slight bobbing of heads. I continued.

"We have a unique cargo that we would like Hart & Swan to deliver, and it is not without its perils. This is why I wanted to meet you all today and explain in person exactly what you as drivers would be carrying. We believe the shipment has the power to change the world, to stop the war, and make Europe a fundamentally safer place."

If my talk was being given to waxwork dummies at Madame Tussauds, I'd be getting the same response, zilch.

"Operation Anchovy," I announced. "You have been specially selected by Leon here for this job because he knows we can unequivocally rely on you, to not only get the job done but to do it with the integrity, passion and with utmost tight-lipped professionalism this assignment requires."

Still, the statuesque faces stared back at me.

I rallied on, giving a full explanation of the cargo to be shipped, the risks involved, its intended effect on the Russian population and its Latvian destination.

Again, my audience was inert.

Seeing that I was promising to end the war in their home country in a matter of months, I expected more from our Ukrainian friends, but they were unperturbed.

"Any questions?" I probed, hoping for at least a little curiosity.

Arkady Kravets raised a half-hearted hand.

We made eye contact; his were dark, unreflective pools that owned up to being the witness of way too much pain.

"You think these arse-wipes will get read?" the weariness in his was voice profound.

"Arse wipes?"

"The leaflets. You think Putin will allow the Katsap's to hand out your propaganda and walk free?"

"The Katsap?"

"Yeah, the Moskal, the Russians." He said elongating the R in Russians.

The other drivers all sniggered.

"It's a gamble, but we are working on a plan for that."

"You better make them with invisible ink," jeered Taras Holab, sardonically.

More laughter ensued.

I reached inside my man-bag and retrieved a handful of leaflets.

"I've had draft copies made in Ukrainian and English. Please take one and read it, but I must have them back before you leave."

Arkady spoke again, "I don't wish to piss on your bonfire, Mr Llewellyn. I really don't, but, I can't bring myself to believe that the pen is mightier than the sword."

Jamie Holdsworth interjected, "Ignore the banter, Mr Llewellyn. We don't need to read your leaflets. What you have told us seems sound. We just provide the transport; the nature of the goods is someone else's responsibility. Just point us in the right direction, and we'll get it there."

His statement stunned me.

"So you've all decided to go then? When did this happen?"

"About ten minutes before you arrived. I think the pay packet did it."

Alison interrupted, "Hart and Swan are picking up the tax and national insurance for the bonus payment, Mr Llewellyn. It only seemed fair."

I didn't quite know what to say. I had come here with no certain expectations.

"Wow, thank you, everyone. This is, erm, very exciting. Erm, well I suppose I'll see you all on the uh, 13th of May then."

Rugged smiles and nods answered my question. I turned to the Harts with a jubilant expression stretching my face, to the muffled sound of chairs being rearranged across the carpet and under the table.

Julian spoke over my shoulder to the departing drivers. "Double up on the shirts, lads."

I had no idea what he meant by that. He explained.

Hart & Swan has a good rapport with the police forces throughout Europe but, as an insurance policy, we always carry a few football shirts in the cabs. It's a wonder what a Man U or Liverpool shirt can do in a sticky situation."

"Bribery?"

"No, not really, just a thank you for helping us out. Trailer looting can be rife on the continent; we find it's best to keep the law on our side."

I nodded, contemplatively.

Shaking the directors' hands, I thanked them once again. A quick glance over my shoulder assured me that the drivers had vacated the room before I raised a burning question with Julian.

"If your guys had already decided to take us up on our offer, why did they sit there and endure my speech?"

"Just wanted to get the measure of you, I suppose; besides they are on overtime this morning." He guffawed.

"Mr Llewellyn." Alison's sultry tone turned my head.

"Yes?"

"Would you care to follow me? I have something to show you."

My mind boggled. How could I resist?

"Where are we going?" I wondered as we walked.

"Out to the trailer park."

"Okay?" I replied curiously.

As we traversed the concrete, I made an attempt at small talk.

"Going somewhere nice today?"

"My son has a polo match down in Epsom. It's his first match in the adult team. We're all going down, and I can't wait to watch him play."

All eyes are going to be on you, I thought.

We reached an idle, curtain-side trailer, standing apart from anything else, close to one of the hangars. It looked brand new.

"We've been busy," she informed me. "Practicing your instructions."

In one swift, easy motion, she unclipped a strap and slid the PVC curtain back like it was of little consequence, which I knew it must have been.

On the bed were two pallets, stacked with polystyrene blocks to represent the leaflets, on top of which, imitating the office furniture, were sheets of cardboard about six inches thick, and on top of these were rows of traffic cones, surrogates for the trees. All of which were tightly bound in pallet wrap.

"We can unload a trailer packed with these in ten minutes," she boasted. "We'll easily get all the trucks unloaded in the period you've allotted us."

I pursed my bottom lip.

"Impressive. That's exactly what we need."

"Thought so," she said, cockily.

I arched my eyebrows. This woman was a whirlwind.

"Have you arranged a date for us to collect the trees yet?" she asked.

"Er, no, not yet, but I think, for the health of the plants, they'll be better off kept at the nursery until the last moment, rather than drying out in the back of a container for a week or two. So maybe on the 11th, that should give them a chance."

"Cool, if you could sort that out, and let us know. I gotta run now, but I'll see you very soon, Abel."

She turned on her pink heels and swaggered across the yard towards her waiting, chauffer-driven, bronze Bentley.

I watched her go for as long as was prudent, and without getting caught. She'd called me by my first name, something she hadn't done before.

It made sense for me to drive straight to London, rather than head home, dump the car then catch a train back into the Smoke.

I'd booked yet another day off work and wanted to tell Milana and Andrei the good news personally.

On my journey down, I pondered over the reaction the Russian people were going to have on receipt of the leaflets, or seeing the posters. Would they believe a word of it, or would they just consider it Western bullshit and bin it? After all, from what I'd been led to believe, the majority of the citizens bought into the State narrative and were too scared to even think otherwise.

Yet, I reasoned, surely, they are not all subjugated sheep. The Fox and The Scalpel have proved it to be otherwise, as do all the dissidents who have fled, and our own Oleg Stepanov and the opposition politicians who are now in prison. And all of the murdered prominent people who'd dared to speak out against the regime, or the jailed journalists who sought the truth.

No, I was convinced that what we were doing would stir up enough free thinkers to have the courage to do the right thing.

If they did it en masse, there would not be enough judiciary to stamp it out.

Arkady Kravets' words still haunted me. 'I don't believe the pen is mightier than the sword'. Maybe not on its own, but together with the Ukrainian counterattack growing in momentum at the moment, and causing Russian casualties, the two forms of attack might be enough to sway the Russian general public and bring about an end to this abominable empire-seeking government and this despicable war.

***

The office had three parking spaces in an underground facility close to Haymarket. It was only a couple of minutes' walk away, so I decided to see if it had a space available, before searching for an extortionate NCP to put the Volvo in for the afternoon.

Luck would have it, only Jim's Harley Davidson was occupying one of the spots.

"Yes!" I vocalised.

I backed in beside the immaculate machine. I'm not into bikes much at all, but even I had to admire the quality and craftsmanship that had gone into the manufacture of this beast, and, of course, the fabulous condition Jim kept her in. She was a beauty.

She reminded me of a nugget of information Jim had outlined. The Russian motorcycle fraternity was not best pleased with the war in Ukraine, not just because of its foolhardiness and the carnage it was causing, but the situation it had bestowed upon them. For now, they couldn't get hold of any spare parts for their machines or go on any tours outside the country.

Plus, a good majority of bikers were ex-servicemen, and they were being called up for national service, or face the consequences if they didn't conform.

It bolstered my resolve to think that we would surely have their vote when it came to it.

Off the bustling street, the building's glass doors closed automatically in my wake, hermetically sealing me in climate-controlled comfort.

A quick hello to Irina at reception, and I bounded up the stairs two at a time like I was eighteen again.

The lobby was library quiet. If it weren't for a few visible heads transfixed to their computer screens through the glass walls of the lower offices, I'd swear we were closed.

Deciding that I'd completed my exercise for the day, I took the elevator up to the next level.

Andrei and Vanya were bent over a chess board in Andrei's office, each considering their next ten moves. It appeared it was sacrilege to interrupt, but I did anyway.

"Milana not here?"

Andrei turned to me and screwed up one side of his face.

"Gone for a power nap. She is exhausted."

He went back to his game, and I got the hint.

A few offices down, five workers, The Scalpel and Vladimir, were busily attending to their own schedules. No banter or skiving in attendance whatsoever.

I was definitely not in a British office.

The Scalpel looked up. "Ah, Abel, how did it go?"

I relayed this morning's events with great enthusiasm, to which all seven of them paid the closest attention.

"Excellent," The Scalpel clenched both fists and shook the air in front of him.

"I also have good news. I have managed to find four friends who are more than willing to help with the loading at the farm. Two of them, Grisha and Matvey, are going to take a crash course in forklift driving this weekend, which will speed things up dramatically at Petrov's."

"Brilliant," I said, then relayed to him Arkady's concerns over the welfare of the leaflet distributors on the streets of Russia.

He lowered his head.

"Of course, of course, it concerns us all. Even though The Russian White Rose Party will make it overtly clear that we advocate a non-violent policy at every stage of our campaign, it will make no difference. The police will be under pressure to squash any demonstration of disloyalty to the Putin regime.

"The leaflet distributors will, without doubt, take the brunt of the intolerance of the state, but with a leaflet drop of this magnitude, the authorities will be hunting for the ring leaders."

"Our agents, you mean?"

"Yes, they'll use any means at their disposal to extract the information they need."

"You mean torture?"

"Of course, torture, intimidation, the threat of long jail sentences, anything to get them to talk."

"And will they?"

"Probably. These are young people, students, political activists, they'll only hold out for so long."

"So, our agents will be exposed?"

"Maybe, maybe not. Let me explain how it is set up. Once loaded, our twenty Russian lorries will depart for their designated areas and meet with the first agents in secret locations and dispense their cargo.

"Within two days, all one thousand and four second agents will collect their quota and contact their four, third agents. Who will, in turn, split the leaflets and posters up into twenty lots. Are you with me so far?"

"Oh, yes, I'm following you."

"Good. Each distributor will receive a freezer bag, you know, the type you get in a supermarket, containing fifteen hundred leaflets, six posters, glue, drawing pins, Sellotape and a map of the streets they need to cover.

"The bags will be left in hidden places, and the distributors will receive a phone call and instructions on where to find them."

"All this has to be done in two days?"

"Yes, it's going to be tight, but our agents are dedicated to the cause, and they will get it done."

"Hold on a minute. Are these guys getting paid? Only, I reckon there'll be more than eighty thousand distributors; we're only sending a hundred grand to cover the wage bill. What are they getting? A pound each?"

"The Russian people suffer well; they endure anything for their freedom. The money is going to be split between the drivers and the top agents. That's where the costs are."

My head bobbed on my shoulders like a nodding donkey, considering the expenses of running trucks, paying drivers and funding a network. It would easily eat up a chunk of money.

I voiced the obvious. "So, if they get caught, the distributors won't know the agents who gave them the bags?"

"Exactly; our biggest worry is that nobody up the chain gets caught before the 20th. That would fuck the whole enterprise up."

I'd always imagined that Friday and Saturday would be the most dangerous days, but The Scalpel let me in on another simple safeguard.

Each distributor would be encouraged to share their workload with friends and family. Not only would it get done quicker, but a tsunami of leaflet circulation would hopefully overwhelm the local police forces and they would step back, realising they couldn't stop the tide of popular opinion.

In an ideal world, this sounded good, but this was Russia we were talking about, a different syntax, a different mindset, and a very different agenda.

He went on to tell me that my help was required here at HQ from the 16th to the 24th, in the operations room. Information, coming through from Russia twenty-four-seven, needed to be transferred onto the map and various whiteboards.

Every available member of staff was required, and we would all be sleeping here at the office.

Jim would be sorting out the temporary bedding and The Scalpel was giving up his flat upstairs to kip down here with the troops.

A wicked smile invaded my inner mind. A week of sharing Milana's bed didn't seem too shabby.

***

Wednesday 27th April.

Beau and Victoria had initially volunteered to handle The White Rose's finances and accounts.

It soon became very clear the job was way too vast for the amount of time the pair could allot to the task. And so an accounts department was created and was now well and truly ensconced within headquarters walls.

But they remained as a part of the team who searched for properties abroad in which to set up a remote White Rose office.

Two more such offices were about to be opened, one in Helsinki and the other in Oslo.

Our entire household had gathered in the Raft, to celebrate.

Because the world's media had tagged our remote offices 'The new Russian embassies', we'd learnt from The Fox that Mr Putin was outraged with the term and, indeed, our endeavours thus far.

Whilst prospecting for both the Norway and Finland offices, they uncovered some inspiring facts.

In Norway, reside approximately five thousand five hundred Russian nationals, and in Finland the numbers are far greater, with an estimated sixty thousand.

Both countries share a border with Russia, so people will inevitably migrate for work or family matters, and these significant numbers gave the teams an enterprising idea.

Once the premises were acquired, adverts were placed on social media for staff. The requirements for these positions were that the applicants needed to be bi-lingual and have experience in working at an embassy or government facility.

It was a general consensus that, worldwide, Russian embassy staff wanted to jump ship. So a giant carrot of quadrupling their current salaries was offered.

The plan worked spectacularly. Seventeen of the Helsinki Russian embassy employees left their positions and came over to us. In Oslo, we acquired six.

Milana and Andrei's dream of having a little bit of Russia outside of the regime, that Putin couldn't touch, was gaining force, and probably really pissing him off.

Whilst watching these new offices being unveiled on the news, the Oxford Eight, as we were now affectionately being labelled, came up with a foolproof idea to judge whether the Russian people wanted Putin out of office or not.

Using the sixty-thousand-strong Russian population in Finland as an example, we estimated that forty-two thousand were eligible to register to vote in the motherland, for the forthcoming Presidential election.

Once they had received their registration numbers, the White Rose office could send them a survey form to fill out, containing one simple question with a multiple-choice answer.

'Given the option, during the next Presidential election, would you vote for Putin's Independent party, Oleg Stepanov's White Rose Party, or someone else?'

The surveys could include a return addressed envelope to the Helsinki main post office, where they could be collected and transported to the Chinese embassy, where staff there could independently collate the information, eliminating any accusation of fiddling by one of Putin's allies.

This idea could be replicated in all seventeen countries in which we now have offices, and we were confident that the White Rose Party would receive at least ninety per cent of the vote, sending a clear message to the Russian people that Putin could quite easily be booted out of office.

I called Milana later and forwarded our idea. She resoundingly gave it her seal of approval.

***

Saturday 30th April.

After a gruelling session with Charles on the river, where we really picked up the pace, we sat on the bank taking in some fluids, and talked for a good hour about the forthcoming operation.

His main concern was the number of people now involved, and the risks they were taking, voicing his conclusion with one chilling statement.

"Be prepared for a hefty butcher's bill."

His words underlined the reality of the outcome of this endeavour and grounded me with harsh contrition for being a part of an organisation that was sentencing these brave young souls to imprisonment and at least a severe beating at best.

I had never felt as low as I did at this juncture. But The Scalpel's words echoed in my head, 'Russian people suffer well. They will endure anything for their freedom'.

Charles perked me up. He said that two more Russian oligarchs had contacted him wishing to donate to the Russian White Rose Party, adding that it was a clear sign that Putin was losing his grip.

His face then started to curl, the way it always did before he hit me with one of his self-concocted pearls of wisdom.

"Those oligarchs," he said, "they do like to keep their insurance policies up to date."

14

Lemon Grove, Oxford 13th May.

While I lay dozing in the half-light, somewhere between slumber and sub-conscious, my mobile phone, until now innocuously dormant on the bedside cabinet, suddenly wrenched me violently into the world of the living.

I reached across a floppy hand and pulled the screaming thing up to my face.

Focussing on the caller ID first, and then the time, I inhaled deeply and sat upright. It was six-thirty. Alison Hart was beating her chest.

"Morning, Abel!" she chirped, way too exuberant for this time of day.

The reality of why she was calling faded in like a focusing telescope.

"How's it going? You about to leave?"

"You sound knackered, Abe. Have you just woken up?"

"Yes, my alarm is set for seven. You've caught me napping, I'm afraid."

"Ah, real men get up at five," she ribbed. "We're almost set, gonna leave in twenty minutes."

"Right, right." I struggled, slightly wounded. "What time are you catching the Eurostar?"

"Ten-twenty. It's all booked in."

"Cool, cool. Are you checking in with me tonight?"

"Yeah, when we've used up the Tacho' hours, should be somewhere in Germany."

"Brilliant. Any problems…"

"Yeah, yeah, I'll let you know. Back to bed, snoozy."

I was just about to say that I was getting up now, but she cut me off. Marvellous.

I had a very busy day planned, meeting with some top military bods to discuss the re-wilding of a forest on MOD land back down in Dorset. Ripping out non-native species plantations, turning areas back into heath-land and letting nature run its course. This way, flowering plants would take up residence, helping the pollinators, the invertebrates, and the snakes and lizards. Then, native trees would self-seed and grow naturally, bringing back the birds and mammals, and the diversity that should inhabit our woodlands.

Comatose, I sauntered to the bathroom, keen to empty my bladder, praying it was vacant. I needed to shower and be on the road before eight o'clock.

My luck was in. The door latch snapped back as I approached, and Jack emerged wrapped in a tatty, pale blue towel, followed by a cloud of venting steam.

"Morning, mate. It's all yours," he declared.

"Oh, spot on. I'm busting."

"What time are you back tonight?"

"Why, who's cooking?"

"It's my turn."

"Oh no, not leek and potato soup again?"

"No," he said, feigning hurt. "I'm making a sweet potato Korma, actually."

"Ah, I knew there'd be potatoes in there somewhere."

"Get out of here," he quipped, and then flicked me with an even wetter towel, which narrowly missed as I hurried out of its trajectory, smirking.

As I stood in front of the porcelain, emptying my bladder, my mind drifted from the important task I had for the day. I was too preoccupied with thoughts of our convoy heading for the continent.

I was confident enough with the professionals we had chosen for the transport. It was just that any number of things could go wrong en route and bugger up this entire operation.

It was best to put it to the back of my mind. We'd done all we could this end to ensure those leaflets get into the hands of the Russian people before polling day. Their fate, it seemed, lay with the well-oiled machine we had set in motion. There was nothing more I could do, and certainly worrying about it wasn't going to ensure its success.

At five o'clock that afternoon, I should have received a call from Alison, telling me they were parking up for the night.

But instead, I was coming off the A34 at Oxford, around six, and still she hadn't called.

My day in Bovington had gone well, but I was now getting anxious. Something had gone terribly wrong. I had convinced myself of it.

Not wanting to wait until I reached home, I pulled into the retail park car lot, found a space and switched off my engine to make a call.

Alison answered almost immediately.

"Hiya, what's up?" Her voice was loud, and pitched high above the drone of her DAF's fifteen-litre engine.

"Are you alright?"

"That's nice of you to care. A bit tired and rather hungry to be honest, but we'll be stopping in an hour, then I can get some grub."

I was perplexed by her lack of anguish and also, her apparent use of the phone whilst driving.

"Are you using hands-free?"

"Of course. My phone is connected to the onboard system via blue tooth. You've just interrupted a Kyle tune; so it had better be worth it."

Why she wasn't concerned with the hour of the day was baffling to me.

"I thought you were going to report in at five. I got worried."

"Ahh, no need to worry about me, Abel. I'm a big girl. Nah, we got held up at border force control in Croquells. Bloody two-hour queue, doc' check, plate scan, boring as hell.

"We've made good time since then, though. Gonna be stopping at a Parkplatz near Kreuz about seven."

"Oh, right. So everything is fine then?"

"Yep. Stop worrying, Abel. I'll check in with you tomorrow at about four o'clock."

"Okay, talk to you then."

"Byee!"

Nerves calmed, I headed home.

The sweet potato Korma was surprisingly good. I suspected it was due to the help of Jack's girlfriend, Agatha. Between the two of them, they'd knocked up a huge pot of the steaming brown stuff and an equally large pot of Basmati rice, a mountain of Naan bread and a pile of garlic and herb poppadoms, enough to feed all eleven of us plus the rest of the street.

We slouched in the Raft, all of us too stuffed to move, swigging from bottles of Tiger beer and sipping from tumblers of various spirits.

The question of the White Rose remote offices was addressed. The teams had planned to have thirty up and running by Election Day. So far, we had nineteen, with the possibility of one more opening in time, in Kazakhstan.

Some twenty to thirty million ethnic Russians are estimated to live outside the bounds of the Russian Federation (depending on the definition of "ethnicity").

We planned to capitalize on this by sending leaflets to as many of those ex-pat Russians as we could locate.

The personnel employed at the remote offices had been working like bees to get this task done. Printing and distributing in those countries had not been a problem, just a massive mailing task.

We hoped that being outside the grips of Putin's iron fists, the voters would have more impartiality, less obligation to state rules and a better understanding as to what was truly happening in the world, rather than the spoon-fed bullshit the regime blinded them with.

Twenty million votes in our favour would help tip the scales dramatically.

German-Polish border, A12 crossing, Saturday 14th May 1 p.m.

More than twenty trucks, including all ten Hart & Swan vehicles, were sitting in holding bays beside the border control buildings.

The drivers were asked by the guards to stay in their cabs but to hand over their paperwork.

Spot checks were unusual these days, but did occur occasionally.

Julian Hart was outside his truck talking to the head honcho.

"Your EU import declaration, states that you are transporting printed advertising fliers, office furniture and apple trees to Latvia. A strange combination, Mr Hart?"

Julian shrugged. "We pass no judgement on the goods being carried, Josef. Can I call you Josef?"

Josef slowly nodded in the affirmative.

"We just deliver the stuff."

Josef's face puckered.

"Yours is a very large haulage company, Mr Hart. I see your trucks every day. Do you always drive one yourself?"

"I like to keep my hand in now and again."

"Hmm." The guard looked mighty suspicious. "And it is all going to a farm?"

"I believe they have a transport hub there for further distribution. It's the first time for us."

"Hmm. I'd like to inspect your trailer, Mr Hart. Can you draw back the curtain please?"

"Certainly."

Julian complied with the captain's request, pulling the vinyl sheet back to the rear.

On the bed, strapped together, were twenty identical pallets stacked with a square of leaflets six feet high, on top of which were the desks and the apple trees almost touching the ceiling of the trailer. All were tightly bound in pallet wrap and strapped to the deck, so they wouldn't shift in transit.

It was a work of art, one that Josef was reluctant to disturb.

"Do you have a copy of the flier, Mr Hart?"

"All bound up I'm afraid. Besides, they're in Latvian so it'd be of little use to me as reading material. 'Ere, do you like football?"

Josef squinted.

"Of course, doesn't everybody?"

"You be surprised. Do you follow any British clubs?"

The guard wondered where this was going, but played along.

"I like Arsenal; they had our Wojciech Szczesny playing for them during their heyday. One of the best goalkeepers in the world ever, you know? He still plays for the national team. Why do you ask?"

"'Cause today might be your lucky day, old son!"

Julian went to his cab and climbed up inside, coming back down moments later with an unmistakable red and white number seven, Arsenal shirt, with Bukayo Saka's name on the back.

Josef appeared apprehensively curious.

"Are you trying to bribe me, Mr Hart?"

"What? No, just a gift, from one Arsenal fan to another. It's this year's design."

"You follow Arsenal too?"

"Since I was a boy, like my dad and granddad, a family tradition."

This made Josef smile. He looked around to see that none of his colleagues were watching, then took the shirt and hastily stuffed it inside his Hi-Viz jacket.

"Thank you, Mr Hart," he said. "I believe all your documentation is in order. You may proceed through Poland. I wish you a safe journey."

"Thank you, my friend. I hope you get to enjoy wearing the shirt. See you again."

With that, Julian rolled back his curtain and secured the straps.

He then walked back to Dean's truck and gave him a wink.

"We're all set to go, son."

"Did I hear you telling him you were an Arsenal fan?"

"Needs must, son."

Dean chuckled. "They'll string you up at Olympic Park if they hear you've said that."

Julian smirked as he walked back to his truck, holding his hand aloft, pointing his forefinger skyward and rotating his wrist.

"Let's roll," he said.

Again, she was late checking in. But, I worried less than I had the day before, deducing that things happen on the road that simply couldn't be predicted, and that timing the route to perfection was a wasted exercise.

At ten past five, Alison finally switched off her truck after re-fuelling at a Lotus station on the E30 near Brwinów, northeast Poland.

She explained to me the cause of the delay and the football shirt business, assuring me that everything was indeed fine.

Some of the guys were getting a taxi into Warsaw to have a few beers for the evening, but she was staying put, along with Dean and Julian, to keep guard on the cargo.

She wished me a good night and scheduled another call for tomorrow. Her voice was weary, not her usual buoyant, confident self. I guessed the road was taking its toll.

Milana and I hadn't cemented our relationship in traditional ways. We'd never been out on a date, I hadn't even wooed her or plied her with gifts, and we found very little time to be alone together, other than sharing a bed at weekends.

The sex was great, intense at times; it felt like a release most of the time, from the immense stresses she was under.

I therefore felt a little bit like a facility, rather than a partner.

Ultimately, if everything went to plan and the White Rose Party won the election, we could end up on very different trajectories.

I hadn't dared to dream what life could be like if I quit the UK and followed her to Russia. Would she even have the time for me, or the inclination?

We hadn't proclaimed undying love for one another, and there was certainly no talk of wedded bliss on the table. So, however our strange relationship played out, we'd just have to wait and see.

I'd like to think that we'd always remain friends, but who knew what strain the world of international politics placed on an affair.

For now, I was just going to go with the flow and enjoy the next week with her as much as I could. Support her, and do my best for the party.

By circumstance, more than planning, we found ourselves quite alone this evening.

It was the lull before the storm. Most of the staff members were absent, doing whatever they needed before the expected chaotic week ahead.

Scal', Andrei and Jim had gone down to the Gnat's Racker for a drink. And, there were just a couple of security guys milling around downstairs.

So, we decided to have a date night after all. But not go anywhere, just order a Chinese meal and sit and chat like a proper couple over a few glasses of wine.

The next three hours turned out to be the most informative, extraordinary, heart-warming conversation I'd ever experienced.

I got to know a glimpse of the real Milana and her perception of a new modern Russia. The passion she had for its people was inspirational. If anyone was born to do this job, it was Milana Fyodorova.

She'd kept hidden the amount of pain and suffering her and Andrei had endured. How they were sent away at a very young age to protect them from persecution. Moved from pillar to post in secret until eventually, as teenagers, they ended up here in the UK as asylum seekers.

Even now, as their fame and popularity grew, Milana knew that it would have dire consequences on the way her parents were being treated in prison. The anguish was almost unbearable, but put it aside she must, because they would never be freed unless the White Rose Party came to power and put an end to the archaic, totalitarian, doctrine of imprisoning political opposition.

I wanted to show my appreciation and the respect for her she had instilled in me. I offered to buy her a gift. She didn't want a ring or jewellery or anything fanciful, but did accept a new outfit to wear on her next TV appearance, when she would stand atop the steps of the garden patio, here at headquarters, and address the world's media as the new interim president of the Russian Federation.

This was acceptable; she liked that idea very much.

Sunday 15th May, 10 a.m.

The Scalpel and I were in his office, going over the plan. The rest of the team was absent and I intended to make the most of it. After today, and for the next nine days, this place was going to be frantic.

All thirty-nine employees were going to be here, working, eating, sleeping, farting, twenty-four-seven, hopefully collating good news.

We hadn't had the chance to talk on a personal level before, so now seemed like the perfect opportunity to get to know the man.

All I knew of him was that he was a Russian citizen. Who had until recently lived in that country, but fascinatingly, he spoke perfect English with a West Country accent.

I was more than curious.

"Where did you learn your English, Scal'?"

He stopped arranging the boxes of pins he was lining up and gently smiled at me. I got the feeling I had awoken a warm memory.

"I came to England in my mid-twenties, to work for the NHS as a nurse in Exeter Hospital. I had some English already that I'd learnt at college, but it was quite pidgin.

"It was at Exeter that I met Danil. He was also a nurse, British, but his father was Russian, his mother came from Cornwall."

"Oh? And how did they meet?"

"Danil's father was the chief officer of a Russian merchant ship that ran aground and sank off Porth Nanven during a storm. He was picked up, along with several crew members, bobbing about in a small lifeboat, by the RNLI and brought ashore.

"Danil's mum worked at a hotel in St Just, where the sailors were boarded, and that's how they met. Kirill liked the country so much he stayed and eventually they married."

"And Danil, he was your partner?"

"Yes, for seventeen years. We both had family in Russia and would periodically spend time over there.

"We became heavily involved with Russia's Anti-Gay movement, until three years ago, when Danil was arrested for simply holding a placard during a peaceful Pride march in Moscow. He was sent to prison for three years."

"Three years! For holding up a sign?"

"If he hadn't had dual citizenship, we're convinced he would have received a ten-year sentence."

"So, is he out now?"

Scal's gaze fell to the floor as he embodied the saddest soul alive. I instinctively knew what was coming.

"One year, three months and two weeks into his sentence, I received a phone call from Kirill. Danil was found dead in his cell, cause of death, suicide."

He became stoic, emotionless, and tempered by grief.

I gave him a moment before asking if they suspected foul play.

"Absolutely," he spat. "I knew Danil better than anyone; he most definitely wasn't the type to take his own life. He loved life and fought hard to better the lives of all of us, especially the many thousands who can't find their own voice."

The Scalpel's eyes locked onto mine like tractor beams.

"That's why I'm sitting here, Abel, to avenge Danil's death by destroying the evil that murdered him."

We both took a minute, letting the ribbon of conversation fall softly to the desk.

Scal' picked it up again.

"It'll take one of several things to kick-start the decline of that piece of shit," he declared.

"One: losing the support of the Russian people, obviously the one we are gunning for. Two: losing control of the Armed forces. Without them, he's well and truly buggered. Three: his oligarchs, who we know are already jumping ship. It won't take many more failures for them all to follow suit.

"Four: his allies. If they all turn their backs on him, he will soon run out of munitions and vital supplies. And five: his health. If he has a terminal illness like we think he has, then why carry on? He could leave office and spend the rest of his days soaked in luxury on one of his super yachts or in one of his palatial villas.

"Surely, no sick human being would opt to be under the mega stresses he's pulled on top of himself, not even a narcissistic megalomaniac such as Putin.

"Deluded and lied to as he is, his blood pressure has gotta be through the roof!"

I said nothing, just swayed in my swivel chair, drowning in pity for The Scalpel and all those who have lost loved ones due to that brutal paranoid dictator.

Anastasia, one of the staff, poked her head through the door. "Drink, anyone?"

"Oh!" Her words jerked me back to the present. "I'd love coffee, please, Anastasia, if that's alright."

She inclined a nod and waited for The Scalpel's reply.

"Do we have any Vodka?"

She grinned. "*Da, Konechno.*" As swiftly as she had entered, she was gone.

"Never too early," I ventured, giving him vindication.

"Not for a Russian," he agreed.

I grinned.

"So, Scal'," I said, wanting to drastically change direction. "What's with all the coloured pins?"

"Well, you know the map in Milana's office with all the black pins representing the whereabouts of our agents?"

"Yes."

"When they have received their quota of leaflets, they'll let us know and we'll replace those black pins with red ones, and a red tick next to their number on the whiteboard."

Anastasia barged in carrying our drinks.

"Here you are, guys. Don't get too pissed, Scal'. We need you on the ball tomorrow."

She placed a large mug of white coffee on the table, along with a glass, and a half-full bottle of Smirnoff.

The Scalpel barked a laugh.

"It will take more than that. But don't worry, Anastasia; I'll just have the one glass, a big one."

She smiled and left the room.

Scal' continued. "When the first agents have divvied up their supply to the second agents, and let us know, we'll replace the red pins with yellow, and a yellow tick.

"Likewise with the distributors, once their leaflets and posters are gone, and they are still at liberty, their reporting back will cause us to change the yellow pins for blue ones."

"So, this way will show us at a glance just how successful the distribution has been?"

"Exactly."

"And, if any areas have failed?"

"Yes."

It was simple World War II technology, albeit with internet communication.

"So, what are the orange and purple pins for?"

"Orange is to indicate that the Russian people have come to their senses and worn something white over the weekend, and purple if they actually down tools and go on strike."

"When will we see evidence of that?"

"On the 23rd, starting at four or five in the morning."

Scal' inhaled for a good five seconds.

"This will be the most nail-biting time of the whole operation, waiting for that information to come in. It is the apex of the mission. If people go on strike in numbers, we have them; we know we're in with a chance of winning this thing."

He then said something quite profound. "Nothing gives the fearful more courage, than another person's fear."

"Meaning?"

"The whole of Russia will be witnessing what we see, and Putin will be shitting himself, adding to the snowball effect of contempt for his office."

It made sense.

The massive question was. Would the Russian multitude be swayed enough to unite behind us, by what is effectively words on a piece of paper?

The Scalpel, as always, provided a positive perspective.

"Everything on that leaflet is true and can be verified. However much it hurts, you can't argue with the truth."

"But I've heard many times, from Russians themselves, that your people are suspicious by nature. Would they know the truth, even if it was staring them in the face?"

"This is our gamble, Abel; we've gone all out to be as honest as we possibly can. Nikolay has done a fine job with the context of this leaflet; any reasonably intelligent person can see that it is not bullshit."

"I agree, and the actions requested within it are all very clear."

I sipped my exceptionally strong coffee and thought for a moment.

"What do you consider the magic number for people taking to the streets, to make a difference?"

The Scalpel lent back in his leather recliner and brought his left foot up to rest on his right knee.

"I don't want to commit to a number, Abel, but it has to be over fifty per cent."

I nodded contemplatively, before saying, "What about the peaceful protests outside the jails where the political prisoners are being held, including our party leaders, are they still going ahead?"

"I sincerely hope so. The Fox tells me he has all this organised. Rattling those cages will absolutely rattle Putin's."

"How many political prisoners are we talking about? How many has he put away?"

"The latest information says that there are nearly five hundred incarcerated. Some of them have been given fifteen-year sentences."

"Five hundred? That's a lot of political opposition to have on our side. Is there any way to get leaflets to them?"

"Near on impossible, I'd say, but worth a thought."

The day wore on; preparations were well underway for the entire staff to be billeted here for a week.

Jim was putting in a gargantuan shift to make sure we had enough camp-beds, blow-up mattresses and washing facilities.

The kitchen staff had stocked the larders with plenty of food and drink, and right now, as people were coming in, burdened with backpacks and holdalls, there was a jovial camp-site atmosphere. No doubt, that would mellow as the week progressed.

It had been decided that during the operation there would be three shifts of eight hours a piece, doubling up if the job demanded it.

The time for the operation room to jump into action was dictated by the last Russian lorry to leave the Petrov farm arriving at his first drop because he would have the least amount of distance to travel.

We estimated that the second agents would receive their quota two hours after the first. So those second acknowledgments should start coming in around ten o'clock in the morning.

It was gonna get hectic.

I was just about to tuck into a healthy portion of Beef Stroganoff when my phone chirped into life. It hadn't made a sound all day, and I was pleased to know it wasn't broken.

Alison's ID made me smile. They were fifty-two miles short of the Septini lorry park in Latvia. The roads were a lot smaller in this neck of the woods and the fuel stations tiny. The journey had been vexing, but uneventful.

They would get to the lorry park in the morning and lay up for a day and a half until the first two trucks peeled off for the farm at around five in the afternoon, on the 17th, an hour's journey.

"Are you feeling alright, Alison? You're not as sparkly as you normally are."

"Hopefully I'll be spark-out in a couple of hours. I'm not used to all this driving. I'm knackered."

"Can you take a break before driving back to Britain, rest up?"

"I'm gonna do better than that Abel. Dad, Dean and I are gonna leave our trucks at the hub in Riga and fly home. There's business to attend to. The trucks can be picked up at a later date by shotgun riders."

"Ah, good for you. I hope you have a good night's sleep. Check-in tomorrow as planned when the mission is complete."

"Will do, Abel. Speak to you then."

The call ended, and I went back to my lukewarm dinner.

On the 16th, nothing much happened in the office. The staff had all successfully transited into the building. The ambience was party-like, and expectations were high.

Milana was calm, uncharacteristically openly loving towards me in front of the crew, causing many to smile.

Everyone knew about our relationship, of course. We just hadn't displayed any affection toward each other within the working environment.

Alison confirmed the convoy had reached Rezekne, with a phone call at nine o'clock.

Now the big wait began. We would be radio silent until all of the trucks had been unloaded and were on their way back to the UK.

15

Tuesday 17th May

A day that would go down in the history books as the end of a momentous siege and an immensely selfless last stand.

The remaining exhausted soldiers at the Azovstal steel works finally surrendered to Russian and DPR troops. Delivering Mariupol into Putin's grabbing hands.

Ukrainian Deputy Defence Minister Hanna Malyar said, "Thanks to the defenders of Mariupol, Ukraine gained critically important time to form reserves and regroup forces and receive help from partners. And they fulfilled all their tasks. But it is impossible to unblock Azovstal by military means." Two hundred and eleven soldiers were evacuated via a humanitarian corridor to Olenivka, a town in the DPR. Another two hundred and sixty soldiers, including fifty-three seriously wounded, were taken to a hospital in the DPR town of Novoazovsk.

North-East Latvia, 6 p.m.

Julian's burner phone rattled on the dashboard, accompanied by an unfamiliar tune. It was the first time it had made a noise since he'd taken possession of it, and it broke the monotony with curious relief.

He had been going stir-crazy in the cab with Arkady. Travelling the whole journey together, they had run out of things to say.

On the other end of the line, a female voice, tinged with a light East European accent, gave him the all-clear to proceed towards the farm gates.

"Two trucks only, please," asked Stasya. "The lane is single track and is impossible for vehicles to pass coming in opposite directions."

"Righto, love, no problem."

He ended the call and turned to Arkady.

"Chocks away, Arky. You have the coordinates?"

"Plumbed in already, boss."

"Good, let's go."

Julian phoned Jamie in the next truck and informed him they were leaving. They set off northeast up the A13, a pencil-straight road which cut through a predominantly flat landscape, a road bordered with immature trees boasting lush spring coats, tossed into turmoil by the passing trucks.

The country here was a patchwork of small-holding farms, glades of pasture and pockets of forest, not too unlike parts of rural Norfolk in appearance.

At Karasava, they turned left onto the P45 and headed further north along the gentle, narrow, tree-lined avenue of the Ludza Municipality.

Traffic up here was sparse, and it was a pleasure to travel the almost empty road, rather akin to driving in the 1950s when family cars were an exception to the rule.

Four kilometres up this road, they were running parallel to the forest-lined Russian border on their right, no further than five hundred metres away.

Flat, wide, open plains of wheat fields stretched out to the left and ahead of them under a baby blue sky, and not a sign of a country divide whatsoever, apart from one solitary, galvanised, metal-legged watch tower, twice the height of a telegraph pole, at a point where the border was less than a hundred metres from the road.

Russia, thought Julian. It looks no different here to the rest of Europe. Yet, cross that line, just step across, it would be simple, and he would be in a very different world.

They entered the quaint, rustic town of Baltinava and were required to slow down considerably. The road narrowed to virtually a single lane's width, reducing their speed to twenty mph.

No sooner had they begun to turn right at a T-junction, in the direction of Vilaka, Arkady had to brake to a stop violently, due to an oncoming white Scania, transporter, flying around the bend on the wrong side of the road. The Ukrainian sounded his horn in protest to the reckless driver, who ignored the objection, continuing to hurtle down the rural street like he owned the village.

"Fucking loony!" spouted Arkady.

They set off again, slowly, through the low gears.

The dwellings through here were mostly timber-clad bungalows with corrugated tin roofs, humble, some unmistakably Backwater, but not one of them untidy. The entire village was immaculate and weirdly void of any visible occupants.

Perhaps they were simply at work and school at this time of day.

A building that did stand out was a formidable stone Catholic Church, one that would look very much at home in any part of the UK.

Once through Baltinava, they picked up speed, and a kilometre later they reached the fork in the road they were after.

They went right, onto a single-track dirt road.

Five hundred metres in, they met Stasya on the corner of the Stevens farm drive. Finally, they had arrived.

The woman wore a washed-out mid-blue, jumpsuit style overall and heavy work boots, her black hair was tied up functionally with a red headband. With her sleeves rolled back and her trouser legs turned up, she resembled a Land-girl during the war, but donning a brick of an iPhone in her left hand.

Arkady drew to a halt and lowered Julian's window, so he could speak to her on his side of the truck.

"You must be Stasya," he said.

"Mr Hart?"

"I am."

"Welcome to Latvia, Mr Hart. I trust you had a safe journey?"

"We are all in one piece, my dear. Thank you for asking. Which way do we go?"

Stasya pointed down the track towards the farm buildings some four hundred metres away.

"Follow the drive past the house and into the courtyard. My brother and sister are waiting for you there. I shall call Alison now and tell her to send the next two trucks up."

The first two did as instructed, past the stone-built house with a red tiled roof and into a cobblestone square, flanked on three sides by more stone buildings all with corrugated red tin roofs.

Four people identically clad in the same blue work overalls as Stasya, were standing attentively by a collection of vehicles. The anticipated JCB Telehandler, two Claas tractors and four, long flatbed trailers.

The trucks parked one behind the other and all three men climbed down from the cabs.

Both groups met in the middle of the courtyard. Sergei was the first to speak.

"Welcome to our humble abode, gentlemen. I am Sergei, and this is my sister, Pipene, her husband, Karol, and Stasya's husband, Rurik."

Handshakes were exchanged.

Julian spoke, introducing himself and his guys.

"Your English is spot on," he said.

"And so it should be, our father was from Somerset," replied Sergei with a wry smile.

"Ah, that'll explain it. I have something for you, just a moment."

Julian strode back to his cab and climbed in the passenger side. Under his seat, there was a secret compartment, a hollow void about the size of a house brick. The webbing was fastened with a black metal zip.

He reached in and retrieved a pallet-wrapped block containing more than eleven and a half million Roubles. Fortuitously, the Bank of Russia made a five-thousand Rouble note, otherwise, the stack could have been hard to conceal.

He walked back to the Latvians and handed Sergei the package. "The Spondoolicks, old boy."

Sergei smiled at the funny English colloquialism. "I'll see that it gets to the right people."

"Right." Julian clapped and rubbed his hands together. "I understand time is of the essence, guys. Shall we crack on?"

Sergei inclined his head. "Absolutely. The plan is to unload all of the pallets onto the ground, where we will all take part in unwrapping the apple trees and the office furniture and forklift them into the big barn at the end there.

"Then, we need to load the two hitched flatbeds with as many leaflet pallets as is reasonable, at which point Karol and I will take them across the border, through the woods beyond that field.

"Am I right in thinking that you, Mr Hart, are staying with us to manage the JCB?"

"You are. I'm good for that. Tell me, Sergei, is your route into Russia a recognised one?"

"Not at all, Mr Hart, but we are pretty remote here. We've been using it for years, and nobody has ever questioned us."

Julian rubbed his chin and nodded.

Sergei addressed Arkady and Jamie. "When your trucks have been unloaded, guys, you can exit through that gap in the buildings."

He pointed towards the right-hand corner, where the two buildings shared a distance of around ten metres, and a dirt track disappeared round to the right.

"It's a second entrance that will bring you back out onto the track you came in on."

"Cool," said Jamie. Arkady just nodded.

"Before you leave, I will let Stasya know you're coming, and she can call Alison to let her know you are on your way back. By the time the next two trucks get here, hopefully, we will have transferred the first lot of pallets over to the Petrov farm across the border."

"And over there," said Arkady, "what happens over there?"

The look of distaste towards Russia was evident.

Sergei took a breath. "Over there, if all goes to plan, Old man Petrov will be waiting in his forklift to offload the flatbeds into twenty box wagons, which'll leave as soon as each one is loaded. They have many kilometres to travel, and all this has to be done, and all vehicles gone, before five in the morning. Before our workers arrive."

"Sounds like it's gonna be tight," proclaimed Julian.

Sergei sighed. "Indeed, it is, and exhausting."

"We better get to it then, lads. Un-strap those trailers," instructed Julian.

He climbed aboard the JCB, familiarised himself with the controls, started her up and set about the task at hand.

Within half an hour, he'd unloaded all forty pallets, which were feverishly being dissected by the family.

These two empty, the drivers secured the curtains back into place, bid the party farewell, got into their cabs and took off down the dirt track, leaving a rolling cloud of dust in their wake as a parting gift.

Julian loaded the flatbeds as the pallets became available. At a squeeze, he managed to get ten on each trailer, with about six inches of pallet hanging off the back. He couldn't see a problem with that, as long as the tractor drivers took it easy.

Sergei and Karol jumped into the tractors and set off in a single file, leaving the others to load the two remaining trailers.

By the time they get back, which he estimated would be forty-five minutes, Sergei hoped that the next pair of artic's would have arrived and be in the process of being unloaded.

They entered an open pasture, void of any animals, and traversed its wire-fenced perimeter across to another grassy field. All the gates en route had purposefully been left open, contrary to countryside practice, but necessary for tonight's clandestine activities.

After a further field, they turned left onto a dry, heavily rutted track, which wasn't a road by any means; just a passage made by their vehicles through the baked mud, but would lead them into a forest that bordered the two countries.

The tractors, positioning themselves over the dry ruts, rocked violently, making the trailers twist on the towing bar, shifting the loads.

A rear pallet on Sergei's lead flatbed decided it was time to get off, and bounced its way to the deck, landing on its side with an audible thud.

Both tractors came to an abrupt halt, causing a quick exit from both men to inspect the damage.

Thankfully, the load was so densely wrapped with the film that nothing spilt from its bounds. But now they were left with an extremely time-consuming dilemma. The incredible weight of the pallet made it impossible to move, let alone upright.

There was only one option open to them. Sergei called Pipene, to ask Julian to stop what he was doing and drive the Telehandler over to the forest.

This was going to set them back half an hour that they didn't have.

Whilst Julian was making his way over, guided by Rurik, Sergei and Karol re-positioned their trailers so that the forklift could get in between them.

First Julian righted the pallet and then picked it up and placed it back onto the flatbed.

The men then used bailing twine to strap the load to the trailer as an insurance policy against further spillage.

Julian said that they had some ratchet straps on his lorry. They would be much quicker to use and far safer. They agreed to use them on all future loads.

Once loaded, Julian and Rurik took off back to the farm, whilst the tractors headed towards the forest once more. The window of opportunity had narrowed considerably.

The forest, unmanaged, was thick with spring growth, even though the men had been through it of late and cut back the brambles and overhanging branches, the sides of the tractors received some serious scratches scraping past the vegetation.

Time and again, taut limbs slapped the cab's glass, threatening to break it in outrageous defiance; the trees were aggrieved at the peace being disturbed.

Half a mile later they were in a clearing and in Russia.

Now they just had to skirt two fields planted with barley and rye, then come out onto another dirt track which ran for three-quarters of a mile with limited passing bays, so Sergei phoned ahead to old man Petrov, to make sure nothing would be heading their way.

He assured them there wasn't and enquired what had kept them. Sergei gave him the run down; they'd be there in five minutes.

This portion of the Petrov estate was quite dilapidated. The house hadn't been occupied for at least twenty years and reflected the neglect.

It did, however, have a huge metal-construct open-sided barn, which was put up three years ago to store its machinery. Such as the Manitou 625 he was sitting in, a compact little telehandler with a lot of punch.

Petrov was scrawny, with a sunken-cheeked leathery face, hollow eyes and a scraggy grey goatee beard complimented by a longhorn moustache.

He'd taken a battering from life, absorbed all its nastiness, weathered harsh winters, the harsher Soviets and their crippling state ownership and suppression.

What took its toll most of all though, was the loss of his two sons in the Afghan war. The two people who should be running this farm now, not this wizened shell of a man who should be lazing in a hammock under the shade of the cherry trees that grew beside his house. Not toiling through a thirty-six-hour shift at seventy-nine years of age.

Still, he reasoned with himself, if his small sacrifice tonight would help end that Soviet-bent despot in charge at the Kremlin, it was a price worth paying.

The two Claas tractors turned into Petrov's wide yard. He greeted them through the glass cab with an upward nod.

Leaning against the Manitou, drawing on a cigarette, was a man dressed head to toe in black. The collar of his three-quarter length leather jacket turned up, and his leather cap pulled low down onto his manicured eyebrows.

Sergei recognized him immediately. It was the same guy who'd helped the Plotnikovs escape at the beginning of the war.

Pulling his tractor up beside the forklift, he got out. They embraced warmly.

"Mr Fox, good to see you again."

"It is my pleasure, Mr Stevens."

"I have something for you," said Sergei, reaching back into the Claas and retrieving the money block, and then handing it over.

"Ah, the motivation tool. I'll pass it on to the drivers."

The Fox peered through the wrapping.

"Five-thousand Rouble notes. You couldn't get anything smaller?"

Sergei held out his palms submissively.

"It was not of my doing."

The Fox gave a resigned smile, turned, and headed off towards the gaggle of drivers.

Twenty box wagons of various sizes lined the far end of the concrete courtyard, their drivers mostly asleep or congregated at one end, smoking and shooting the breeze with the other helpers.

Sergei and Karol wasted no more time, unhitching their trailers close to the wagon being signalled to by one of the drivers.

They then raced over to two empty trailers, hitched them to the tow bars and shot back out of the yard to retrace their steps and repeat the process.

Petrov wielded his Manitou with deft precision and soon had the trailers bereft of pallets, instigating a rush from the Russian drivers, who rallied to cut free and load the reams of leaflets onto the first trucks to be setting off.

The farm not only grew grain and crops for human consumption, it also produced animal feed. This section of the farm had a moderate-sized packaging plant for just that market. Loading a couple of pallets of mixed corn onto the back of each truck would give the drivers an extra layer of cover, should they happen to get inspected on the road, and an excuse for having been to the farm today.

Petrov agreed to swallow the cost for the good of the party.

First truck loaded, it left the farm yard, with the longest and most undesirable journey ahead of it, Yakutsk, in central Siberia.

"*Idi s Bogom*," whispered Petrov. Go with God.

When Julian got back to the Stevens farm, he helped move the saplings into storage. It wasn't long before Danylo and Sam hissed to a stop in the yard and the whole process started again.

Sergei and Karol returned with empty trailers, unhitched them and then attached their tractors to the waiting loaded trailers.

At last, the operation was in full swing.

Dusk was settling in, subduing the yard in an orange-ochre diffusion. As Julian unloaded the second truck, his mobile phone vibrated in his breast pocket. It was Alison.

"We got a problem."

"What's that?" he said incredulously.

"There's been a crash."

Julian's heart sank.

"One of our guys!?"

"No, no. A nutter in a transporter tried to pull into the lorry park at a ludicrous speed. He side-swiped a Mercedes Sprinter coming in the opposite direction, and smashed it to bits."

"Ye Gods. Anyone hurt?"

"Yeah! The Mercedes driver is unconscious and bleeding from the head. The guys are all over there trying to get him out. Looks like he's gonna have to be cut free."

"Jesus," said Julian, pinching the bridge of his nose. I take it you can't get out of the park yet?"

"Nope, the exit is completely blocked with a jack-knifed transporter. It's gonna take a while before the emergency crews get here."

"Fuck," murmured Julian.

"That idiot transport driver is probably off his tits on something. He can't keep still. He's flailing his arms about and protesting his innocence. Jamie's trying to remonstrate with him in pidgin Latvian."

"Is it a white Scania transporter?"

"How did you know?"

"Cause he nearly ran us off the road in Baltinava. I bet it's the same guy, arrogant shit."

Pipene noticed Julian on the phone and went over to him.

"Everything alright, Julian?"

He held up a hand, asking her to wait a moment, then ended the call to Alison by saying that she should call him the minute the exit was clear and the next two trucks could get moving.

Julian relayed the bad news to Pipene. She sighed and her shoulders slumped.

"This is not good, not good at all."

"We just have to carry on with what we've got and hope the hold-up isn't too long."

The woman blew air through her lips and then slouched off to let Rurik know.

When Sergei and Karol returned, they already knew the score. Pipene had phoned them.

The yard was devoid of lorries; the trees and office furniture had been stowed away and the JCB was on the cobblestones, cold and idle. Julian was on his phone talking to Dean.

The fire brigade had extracted the van driver. He didn't look good. An ambulance had taken him away. The Police had arrested the transporter driver and were now interviewing witnesses. A tow truck had just arrived and was attaching steel ropes to the wrecked cab, to pull it out of the way.

Dean thought the road might be clear within half an hour.

"This setback is going to balls the whole thing up Julian," affirmed Sergei. "It's gonna push it right to the wire."

"Out of our control, my friend. We just gotta sit here and cross our fingers."

"Yes, yes. Drink?"

"Don't mind if I do. Have you any brandy?"

"We certainly do."

Sergei strode off to the farmhouse, mobile phone up to his ear, informing Petrov of the situation.

Stasya rode up from the gate on a quad bike. She'd heard the news.

"We might as well use this break in activities to eat something. We may not get another chance," she announced.

She and Pipene also wandered over to the house, leaving just their Russian husbands and Julian in the middle of the yard.

"Either of you guys speak English?" ventured Julian.

Karol rocked an outstretched hand.

"A little," he said with a thick accent.

"Tell me, lads, do you like football?"

At nine forty-three, Alison Hart called her dad again.

"Road's clear, Pops. Kyrylo and Dean are on their way."

"Nice one, sweetie. 'Bout time. Everyone's getting real twitchy this end."

"And bored this end. Speak to you soon, Pops, Bye."

They had just under an hour to wait; thankfully, it would be spent in the warmth of the Stevens' kitchen, playing five-card brag and drinking coffee, laced with brandy.

Alison's truck came in last. By the time it was unloaded, it was approaching three o'clock in the morning.

Stasya made more coffee, the last of the trees were stored away and a very weary father and daughter hugged the Latvians and the Russian husbands and bid them all good luck and goodbye.

They left together, accompanied by Filip Jankowski in his truck, so grateful to be out of there and heading for some well-earned sleep back at the lorry park.

Julian forced himself to stay awake, to give his daughter company and keep her lively, but as they neared Rezekne, his head was warming the glass of the passenger side window.

She would sleep until eight, and then give Abel a call to let him know their part in Operation Anchovy had been completed.

The last truck to trundle out of Petrov's farm did it at daybreak on the 19th, heading for Pskov.

Bogdan Melnyk, the farm manager was always first to arrive. He passed the truck on the track coming in, with more than a curious glance.

Seeing Petrov in the yard, his suspicion grew wilder. What was this he knew nothing about?

"Who was that?" Melnyk asked with a grain of salt.

"Chicken feed," replied Petrov. "Got a frantic call late last night from a poultry farmer in Velikiye Luki, totally out of grain, a clerical error."

"Huh." Puffed Melnyk, not believing a word of it.

White Rose Party headquarters, Haymarket, London, 5:42 a.m.

I couldn't sleep, multiple thought trains running at oblique angles through my station.

I got up. Milana stirred under the duvet but didn't wake. How she could switch off and snooze at this juncture was beyond me. I was too trepidatious to embrace oblivion. Plus, I was angst ridden as to why Alison Hart hadn't reported yet with news of the leaflet drop; it should have been accomplished hours ago.

Something must have gone awry. Unless she had forgotten to call, but that was unlikely.

In Milana's office, which had now become the operation room, six people had congregated, including The Scalpel.

Like me, he couldn't sleep and, having confessed to me that he felt the weight of responsibility for the success of this operation to be overwhelming, it was a wonder he was holding it all together as he was.

On the exterior, he appeared as cool as an Arctic cucumber.

"Good morning," I said, as I sat down with a fresh mug of java in my hand.

I received a subdued response.

"Anyone heard anything from Alison?"

Silent shakes of the head were their reply.

This was concerning.

"Scal', if it's all gone to plan, what time would we expect to hear from the first agent to receive their cache?"

"It should have happened by now; Pskov is only about three hours away from Petrov's farm. They're either running late, or the whole thing has gone tits."

"Can't we just call The Fox and ask him what's going on?"

"As a last resort, but we don't want to use mobile phones and break our security measures. The secret service will be monitoring our calls to and from Russia, you can bet your life on it. The encrypted messages will come through on the dark web as planned; we stick to that for now."

I leant back in my recliner and snorted.

The big clock on the wall ticked by, relentlessly marking off the seconds of my life. It was so quiet in the room; the clock's strokes were annoying.

"Wish I was out there doing something positive, rather than sitting here, twiddling my thumbs. It's like waiting to be hung."

The Scalpel was unmoved by my sentiment.

"You've done your bit to get the leaflets out there, Abel. It's been a heroic effort by everyone involved just to get this far. Now it's up to the Russian people to play their part in getting that monster removed."

Andrei came into the room, yawning and scratching his head.

"Anything?" he probed.

"Not yet," informed The Scalpel.

Andrei glanced at the clock, six-fourteen.

"Fuck," he said resignedly. "It's all gone to shit."

"We don't know that yet, Andrei, There may have been some problems. Let's be patient and wait it out," declared The Scalpel.

"Sure," he responded dejectedly. "I'm getting a coffee. Anyone else want one?"

Seven hands went up in the air; he wished he hadn't said anything.

Sluggish minutes passed. I wanted to go outside and breathe in something tangible, but felt compelled to be adhered to my seat, in this pressurised atmosphere, in case things started to happen.

The room had the tension of an immobilised submarine, the anxious crew, floundered on the ocean floor, praying for salvation.

More people arrived; Jim, Vanya, Ekaterina, and Ksenia, all concerned with what was happening. Then eventually Milana, as radiant as ever, fresh from the shower and well-rested, waltzed in like a flight attendant on her first long haul trip.

She halted in front of the map, puzzled, and then said, "Why aren't there any red pins in here yet?"

The room went even more silent than before, and then Scal' spoke up. "Because, no one has reported in yet, Milana."

Our leader spun around to face us and inhaled sharply.

"It is early still. Give them time, it will happen," she assured us.

Computers hummed a background noise that you normally wouldn't notice. Their screens showed a frozen image, unchanged from the last two hours.

Some of the staff stared at the monitors, lost in thought, willing something to happen. Others were fixated on their phones, scouring social media or playing muted games.

I went and sat on Milana's desk in front her, whilst she swivelled listlessly in her chair.

"You okay?" I murmured.

She closed her eyes and nodded. I reached for her hand. If only it was love that had rendered her so restless.

Six fifty-seven, the ping indicating a message had arrived on Scal's computer screen made everyone jump. We were that subdued.

It was from Jellyfish, agent one's call sign. All it said was Red.

The room erupted like we'd just put a man on the moon. Chills went through me; Milana got up and squeezed me harder than she should have had the strength to.

"See!" she said. "You just have to have a little faith."

The Scalpel handed her the red box of pins so she could do the honours. And to great applause, she exchanged Jellyfish's black pin with a red one. We were off.

Alison called, bang on seven o'clock, with the pre-emptively arranged code, "The anchovy has landed."

"I know," I replied. "We've just had an acknowledgement from our first customer."

"All good then?"

"So far. Any problems your end?"

"I'll tell you about it over a dry Martini. You're buying."

"Oh! Okay." That flummoxed me.

"I'll give you a bell when I'm back in Blighty. Bye for now."

I would have said bye, but she'd already hung up.

The fact that she wanted to have a drink with me was unexpected. I didn't think Milana would appreciate it, but I would like to know what had happened out there, what held up the delivery. I'd give it some thought; maybe I would just ask her on the telephone.

As the day wore on, more and more affirmative responses trickled in. By lunchtime, ten per cent of the map had red pins in it. The system was working.

Around two o'clock, I received a call from Sergei. He thanked me for the apple saplings and said they were going to make a start on the orchard this afternoon.

I told him because they were less than a year old, they didn't need staking and that he should plant them four and a half metres apart and leave six metres between rows. He appreciated the advice.

Asking how my latest project was going, all I said was the trees are bearing fruit. He grasped my meaning without further question.

I thanked him again for his assistance and ended the call.

The Scalpel received a call from his close friend Grisha.

Scal' had been concerned that this fella hadn't checked in yet. He was one of the helpers at Petrov's farm and should have called hours ago.

His conversation was generic, and unrevealing in its content. But it did contain a modicum of mirth.

He said that he had been to an all-night rave with his boss and his work colleagues. The boss was not supposed to be there and had told his wife that he had gone night fishing.

To cover his arse, the boss had bought three whole brown trout from the fish mongers and kept them in a cool box, so that come the morning he could produce the labour of his night-long efforts.

The Scalpel was laughing into his phone, surmising that this was exactly what Petrov had done.

Everyone got home safely after a very long and weary night.

After two days, a few black pins remained defiant on the map, which was now bristling with yellow but, disappointingly, several red pins also kept their place.

It would have been far-fetched to expect every agent to have shown up and fulfilled their promise, especially in the furthest reaches of the country, but, the amount of distributors who were now in possession of their quota was a staggering feat.

Even better, neither the Russian police nor the security services, as far as we could tell, had any idea what was about to hit the streets.

This was due to change, though, starting at five o'clock Friday morning.

Pictures of the posters began to appear on Telegram, pasted to buildings, trains, and busses and pinned to posts and trees in parks and city centres, creating a fervour that soon went viral around the internet.

By the time the security services were out ripping them down, which was also being caught on camera and broadcast on news channels across the globe, more than half the leaflets had already been handed out.

We were getting information back that said the distributors had enlisted the help of family members and friends, sometimes to the power of ten, making a possible eight hundred thousand people giving out leaflets; overwhelming odds for the police to control.

It was a staggering convergence, a humbling concord which in itself only suggested one prognosis. The Russian public was indeed ready for change. And we still had another day left for further distribution, although now the police were ready for it, in full riot gear and on the streets.

Anyone caught handing out leaflets would be dragged away, beaten up and slung in jail.

Crowds were gathering outside the eighty-seven prisons earmarked for silent, candlelit vigils, and news crews from around the world were picking it up and broadcasting the events while they still could.

By ten in the evening, the blue pin box had been raided, confirming fifty per cent of the leaflets had gone out.

It was so encouraging, yet, the real test was going to come on Monday, on strike day.

Sunday 22nd May

Every news channel worldwide was running the story, the potential game changer, and the bold and brazen act of rebellion against the totalitarian dictatorship.

Some channels went as far as calling it a revolution.

We watched from the offices, awestruck, as news footage showed our operatives blatantly handing out leaflets in the streets, with the police weirdly taking no action at all.

It was utterly against the reaction we had all believed would happen.

We could only surmise that the whole thing was too big to contain and that the authorities were just letting it run its course, confident that it would peter out and come to nothing rather than intervene, cause unrest, and even more resentment towards a government hell-bent on an isolationist ideology.

Or maybe the police force itself was sympathetic; perhaps the wind of change was guiding their lack of action. It stood to reason that members of the force would have relatives who have suffered due to the invasion of Ukraine, and there must be disillusion amongst the ranks, despite the hard line indoctrination and propaganda forced upon them.

For us, it was a day of waiting. By mid-afternoon, eighty per cent of the blue pins were up. We couldn't expect any more due to the pyramid effect of there being still some black, red, and yellow pins on the map.

But eighty per cent, it was a fantastic result, ninety-six million leaflets handed out, it had to provoke a response.

Yet still the Kremlin remained silent.

At three o'clock that afternoon, The White Rose Party put out an announcement.

Milana Fyodorova would deliver a statement from the steps of the London office at midday on Monday the 23rd, concerning the party's status and its full intentions.

Speculation was rife over the airwaves. What was Putin going to do next? He hadn't been seen in public for three days. Was he waiting to see what the citizens of Russia would do tomorrow? Were his actions dependent on Milana's announcement? The conjecture was swamping the global media circus.

We debated well into the early evening as to what the despot was going to do next. Some suggested that perhaps he had done a runner, but Milana, Andrei, The Scalpel and I thought that highly unlikely, for the simple reason that if the Russian masses did not support us, not go on strike or wear something white tomorrow, then he had won without one vote being cast.

Our defeat would be absolute and irrevocable, damning any future party from posing effective opposition to the tyrannical federation, because they would not receive the support of a people who couldn't be swayed by the truth. The very people we were fighting for.

Tomorrow seemed a long way off, and we all needed some sleep.

I'd volunteered to man the desks for the midnight shift along with others. Milana and Andrei said they would join me.

Moscow is two hours ahead of London, which meant that the results of our endeavours should start to become evident around eleven o'clock our time.

We all prayed to whoever might be listening, that we'd spend the whole of Monday pushing in orange and purple pins to that perforated paper map on the wall, and that enough Russian people would summon the courage to overcome their fear. For courage is the complement of the frightened and without fear, you can not possibly be brave.

16

On the leaflet, we kindly asked the people of Russia to go on strike from midnight Sunday, and run it for twenty-four hours.

Two massive clocks on the wall of the operations room, set with London and Moscow time, helped to give us a perspective at a glance, to where we were at any given moment.

Eleven fifty-three, Moscow time.

Milana, Andrei, Jim, The Scalpel and I, stood like resting zombies, staring at the clocks, entertained by the second hands marking off the countdown.

Why we were waiting for midnight was anyone's guess. Nothing was going to happen immediately. The majority of people wouldn't be expected at work for another eight hours. But night shifts were obviously in place, so if the call was answered, then we should start to see some action within the first hour.

The task now for our agents on the ground was to report back with news that there were workers downing tools, forming picket lines and or, walking the streets wearing something white.

This process of reporting would go up the chain from the distributor to the second agent, to the first agent and then to us. It was going to take a while.

Three minutes to twelve, we waited with bated breath.

This was the most anxious I'd ever seen Milana. Her body was experiencing involuntary muscle spasms in her arms and legs, and she was cold to touch.

I put my arm around her waist to comfort her. It had little effect.

Andrei appeared nonplussed yet he knew as well as everyone in the room, that these next twenty-four hours were either going to make or break us.

He stroked his moustache with his thumb and forefinger, contemplatively.

At twenty-one minutes past twelve, Vavara's computer screen pinged, indicating a message arriving from the web.

She quickly scanned the text, and then swivelled in her chair to face us, as we waited in a state of high expectancy.

She spoke like an automaton.

"Lemur, agent fifty-two, Central Moscow district, all underground, railway and bus stations in the district are reported closed.

"Notices on gates say a twenty-four-hour strike is in place, in support of The White Rose Party.

"All notices include a white ribbon attached to them, and staff who are erecting the signs are reported to be wearing white armbands."

An all-mighty cheer erupted, followed by clapping, which spread throughout the building like a Mexican wave, as the entire staff cottoned on to the news we had been depending on.

But Milana wasn't right. Her eyes rolled back into her head, she went limp and fell into me. A dead weight that I wasn't ready for, and we both collapsed sideways onto the floor, launching an office chair on castors across the carpet.

The Scalpel was on us straight away, as was another staff member, Olga, our eldest employee with many years of front-line nursing experience in St Thomas' hospital.

The pressure and relief had overwhelmed Milana. She'd fainted.

Olga laid Milana on her back and raised her legs onto the lip of another, more obedient, office chair. Twenty seconds later our boss came to.

"What happened?" she said, mystified.

"Too much excitement, I think," said Olga, authoritatively.

"Are we winning?"

I smiled and held her hand. "Well, we've made a start."

"Come on, Abel," ordered Olga, "Help me take her upstairs. She needs to lie down for a while."

I did as I was told, and between us, eventually, we got her onto her bed, gave her a glass of water to drink, and then laid her down, covering her with a fleece blanket to keep her warm.

I stayed with her until she fell asleep and then slipped back downstairs to see if we'd scored any more goals.

We had. So far in St Petersburg, the ports and shipyards were closed, as were the aluminium plant, the Baltika brewery, and the mint.

And in Voronezh, the international airport and the bus and railway stations were rendered inoperable.

It was happening; the Russian people were rallying to our cause.

Milana had prepared two separate speeches for today. One, should we only receive a fifty per cent turnout, the other for anything above seventy.

When she made that speech here at HQ, it would be two o'clock in the afternoon in Moscow, plenty of time for us to evaluate which speech she was going to use.

A steady stream of reports came in, letting us know that tower blocks in residential areas in many cities were hanging white bed linen out of their windows. White balloons were festooning railings and phone boxes.

The morning rush hour was still happening, but instead of vehicles making their way to work, they were just rallying around the circuit streaming white ribbons and flags, and honking their horns.

Adults and children were in the streets, adorned in white shirts, dresses, or hats and armbands. It was an unstoppable tide of solidarity.

We couldn't believe the enormity of it. All the news channels were now solely focussing on this one story, the wind of change expanding into a hurricane.

The Fox, naturally not at work today, had toured Moscow's central bars and cafes and was delighted to check in with glorious fervour that they were all open, but everything was free today in support of the party, to feed the people of the Rose.

All thirty-four desks at HQ were busy taking encrypted messages from our agents, all reporting the same thing, the length and breadth of Russia, there was hardly a citizen or building not displaying something white. It was an incredible achievement, and Milana was still in bed, missing it all.

Reports were also suggesting that today was going to be the hottest of the year so far.

I lent back in my recliner and closed my eyes, exhausted, humbled, yet extremely happy. The response, so far, way exceeded my hidden, low expectations.

I pictured a typical residential complex in the heart of any Federal city, like the one in Kira Smirnova's letter to Milana. A square bordered with high-rise blocks, kiosks on the corners, children playing on the swings and roundabouts, old men playing chess, and how the population, after years of oppression and subjugation, might dare to believe that very shortly, they no longer would have to walk on eggshells in their daily life.

The press were gathering in the garden. Once again, the media circus was clambering for a ringside seat.

Jim was out there with security, organizing the ranks. MI6 were involved, their agents would be somewhere in the crowd. A team had been in over the weekend to coordinate their efforts with Milana and Andrei. I hadn't been privy to that conversation.

The police were also outside en mass, directing traffic, cordoning the side entrance and providing extra security on the grounds and surrounding rooftops.

When Milana made her speech from the rear steps this afternoon, there was always the possibility of an attempt on her life.

Andrei had been up to Milana's apartment and had given her the good news. It was eleven o'clock and a huge swathe of the map was bristling with orange and purple pins.

If an election was held tomorrow, it appeared we'd have a landslide victory.

She came down to the operations room half an hour later looking resplendent. Radiating like a beacon in one of the outfits I had bought for her, a two-piece lilac beaded/sequined jacket and skirt and a white silk blouse.

She was going to dazzle the throng that was waiting for her with more than just her words.

I was beguiled by her presence. Smiling warmly, I just said, "Perfect."

Andrei took her hand and led her down the corridor, lined with our people, towards the rear garden. Each member of staff touched her shoulder as she passed, a sign of respect and unity, affirming we were as one.

Vanya opened the patio doors, revealing a massive crowd and igniting a spangled eruption of flash photography.

The calls from the press were a cacophony of madness, impossible to discern. It died to a whisper the moment she reached the lectern.

Milana placed the papers was carrying down, looked up at the Wedgwood blue sky, took in a lungful of spring air and then faced her audience.

She began, "Thank you all for coming here today. I am honoured. And thank you for letting me make this speech.

"If I were to do the same in my own country, I would be promptly arrested and most probably imprisoned for a minimum of fifteen years.

"At present in Russia, there are five hundred political prisoners incarcerated in cells twenty-four-seven, including White Rose leader, Oleg Stepanov, our deputy leader, Grisha Tarasova, and party secretary, Nadia Guseva. Their crime was to simply speak out against the ruling party; sentiments which we believe are shared by ninety-eight per cent of the population.

"It is clear from the actions taken today by the majority of Russian citizens, that they agree with The White Rose Party policies, and obvious to us that we must act in the best interests of the Russian people. That is to oust the current regime, end this futile, wasteful war with Ukraine, and reinstate a stable, geo-political, ecologically based government, with good international relations and trade deals."

A deafening round of applause burst from the crowd, along with wolf whistles and whoops.

She continued, unabated, "We will, as of this day, be pursuing a method to bring forward the date of the next Russian presidential election from its current date of 17th March 2024.

"We have informed President Putin of our intentions, and he only has to put his head out of the window to see just how that vote is going to go."

More cheers.

Milana waited for them to subside.

"President Putin, so far, has not replied to our correspondence, and neither has anyone at the Kremlin. However, this is to be expected. This administration is too egotistical and bigoted to be bothered by a new opposition party calling for its resignation from overseas. They probably feel quite invincible and despotic.

"But mark my words, Mr Putin, the people have spoken, and your days are numbered."

More cheering.

"Our party, The White Rose Party, is unequivocally non-violent. We will not resort to thuggery, brutality, or the subjugation of our citizens to get what we want. We believe in absolute democracy and respect for international borders and foreign lands.

"That is why we are insisting that a declaration of a ceasefire, and a withdrawal of troops from all unlawfully occupied lands, be put into place today, and remain until after the presidential election, when a peaceful and practical solution to the conflict can be found.

"We also insist on beginning the process for the immediate release of all political prisoners within the next day or so."

She stopped for a few seconds and then spoke in Russian.

The Scalpel, by my side, translated it verbatim.

"I now speak directly to the Russian armed forces, the police, the security, and prison services.

"It has been demonstrated today what the citizens want for a future in Russia.

"Your role in the country's evolution is critical. It will be up to you whom you stand with. Choose wisely, and our nation will be stronger together.

"I pray that you do the right thing.

"Thank you."

The crowd redoubled its applause.

Milana then walked down the steps, towards the same young girl who had given her flowers at the last garden speech. The daughter of Vadym Prystaiko, the Ukrainian ambassador to the UK, in her sweet little white dress, excitedly held out a posy of white roses.

The metal barrier erected to hold back the swollen throng prevented the girl from physical contact with Milana, so her father scooped her up and held her in his arms so that the girls were at head height with each other.

It was a gooey moment and the press lapped it up.

Photo opportunity over, our caretaker leader retreated up the steps amidst a deafening volley of media questions, which she ignored until she was back behind the lectern, whereupon she gave one more brief comment, promising to keep them informed of developments over the next crucial twenty-four hours.

Thanking everybody once more she turned and climbed the steps back into HQ.

The appreciation followed Milana into the building. With staff members gleefully welcoming her triumphantly back inside.

It was pure justification. She had got right.

Thanks to modern technology, her speech had been broadcast around the globe, and the world's population now waited intrigued as to its effect.

The feedback from The Fox came in almost immediately. Russia had stood still for ten minutes and watched.

Milana had not minced her words. She made it quite plain that she expected those in uniform to keep the equilibrium and help with the transition, and she wanted their decision within the next twenty-four hours.

As everyone returned to their posts, Milana and Andrei headed for the conference room, where they were joined by Vadym Prystaiko and his crew.

A Zoom meeting had been set up to take place in half an hour, with the Ukrainian President, Volodymyr Zelenskyy, and it was going to be a closed-door affair.

How Milana was composing herself was a testament to her strength of character, but I was enamoured. Only three months ago she was stacking shelves in Lidl. Now she was at the pinnacle of a career which held the keys to the world's stability.

It wasn't necessary for The Scalpel and me to return to the operations room. Apart from a dozen or so orange and purple pins left unemployed in their boxes, most of the areas we had canvassed had answered the call superbly.

Scal's phone chimed in his pocket; he took it out and peered at the screen, put his hand up apologetically, and then hurried away down the corridor and back out into the garden.

I was dead beat. Having been adrenalin-fired since midnight, I was now coming down and fading fast. I needed an afternoon nap and soon.

Sauntering towards the rear stairwell, I almost bumped into Scal' marching in the opposite direction.

"What time's that meeting with Zelenskyy," he asked frantically.

I looked at my watch.

"About twenty minutes. Why?"

"Come with me. I have to talk to Milana and Andrei before it happens."

He'd got my attention even though I was exhausted.

We traipsed back to the conference room. The folks inside were all standing and chatting and were in good spirits, it seemed through the glass.

The Scalpel knocked and then entered rather determinedly.

They spoke in Russian, the incredulity ever-growing on their faces. I had no idea what was going on.

When they had finished, Milana turned to me.

"Abel, darling, Scal' will tell you what we have just discussed in a moment, but after that, could you possibly call Charles for me and ask him if he could shed some light on the situation, and also if he can attend a meeting here, tomorrow, around nine o'clock?"

Her pleading eyes meant that it was imperative.

"Of course, no problem. I'm sure he will oblige."

Milana and Andrei respected my friend Charles' opinion emphatically.

Scal' and I left the room and headed for the lobby; en route, he began to divulge the contents of his phone call.

It was from The Fox. He'd told Scal that a friend of a friend, who works in the laundry at the Kremlin, had noticed something unusual.

There are six palaces within the fortress's walls and, in all, it can accommodate around two thousand people.

Putin and his entourage occupy the Grand Palace, and we understand that many of his inner-circle live within the walls as well.

The bed linen is changed religiously, every Friday, whether it has been slept in or not, unless there is a definite need for a bed linen change during the week, which is a huge undertaking.

Yesterday, sixty-four rooms had a linen change, and with it being a Sunday, unless sixty-four people had shit the bed, it very much shouts of something suspicious going on.

Not only that, but Scal' also had a call from a friend called Losif during Milana's speech, which he didn't pay much attention to at the time, but added to The Fox's call, making it very important indeed.

Losif works as a porter at The Blokhin National Medical Research Centre. He told Scal that although many of the staff were on strike today, all of the major operations were going ahead as scheduled, but, two surgeons, a nurse and an anaesthetist who are assigned to the Kremlin first and foremost, didn't show up for work at all.

Four operations booked in for this morning, with no relation to the government, had to be postponed.

Scal was staring into my eyes.

"Abel, it's too much of a coincidence. One thing on top of another, plus Putin hasn't been seen or heard of for thirty-six hours."

"You think he's done a runner?"

"It's a possibility. If I was a man in his position and dying of lung cancer, I'd want to fuck off with some medical insurance."

I protruded my bottom lip and nodded slowly.

"Fucking hell, this is immense."

Scal' nodded too.

"If it's happened," he said, arching his brow.

"We need more proof."

"We do. I believe Milana is right, I think some of Charles' clients might be able to shed a modicum of light on this. I'll give him a call right away."

Within half an hour, Charles was back in touch.

He had spoken to an oligarch who owned a super yacht, currently impounded in Tenerife and waiting out the war.

According to Charles, it usually has a crew of about seventy personnel, but right now there's only a skeleton crew of six, held for maintenance.

The owner spoke to the captain today, and the rumour going around the nautical fraternity is that Putin, who has two super yachts currently anchored off Hong Kong, has ordered no shore leave for his crew, for the next three months."

"And these super yachts are they big?"

"Massive! Helicopter pads, swimming pools, cinemas, and twenty-eight luxury cabins a piece, like the one in Tenerife, a crew of seventy, they're like floating hotels."

"What are they called? I'll Google 'em."

"I think he said *The Pride of Russia* and *The Pride of Moscow*."

Scal rolled his eyes. "Ha, original."

"The captain who fed us the information has a brother, who is a steward on one of Putin's boats, also said that the cabins are being prepared to receive a full complement of guests."

Charles made me smile by turning an adage around. He said, "Looks like the rats are boarding a sinking ship!"

He also said that the Kremlin keeping shtum about anything happening at all was a good indication that something definitely was. And that a person who was wanted internationally for war crimes had very few places to run and hide.

He agreed to the meeting tomorrow at nine o'clock. It was going to be a very interesting one.

I caught up with Milana and Andrei in the top-floor corridor; we were all heading for the apartments.

I asked them how it went with the Ukrainians.

"I'll let Milana explain," said Andrei. "I'm deadbeat."

And with that, he shuffled off to his rooms.

We walked together as she talked.

"Very well indeed. We have come to some extremely cordial agreements should The White Rose ascend to power, with solutions to both the Crimea and Donbas annexations, without any need for a conflict whatsoever.

"Mr Zelenskyy was a complete gentleman; an immediate ceasefire would be our first instruction, but without some form of divine intervention, we're going to have to wait and see how the people vote during the election.

"How did you get on with Charles?"

"Err, we may not have to wait that long…"

I went on to reveal what The Scalpel and I had discovered. Milana was more than a little wide eyed.

Balakliya, Kharkiv Oblast, Ukraine.

They didn't know what the worst job in the world was, but theirs must be a strong contender.

Pavlo Karalenko and Orest Sokolov both came from a long line of undertakers based in central Kharkiv and had dealt with death their entire working lives.

Contracted to the Ukrainian army, the men were at present officially and morally obliged to retrieve corpses, and bits of, from the battlefields, roadsides and ruins, when the fighting had subsided. Sometimes weeks after the bullets and white-hot shrapnel had stopped ripping people to pieces.

There was no prejudice in their task. It mattered not whether the bodies of the fallen were Russian or Ukrainian. Their job was too simply to clear the dead, military and civilian, and return the remains to their respective sides.

Pavlo and Orest had been somewhat desensitised to the horrors of human demise, but the grim tasks presented to them, now daily, would destroy the resolve of the most callous human being on the planet.

On an average day, they would pick up between thirty and forty individuals. Ninety per cent of them were Russian soldiers, and it was rare to find a body intact, un-savaged by munitions or mutilated by the wild and decay. Incinerated husks in burnt-out tanks, torsos without limbs or heads, or just a head in a helmet thrown into a field by a massive explosion, their bodies having been turned to pink mist.

Most sickening of all were the civilians. Children caught in the carnage, in bombed-out houses or lying in yards, innocents who had no argument with those who terrorised their village, defiled their human rights, and obliterated their homes.

There were also the executed, mostly men, but some women. Hands bound behind them and shot twice in the back of the head. These were despicable, atrocious, inconceivable acts, which would remain indelible in the minds of the undertakers and tarnish the entire Russian army with a broad stroke, as savage, ruthless barbarians, without a drop of empathy in their blood.

Yet, the respect and integrity that Pavlo and Orest afforded to each soul soon became respected by both armies, who would lay down weapons at their approach and allow them passage through the lines to perform their unenviable task, no matter what the circumstance.

They drove a public transport bus, which had been painted white and had the windows covered, and red crosses on all four sides.

Two metal vases had been attached to the front, permanently containing road-weary bouquets of artificial flowers.

The vehicle, affectionately known as The Compassion Bus, could carry up to forty cadavers at a time, and before the body bags were returned to their units or the morgue, they were each adorned with flowers and any personal belongings or id tags, placed in clear plastic bags and attached to the outer bag.

Today they had twenty-seven soldiers belonging to the Russian Airborne Forces laid in the back.

They had earlier contacted the unit commander; Podpolkovnik (Lieutenant Colonel) Yegor Kuznetsov who was camped near Verbivka, to let him know they were coming in with his men. They had sadly met before, on several occasions.

The bus hissed to a halt outside one of the larger houses in the suburb, requisitioned by force, no doubt, by the advancing army.

Kuznetsov greeted the undertakers personally and invited them into his makeshift headquarters.

Secretly, he'd been opposed to invading his neighbours; he had relatives in Ukraine and wasn't fooled by the regime's false narrative of demilitarisation and de-Nazification. He knew it was just a glorified land grab, but he was a career soldier and took his orders without question.

After three months of needless bloodshed, in which his battalion had sustained eighty per cent casualties, he was down to just one hundred and sixty men.

The Ukrainian army was on the offensive, gaining ground, and his supply lines were sporadic at best.

He felt betrayed by his superiors, who'd ordered him here on false pretences, with a flawed narrative and a poorly devised plan.

Now he was out on a limb, ill-equipped to go forward, ordered not to retreat, and sickened by what he had witnessed.

Watching Milana's speech earlier in the day, however, had given him hope. He loved his country and would willingly die to protect it, but the situation he found himself in now wasn't what he'd signed up for, and The White Rose Party was promising a realistic solution.

"Gentlemen, come in, come in," he ushered the undertakers into what was once a spacious living room.

"Take a seat."

The two men cautiously complied.

"Did you happen to see Milana Fyodorova's speech earlier?"

Both men nodded.

"And tell me, what did you think?"

"I'd vote for her," replied Orest sharply. "She'd do a much better job than that fool you have in charge right now."

Kuznetsov raised his brow.

"Lucky for you I'm not his number one fan."

"Look at all the damage he has done. How many more sons and fathers do we have to return to you in body bags? He's got to pay for his crimes. I am ill with it, ill with it!" complained Pavlo.

"As am I," reiterated the Podpolkovnik. "That is why I have decided to initiate a truce. Something that will be looked upon as treasonous by superiors, of course, but, if I can popularise the idea, and enough commanders join me, then perhaps a wave of rationale will prevail."

"A mutiny?" suggested Orest.

"Not as such, just a ceasefire, until a better solution can be found."

The Ukrainians looked at each other with uncertainty.

"Here's what I propose we do…"

"We?" said Pavlo.

"Do not worry, my friends; your part is nothing more than your usual activity.

"I want you to lay out the men you have just brought in on the ground beside the bus, and then stand to one side. My remaining force will form up on parade and several of them will record a message on their phones, which I will provide in front of their fallen comrades, and then they will post that message on their Telegram pages.

"A TV crew from Russia 24 are here also. I will get them to film it as well. Can you agree to do this for me? My men will help you lay out the bodies."

The undertakers shrugged in agreement. If it would help put an end to all this carnage, it was the least they could do.

"What is in your message?" asked Pavlo suspiciously.

"A plea to all Russian people, a call for common sense to prevail, I hope."

The black body bags were laid out on the ground in two rows, each soldier's name written in large letters on white paper and pinned to the front.

A small posy of camomile flowers lay on each bag.

Pavlo and Orest stood by, respectfully, arms in front, palms across fists, as Kuznetsov strode from the house clutching a pre-prepared speech.

His men stood to attention as he passed their parade, thirty of them stood facing the bus, phone at the ready to record, amidst the TV crew of four.

The Podpolkovnik faced the cameras.

A deathly silence fell. Even the birds, it seemed, held their tongues.

"On Thursday 24th February, I illegally drove across the border and into Ukraine with eight hundred and seventy-nine men.

"Including these poor souls behind me, I have just one hundred and ninety-two left.

"Four hundred and eighty-one others have been killed, a hundred and twenty-four have sustained life-changing injuries, fifty-two are in prisoner-of-war camps in Ukraine, eighteen are missing in action and twelve have deserted.

"We entered this war rolling on a tide of false propaganda and outright lies. The campaign was supposed to have taken three days. A show of might, designed to duress the Kyiv government into submission, so that our greedy rulers could claw back a huge part of the old Soviet Union and steal all of its vast resources.

"This was a defective plan from the start, a foolish enterprise. Our president and our military bigwigs grossly underestimated Ukraine's armed forces, the strength of their president and, most of all, the people's tenacity.

"They also misjudged NATO's and the western world's government's empathy towards a sovereign state's unlawful occupation.

"We've been in this country for three months and are now seriously being outgunned.

"A huge part of our military capability has been lost, and the ability to produce more weapons is severely restricted due to worldwide sanctions.

"I have come to believe that this conflict is un-winnable and that throwing more young lives at it is not only criminal but insane.

"I listened to The White Rose Party's spokesperson, Milana Fyodorova's speech yesterday from the steps of their headquarters in London, and, like many of my counterparts, believe that her proposals are a plausible way out of this mess.

"I spent this afternoon conversing with many commanders here on the frontline and most of us have come to the same conclusion.

"Therefore, we would like to initiate an immediate forty-eight-hour ceasefire of all hostilities between the armed forces of both The Russian Federation and Ukraine, with the hope that the ceasefire will escalate into a permanent state so that a solution can be found to the multifaceted problems of citizenship and territorial ownership.

"Today's nationwide strikes and protests prove my point exactly. The Russian people have spoken, and I hear them. Only a change of government will suffice, and I am backing The White Rose.

"I sincerely hope everyone will respect the forty-eight-hour ceasefire; it is a decent thing to do.

"Thank you."

Kuznetsov then turned and saluted the twenty-seven fallen, as did his one hundred and ninety-two remaining soldiers.

As flags fluttered in a keen wind, a crow mourned with a single craw somewhere off camera.

Epilogue

Saturday 16th May 2026 7:00 p.m.

I was doing something I said I never would; watching the Eurovision Song Contest.

There were two reasons.

One, Russia's vice president Milana Fyodorova was presenting the winning act, Poland, with the trophy. As glitteringly glamorous as ever, she stole the limelight, swathed in a figure hugging, silver, fishtail strapless dress.

Her beauty was undoubted and a wave of nostalgia warmed my core as it rekindled the love we once shared.

Secondly, people who just two years ago were hell-bent on slaughtering one another were now performing a finale together, as choirs from Ukraine and Russia united for a song of peace and forgiveness.

It was testimony to what humans can do when uncommon goals are turned into common sense.

It's been four years since The White Rose Party was established, and even though its founding members are all endlessly busy making the world a better place, we do get to meet up on occasion.

As for my seven house mates, they all qualified as doctors and surgeons.

Lukas, who first prompted us to do something about the war in Ukraine, inspired by his fellow countrymen and women who so selflessly stood up to the evil Nazi dictatorship in World War II, is still practicing in Oxford.

He has a partner called Shannon; they have been together for two years and are by all accounts very happy with life.

Safira returned to Spain and married her childhood sweetheart, Agustin. She works in the local hospital in Malaga and they are expecting their first child in four months.

Beau married his long-term girlfriend, Betsy. They are both surgeons at the Oxford University Hospital.

Victoria moved back to Bethnal Green. She and her partner, Louisa, both work in the A&E department of the Royal London.

Jack, the comedian of the Oxford Eight, went home to Brecon and joined a practice as a GP. I received a wedding invitation from him only last week.

Arouna returned to Ukraine to help re-build her country. She wants her own practice, but for now is working at one of the main city hospitals in Poltava.

Two of the nicest stories I've heard to come out of this war came from Arouna.

She told me that before her father and brother were de-mobbed from the army, and whilst in uniform, because her brother was an officer and her dad a sergeant, whenever they met her dad had to salute his son. Which, according to her dad, were the proudest moments of his life.

And as for those three nerdy boys who went off to war to teach others how to operate drones, they are now successful entrepreneurs who have more than thirty retail outlets across Ukraine called Nikoly ne Zdavaysya (Never Surrender), selling toys for boys.

Nikolay, I'm pleased to report, is living his best life.

He and Sergei took up residence in Islington. They both work for the NHS, Sergei as an Ophthalmologist at Moorfields eye hospital and Nikolay an Oncologist at the Royal Marsden.

Sergei's family farm has done a complete U-turn and is now a huge nursery, growing native European saplings for export all over the continent. I happen to do quite a bit of business with them, which is equitable for both parties.

Nikolay's family went home to Moscow, returning to their country house, which I understand was miraculously untouched. Both Maxim and Dmitri returned to their old positions at the Federal hospital like nothing had happened. And to Maxim's delight, his two Doberman pinscher dogs, which he'd unhappily left behind, were returned to him, having been rescued by his neighbours after they heard their distressed howling the day after the Plotnikov's escaped.

The night before my house mates started to go their separate ways, the last night we would be spending together under the roof of Lemon Grove, Safira and Arouna prepared our favourite meal, a thousand men on a raft with the sun coming up, or as normal people call it, baked beans on toast with a poached egg.

It was a name used by truckers in greasy-spoons back in the fifties and sixties, or so my dad told me.

We had perfected the dish by using ciabatta bread, only ever Heinz beans and free-range eggs.

It's also how the Raft got its name.

As for The Fox, he opened his own bar bistro in Red Square with fine views of the Kremlin. Whenever I go to Moscow, I meet up with old friends there, and we dine alfresco and raise a glass to the city's new found freedom.

The Scalpel was made Russian Health Secretary. Apparently, the health service has never been in better shape. I can believe that. The man is as efficient as he is dedicated.

The White Rose had enacted legislation to outlaw bigotry within the country. Prejudice towards LGBT, ethnic, and unorthodox communities would no longer be tolerated, and equal rights for both sexes were being addressed.

Renewable energy industries were being encouraged with government backing, and fossil fuelled power stations all over the country were earmarked for closure.

A hundred billion dollars of Putin's seized personal wealth was being funnelled into re-building Ukraine's flattened infrastructure, towns and villages, and Russia was once again trading with the democratic west.

Andrei ended up marrying Nadia, a member of the team at the Coffee House, who went back home with the gang. She's about to give birth at any moment.

They both work at the Kremlin.

Milana, the celestial body, is working twenty-four-seven, to make Russia and the rest of the world a better place to bring children into. She is tireless.

She found her perfect partner, quite by chance, the man who stepped up to the plate when it was most needed. Lieutenant Colonel Yegor Kuznetsov, now a General and the head of all Russian armed forces, which is comforting for the rest of us.

Milana and I remain the best of friends. If I were to mention the film *Casablanca*, starring Humphrey Bogart and Ingrid Bergman, persons of a certain age will know what I mean. We correspond occasionally.

Jim, I'll probably see more of than any of them. He married a Cornish girl called Jane and together they bought a thirty-two room hotel and restaurant just outside Penzance.

I understand that the restaurant has been awarded a Michelin star recently.

I'm not surprised; Jim had that ability of knowing what everybody's needs were.

As for my oldest friend, Charles, I think everyone knew that his money and contacts played a major role in getting this whole thing started. Without his impetus, the party would not have stood a chance.

The free world owes him a massive debt of gratitude, but he is humble, not seeking praise or indeed recognition. He was just happy to have helped.

At Henley Regatta, we managed a third place in our event and have a silver cup to show for our efforts. A little win, but it means so much to me and my buddy, a testament to all the hours of hard slog we put into the training. Charles lets me keep it; he says that I have very little in the way of ornamentation at home. He's right. The place is quite austere, a house rather than a home. The cup is used once a year. We toast the anniversary of the end of the war. It's a fitting celebration and shows that tenacity pays off.

We meet up every three weeks for archery lessons, which have highlighted the fact that I'm no Robin Hood. But Charles is a dab hand at it and flourishing. I think that he is going to enter a few competitions; I'll be content just to carry his quiver and enjoy the company.

For my thirtieth birthday, I invited a few friends out for a meal. There were just six of us. Charles brought his beautiful girlfriend, Alison Hart. I had the pleasure to introduce them to one another at Henley, and they had hit it off straight away. I think I'll be buying a new suit soon and preparing a best man's speech.

Before the meal, Charles let on that he had bought me not one, but two presents. He handed me an envelope at the dinner table. Inside was a birthday card, a door key and instructions to take my old Volvo to a garage in town, to have it converted into a Hybrid motor.

This was marvellous. He knew how much I loved my old car, yet was concerned about its nasty emissions. This way I could keep the old girl and do a little bit to help the environment as well.

As for the key, Charles had unbelievably bought me a two-bedroom cottage in the Cotswolds, in a village with a lovely little pub just down the street.

I told him that this was way too much, but he leaned in and whispered that I deserved it, and besides, he makes a million pound each day before I even get up for breakfast.

He wasn't showing off. It was just a fact, and a small cottage in the country wasn't stretching his finances one iota.

It's handy having a billionaire friend sometimes.

Fewer than fifty thousand separatist families took up the offer of money for resettlement in Russia. The rest stayed, formally accepting to become fully fledged Ukrainian citizens with a pledge of allegiance.

Construction workers from all over Europe flooded into Ukraine when the war ended. Contracts to rebuild the broken cities, towns and hamlets were rife.

There was no shortage of funds for the projects, Putin's captured fortune, along with European and American aid packages saw to that, and progress was coming along nicely.

But for thousands, of course, the losses incurred during the war ran much deeper and could not be replaced.

Loved ones lost, families ripped apart, displaced people, the maimed and the mentally affected. No amount of money would ever replace the hurt.

I've been to Ukraine on several occasions, with tree planting projects, using Hart & Swan as transporters, naturally. I always offer my condolences to the families and individuals I meet. There is sadness, of course, but I find the Ukrainian people have an immense resolve and an optimistic attitude, which is very infectious and hard to dispel. No wonder they stood up to tyranny so resolutely.

On one superb occasion I met President Zelenskyy, who is still doing a fantastic job.

It was a real privilege to shake his hand. He may be short in stature, but he has huge magnetism, and has set the bar impossibly high for anyone wanting to run a country.

As for Putin, the best way I can describe his fate, is to say that he cheated the hangman.

On the same day that Milana was inaugurated as vice president, his two yachts set sail from Hong Kong.

Between them, they had a crew and passenger capacity of two hundred and sixty-four. Thirty-two of them, including Putin, were wanted for war crimes.

After two months at sea, hindered by an unpaid crew and refused entry to every port they attempted to dock in, a drive shaft on the *Gordost' Moskvy* broke in the middle of the Mediterranean Sea.

The ship was dead in the water and needed to be towed into dry dock for repairs. But no country would let them in, and with food stocks low and a crew with fewer morals than that of the Black Pearl, the game was finally up.

In the end, the Royal Navy boarded the ship, seized it and arrested the fugitive ex-president and his gruesome entourage.

The yacht was towed into Gibraltar, followed by the *Gordost' Rossii*. Both ships were impounded, and the wanted men flown to Brize Norton by the RAF.

After three months in HM Belmarsh prison awaiting trial, thirty-one of the war criminals were transferred to the Netherlands and stood trial for crimes against humanity. They were all found guilty and received sentences ranging from seventeen to thirty-five years.

But not Putin. He never made it to The Hague. Six weeks after his internment, he died in a prison hospital bed, isolated, on his own, in agony, from lung cancer.

And that was that. The man who'd caused such death and destruction, so much pain and misery, stepped out the back door without his comeuppance, without penalty, punishment, or justice being served.

He certainly made no apologies nor offered any recompense during his time in prison; he just withered away, seemingly without remorse.

Wars immortalise the worst possible human beings, and Putin was no different from Hitler, Stalin, Napoleon, or any other despot who viewed the rest of the world with greedy eyes. Empire grabbers who consider themselves divine.

History teaches them nothing. Snatch all you can with tyranny, and you are doomed from the start. No populace will endure enslavement forever.

On the other hand, wars also bring out the best in people, and I am proud and honoured to have worked alongside my fellow men and women for five months, who would lay down their lives for peace and harmony in the world.

As for yours truly, I have spent the last three and a half years planting forests, woodlands and orchards, all over the world, especially in Russia, helping to fulfil Matvei Drozdov's dream.

I also get asked to give lectures at schools and universities on all aspects of tree conservation, forestry and plant cultivation, which I love.

Only last week I was delighted to open three new classrooms and a research centre at an agricultural college in Lincoln.

After making a speech and unveiling a plaque, I answered questions from the students. The last question was an interesting one; it came from a young man sitting in the front row. He wondered how I felt about people who talk to and hug trees.

I had no problem in answering him.

Fifty-five years ago, there was a young man who did exactly that, dedicating his life to recognizing and improving environmental issues that he saw as damaging to the planet.

Maybe if more people followed suit back then, we wouldn't be in such a state with climate change as we are right now.

His name? King Charles.

God save the King.

God bless Queen Elizabeth.

And let's look after our planet, because we all need somewhere to come back to.

Abel Llewellyn.

If you enjoyed reading this book, would you be so kind as to write a short review and post it on either Amazon or Goodreads, or both if you are feeling frivolous. Reviews go a long way to provide some substance to the book's credibility. Thank you in advance,

Anthony and Doug

About the Authors

Anthony and Doug have been writing together since 2002. To date they have published four novels, the three previous, being, *The English Sombrero (Nothing to do but run)* and *The English Sombrero (The little white ball)*. Both books are comedies and 1 & 2 of a proposed series of 4, and *The Fridge Magnet*

They are currently working on three new titles, to be released in due course.

Anthony has released a novel of his own, *Tales of Tucson* volume 1, a sex & drugs & rock & roll extravaganza set in 80s America, and Doug has published a novel in his right called *What goes around comes around*, a story of revenge.

Links

https://mybook.to/EnglishSombrero1

https://mybook.to/EnglishSombrero2

https://mybook.to/TalesOfTucson1

https://mybook.to/Whatgoesaround

https://www.amazon.co.uk/Fridge-Magnet-Hidden-Plain-sight-ebook/dp/B0BDXG2DZX

You can contact Anthony here:

https://www.facebook.com/anthonyrandallauthor

Printed in Great Britain
by Amazon